'A sweet and joyful story about friendship
and celebrating your passions … I can't wait
to see more in the sequel!'
ALICE OSEMAN, author of *Heartstopper*

'The perfect book for bookworms, and should be
read by anyone and everyone who is not
(or is) ashamed to be a bit of a book nerd'
RUBY GRANGER

'An absolute delight'
The Bookseller

'If you're looking for an authentic UKYA voice,
and a story alive with a passion for books –
you won't want to miss this'
MAGGIE HARCOURT, author of *Unconventional*

'A heartwarming, uplifting look at the power of
friendship and the dangers of bullying online'
LAUREN JAMES, author of
The Loneliest Girl in the Universe

JOIN THE PAPER & HEARTS SOCIETY BY USING
#PAPERANDHEARTSSOCIETY ON SOCIAL MEDIA.
IT'S TIME TO FIND YOUR PEOPLE!

the PAPER & Hearts SOCIETY

READ with PRIDE

BOOK TWO

LUCY POWRIE

Hodder

HODDER CHILDREN'S BOOKS

First published in Great Britain in 2020
by Hodder and Stoughton

1 0 5 7 9 10 0 6 4 2

Text copyright © Lucy Powrie, 2020

The moral rights of the author have been asserted.

A CIP catalogue record for this book is available from the British Library.

ISBN 978 1 44494 925 4

Typeset in Wilke LT by Hewer Text UK Ltd, Edinburgh
Printed and bound in Great Britain by Clays Ltd, Elcograf S.p.A.

The paper and board used in this book are made
from wood from responsible sources.

MIX
Paper from
responsible sources
FSC® C104740

Hodder Children's Books
An imprint of
Hachette Children's Group
Part of Hodder and Stoughton
Carmelite House
50 Victoria Embankment
London EC4Y 0DZ

An Hachette UK Company

www.hachette.co.uk
www.hachettechildrens.co.uk

To the authors who came before me,
for paving the way, for making it
possible to read with pride.

Chapter One

Olivia Santos's tutor group was held in the music classroom. Posters of musical instruments and notes and scales littered the walls, and a ring of keyboards ran around the perimeter of the room. Olivia sat up straight in her chair, listening but slightly distracted as she thought about why her form tutor, Mr Joyce, never seemed to get bored of wearing the same green tweed jacket he'd worn every day for the past four years, even during summer heatwaves.

She would miss this school and its quirks when she left at the end of the year. On the whole.

'Welcome back to your final year, everyone! I hope you're ready, Year Elevens: this isn't a year to throw away.' Mr Joyce enthusiastically gesticulated as he spoke. 'This is what you've been working up to, what you've been waiting for. I hope you'll keep that in mind as the weeks go on and we get closer to exams. It's time to take your education seriously.' He'd been saying the same thing since Olivia had started in Year Seven, but this year it felt poignant.

Mr Joyce ran a hand through his salt-and-pepper hair and sat down behind his desk. 'You'll see in front of you a sheet I'd like you to fill out. Properly, mind. I know what some of you are like. I want you to write down five goals for the year ahead, and then stick the sheet to the front of your new homework planners. You've got ten minutes.'

Olivia drew her hand into the middle of the table to take the worksheets and handed them out one by one to the group around her. Next to her sat Tabby, one of her best friends and fellow member of the book club she ran, The Paper & Hearts Society, and, today, new girl at school.

Olivia took a pen from her brand-new pencil case with the floral meadow design – she'd *loved* going on a stationery shopping spree with Cassie and Henry at the weekend – and started writing.

MY GOALS FOR THE SCHOOL YEAR AHEAD:
1) Achieve good GCSE results by putting in the revision time and focusing on my studies.
2) Read twenty-five new books – because reading is one of the best ways to improve your spelling, punctuation and grammar!
3) Do all I can to add to my CV because it's my dream to one day become a book editor.

*4) Get involved with the library as much as I can —
because it's so important to support it!
5) Attend extra revision sessions in physics
and maths to boost my grades.*

'I've never seen anyone so enthusiastic about school in my life,' Tabby said. Olivia could feel her friend's watching eyes on her as she scribbled away. Tabby looked down at the piece of paper as if it were an alien life form. 'I don't know what to put. I never had to do this at my old school; I don't think they really cared if we had any goals or aspirations in life. They just left us to get on with it!'

'I always think,' Olivia said, offering a reassuring smile, 'that if you're unsure it's best to start small. Take one subject, like French, for example, and think about what you'd like to improve on in your lessons, or the other stuff you can do to help your learning outside of school. Don't overwhelm yourself. And teachers are always impressed if we think about personal goals, outside lessons.'

'Where have you been all my life? Can you just live inside my brain, Livs?'

'I've been right here all along, just waiting for you to turn up, my friend!' She laughed. 'And, no, I'd be far too annoying in your brain after a while. You'd be wanting to get rid of me.'

As Tabby got on with filling out her sheet, Olivia allowed herself to think about the promise of the new school year. She loved nothing more than the first day back: putting on her clean uniform, the familiar weight of her blazer wrapped around her shoulders and her tie looped around her neck. She didn't even mind the blisters that would inevitably pain her feet because they meant brand-new shoes, and her parents always treated her to a new bag. This year she'd gone for a brown faux-leather rucksack which fitted snugly on her back. She also loved that first moment walking through the school door: the excitement in the air as everyone crowded into the main corridor, sharing summer holiday stories, squealing and laughing and shouting.

Olivia cast her mind back to this morning when, far too early in the day for pictures, her parents had taken the annual back-to-school photograph of her and her younger sister, Kimberley, standing by the front door in their uniforms. It was the one that would be sent to her grandmother, her lola, as well as her aunties and uncles back home in the Philippines, and would undoubtedly be compared to all her cousins' photos.

'Your ten minutes is over!' Mr Joyce clapped his hands together and stood up. 'Now, would anyone like to read theirs out . . .? No? No offers? Anyone?'

The room had gone deadly silent. Olivia didn't mind

reading hers out, but she didn't want to be too keen. She noticed the looks that her fellow students gave her sometimes, and she didn't think it would be good to go full-on Hermione Granger too early in the year.

'Well, then, I'll have to pick someone. Tabitha, why don't you come up and join me at the front? Everyone, this is Tabitha. She's new to our tutor group this year.'

Olivia felt Tabby bristle next to her and immediately felt guilty for not having offered herself.

Tabby scraped her chair back slowly and shuffled to the front. She stood in front of the wipe board, next to the trolley full of triangles and xylophones and shakers, and took an audible shaky breath in.

If I could have saved her this, I would have done. Poor Tabby!

Olivia felt for her friend: she remembered her own first day at school, when she'd felt the difference between her new life in England and her life back home in the Philippines that she still felt she could return to. At least Tabby knew her and Henry at school; when Olivia had begun, she'd known nobody.

But it wasn't only that. Tabby had struggled with anxiety over the summer. Olivia could see just how nervous she was, one hand knotted in the sleeve of her blazer while the other gripped the paper for dear life. There was a furrow in her brow and a tightness to her jaw, and Olivia tried to psychically send her good vibes, just to ease her discomfort. She hoped it would work.

'Hello,' Tabby said squeakily, clearing her throat after she'd spoken. 'Um, hi, I'm Tabitha, but you can call me Tabby. My goals for the year are to improvemyFrenchaccent and getusedtowhere everything is intheschool and trytodo atleast one afterschoolactivity.'

She's talking faster than me even when I'm at my most excitable! Olivia thought, having to concentrate super-hard to understand even a little of what Tabby was saying.

'And before you go back to your seat, would you like to tell us a little bit about yourself?' Mr Joyce asked. Even he looked like he'd had to focus more than he'd expected.

Tabby fixed her gaze on Olivia, and she slowed down. 'Well, I'm originally from Cheltenham,' she said, 'but I moved here over the summer, which is when I met Olivia. We had a summer full of bookish adventures with our book club!'

At Tabby's words, Olivia could almost feel the hot summer sun on her skin, hear the rumbling of Ed's van as they'd travelled around the country, immersed in literary culture. A soft smile tugged at her lips in remembrance.

Mr Joyce laughed. 'That sounds very much like our Olivia,' he said. 'Lovely, thank you Tabby. Take your seat. And now I've got some news I've been asked to share, so listen up!'

'Was that okay?' Tabby asked as she slipped in next to Olivia, her cheeks flushed a brilliant red.

'You were amazing,' Olivia whispered, patting her on the shoulder. 'I promise. Just . . . next time maybe take it a little slower? I thought you were going to take off, you were talking so fast!'

'Ugh, I knew it,' Tabby groaned. 'I hate speaking in front of people! I wanted the ground to swallow me up!'

'Honestly, you were great. You have nothing to worry about.'

'. . . And if there are any students who wish to take books out of the library this year, new library rules require you to fill out a permission slip signed by a parent or guardian, which should be returned as soon as possible. The library is open from break-time today, where you can collect your permission slips.' He scrolled down on to the next slide. 'There will be a business and careers fair at the end of—'

What's that about permission slips? We've never had to fill them out before. It was a given right that everyone had access to the library and its collection, whether reading for pleasure or for academic studies. They'd had to sign student declarations when they'd first started at the school to promise to return all books and look after them, but that was it.

'That's weird,' Olivia muttered to Tabby. 'That's really weird. Why do we need a permission slip to take books out of the library?'

'Olivia, is everything okay?' Mr Joyce interrupted, pausing his reading. 'I gather you might be talking Tabby through everything, but please stop a moment while I finish what I have to say. Thank you.'

'Sorry, Mr Joyce,' Olivia said, scribbling, *We need to investigate* on Tabby's school planner.

The bell went for the first lesson.

'You are dismissed. Remember what I said – start as you mean to go on. It's time for your final year at secondary school!'

'What have you got first lesson again?' Olivia asked, heading out with Tabby. They'd planned to meet Henry, Olivia's friend and Tabby's boyfriend, at the end of the music corridor, so he could show Tabby to her classroom.

'PE, followed by chemistry. Talk about being thrown in at the deep end!'

'I commiserate with you, my dear friend. That is indeed the worst of luck.'

Tabby shook her head. 'Why do you suddenly sound like Jane Austen? Or is that a stupid question?'

Olivia gave her a smug grin. That was exactly what she'd been aiming for.

They let the passing students crowd and bunch around them as they stood fast, waiting for Henry. It only took a few minutes for him to turn up and he wasn't hard to spot. Taller than most, with tortoiseshell glasses and floppy hair that kept falling into his eyes, Henry was a few heads higher than the rest of the crowd. He waved dorkily as he saw them, and when he approached, leant down to kiss the top of Tabby's forehead.

'Is that allowed here?' Tabby squeaked, looking around her.

'Ah, young love!' Olivia teased, thinking of her girlfriend Cassie, who would probably be in art at the college on the other side of town right now, which she attended with Ed, their other friend. That was the one thing she didn't like about school: that Cassie was no longer here with her. Hopefully things would improve now she had Tabby, as well as Henry, to keep her company.

'I bet I make a fool of myself, *numerous times*, by the end of the day. I'm bound to, aren't I?' Tabby closed her eyes. 'This is going to be a disaster.'

'It will be fine!' Olivia consoled. 'We'll look after you and show you where everything is and it'll be like you've always been here. Isn't that right, Henry?'

Henry nodded and wrapped his long arms around Tabby's shoulders. 'Of course. We're here for you, silly. Today, I will be your own personal satnav!'

'Lucky me! At least Ed isn't leading me round, I suppose. He told me he got lost once walking from the kitchen to his bedroom.'

Henry chuckled. 'Typical Ed. He'll never change.'

'I feel so new,' Tabby continued. She pointed at her uniform. 'I'm sure this blazer is too big and my skirt feels way too long. And that's not even thinking about these shoes. The blisters are going to kill. I wish I could just wear my Converse.'

Olivia noticed the blue blazer looked even darker on Tabby, contrasted against her strawberry-blonde hair; it was stiff and uncrumpled, the ultimate unworn look.

'You could always go barefoot,' Henry suggested with a smirk, which earnt him a protesting whack on the arm.

It was time for them to move: the corridors were already getting quieter, and Olivia hated being late to lessons. It gave her less time to set up all her stuff and get organised.

'Come and meet me in the library at break-time!' Olivia called as they parted ways. 'You'll see where it is: it's the room with the big sign that says "Library" above it.'

'Very helpful, thanks!' Tabby said, shaking her head to reinforce the sarcasm in her voice.

Olivia giggled. 'See you later!'

Is there anything in the world more magical than a library? Olivia thought as she pushed open the double doors and burst through, free from the last two hours of equations.

Whose idea had it been to schedule double maths for the first day back, anyway? She may have loved first days, but that was pushing even Olivia's limits.

She'd spent many contented hours in this library, ever since she'd walked in that first time in Year Seven and lost herself for the entire lunch-time in the hundreds upon hundreds of books around her. In a library, there were millions of possibilities right in front of you. The key to other worlds, doors to other people and experiences, pathways to understanding the world.

In a library, she was at her happiest: exploring bookcases, finding new titles, running a finger along the spines and conjuring up memories of the books she'd read and loved.

Bliss.

Miss Carter, the school librarian, wasn't strict about keeping the library completely silent because, as she'd told Olivia in the past, she wanted it to be friendly for all students, a refuge of sorts.

'I cater to everyone,' Miss Carter was fond of saying, 'not just the most bookish and studious people, but also to students who might find libraries daunting. I won't force people to be silent.'

For students who did want peace and quiet, there was a small side room with study booths and tables; with the main library and its offshoots, it was the best of both worlds.

Olivia had planned to head straight to Miss Carter's desk, but she was sidetracked by a book she'd wanted to read for a long time – *My Box-Shaped Heart* by Rachael Lucas – sitting right there on the bookcase as she came in! It must be a sign. A sign that she absolutely had to read it. She'd come back for it on her way out.

The wall shelves and individual bookcases ran all down the right-hand side, while on the left wcrc tables for students to work and read at. Olivia followed the route down the middle to Miss Carter's desk.

She was sitting behind it now, her platinum-blonde hair tied back in a chignon, wearing a crisp white shirt, bright red lipstick completing her stylish appearance. Overflowing with piles of paper and stacks of books, strewn with Post-it notes and pens, Miss Carter's desk was notorious for being chaotically organised. She always knew where everything was, even if nobody else could tell among the disarray.

Olivia created a queue by standing behind a girl already at the desk.

'Without a permission slip, I'm afraid you can't take anything out,' Olivia heard Miss Carter say.

Nothing at all? Olivia wondered. *Not a single book?*

She'd have to rethink her idea and come back another day.

'But I only wanted this one book,' the girl said, 'and I'll

bring a permission slip in tomorrow if I have to. I'll look after it, promise.'

She had bronzy brown hair, cropped into a loose bob, and in her frustration she was pulling at the tie around her neck, loosening it away from her half-untucked, somewhat crumpled shirt.

Miss Carter took a piece of paper from the pile on her desk, handing it to the girl. 'No can do, sorry, Nell. I know you'll look after it, and I'd love to sign it out for you, but it's the new school policy and I'll get in trouble if I let you have it without your parent or guardian's permission first.'

'Hold on a minute,' Olivia said. She didn't bother pretending she hadn't been eavesdropping on their conversation. 'I don't get what's going on. Why do we suddenly need permission to . . . well, to read?'

'Hi Olivia,' Miss Carter said. Was it Olivia's imagination or did she detect weariness in Miss Carter's voice? 'It's a long story, but I have to uphold the school's policy and that means carrying out these procedures.' She handed Olivia one of the forms on her desk.

'Procedures?'

The girl – Nell – picked up the book she'd been trying to take out. 'Well, I'll be going then,' she said. 'I'll put the book back on the shelf on my way out. See ya, Miss Carter.'

'WAIT.' Olivia composed herself. 'What does that label on your book say?' Slow, calm. Not at all like the pace of her heart, which had picked up and was booming in her ears as Nell lifted the book high enough so Olivia could read the bold letters covering most of the cover.

WARNING: CONTAINS REFERENCES TO LGBT RELATIONSHIPS. YOU MUST HAVE RETURNED PERMISSION SLIP SIGNED BY PARENT OR GUARDIAN BEFORE YOU CAN TAKE THIS BOOK OUT, WITH CORRECT BOX TICKED.

No, no, no, no, NO WAY is this real! I. THINK. I. MIGHT. SCREAM!!!!!

'But what does this mean?!' Olivia exclaimed, in a voice not exactly suitable for even this liberal-minded, noise-friendly library.

'I'm sorry,' Miss Carter repeated, pinching the bridge of her nose. 'It's the new school policy. At the end of last year, a parent complained because their child took a YA book home that featured two boys in a relationship. The mother was horrified and – I shouldn't even be telling you this, not really. Let's just say it's not been the easiest start to the school term.'

'I can't believe this,' Olivia said, running her hands through her hair in utter disbelief. She took the book from Nell, moving her finger over the label as if it would give her an electric shock any moment.

'This is just wrong.'

Olivia looked up; it hadn't been her who had spoken. It was Nell. Her eyes were wide, her nostrils flaring. 'You can't stand for this, Miss.'

'I'm sorry, I really am. Do you think I haven't tried everything, girls?' Miss Carter kept her voice hushed. 'I'm sorry. I'm doing all I can, but I'm only one librarian.'

Olivia ignored her. 'I just can't believe this! What an affront! An outrage!'

Nell nodded. 'I guess I'll come back for the book another day, then,' she said. 'Once the school has got over its bigotry.'

With that, Nell spun on her heel and stalked out. Olivia watched her back as she left, the double doors slapping behind her.

The library had always been Olivia's sanctuary. She could wander the shelves and know she was amongst friends inside the pages; she was surrounded by knowledge and information, books that offered comfort and support.

But she had to leave – for the first time in her entire life she couldn't stay in the library any longer. Just the sight of it made her feel sick to her stomach.

She put her head down and strode to the door, a sense of relief washing over her as she came out the other side.

'I finally found it!' Tabby said, approaching. 'I feel like I was walking around for hours, up and down basically every flight of stairs and embarrassingly I even went into the lunch hall at one point, but I got here eventually ... Olivia, what is it?'

Olivia shook her head against the imploring look Tabby was giving her.

'I'll tell you when we're with Henry. I can't bear to tell the story twice!'

Cassie: ed, where are you? i can't find your car, i'm waiting outside the art block and i swear if it starts to rain i will never speak to you again

Ed: Have you seen the HUGE GLOWING THING IN THE SKY? It is not going to rain!!! I'm on my way, I just got caught up in geography!

Cassie: hurry up

Olivia: How was your first day?!

Ed: GOOD! How about yours? A GIRL IN MY DRAMA CLASS JUST GOT A NEW KITTEN AND I SAW ALL THE PICTURES AND I ALMOST DIED OF CUTENESS OVERLOAD

Cassie: you can't be hurrying if you're messaging at the same time

Ed: I AM hurrying!! Your carriage will be there to pick you up in a minute I promise OR you can walk home if you'd rather!

Ed: OH NO GOTTA GO I SEE CASSIE AND SHE LOOKS ANGRY

Chapter Two

'Is that you, Livvy?! I'm in the kitchen!'

Shrugging off her shoes and leaving them neatly by the front door, then putting her rucksack on the bottom stair to take upstairs later, Olivia followed her mum's voice to the back of the house, where she found her working on her laptop at the kitchen table.

Mum and Dad were both journalists and so Olivia and Kimberley were used to treading on eggshells whenever either of them had deadlines or something was particularly stressful.

'Hi Mum, how's the deadline going?'

Mum pulled a face. 'Deadline has "dead" in it. That's all I need to say.' She looked so bleary-eyed that Olivia was sure she hadn't moved further than from the desk to the kettle in hours.

'How was your day?'

Olivia grabbed a dog treat from the jar on the kitchen counter and threw it to her tiny wire-haired Jack Russell terrier, Lizzie, who swiftly uncurled herself and bounded out of her dog bed, licking her lips gratefully.

'Fine,' she said. She tried not to tack a huff on to the end.

This time, Mum did look up. 'Just fine?' she asked quizzically. 'I know you, Olivia. Every year you walk through that door from your first day and don't stop until you've told us every tiny detail. And yet, right now, you've turned into a mumbling teenager who won't say a word. Spit it out,' Mum said, and closed her laptop lid.

Feeling like the mumbling teenager her mum had accused her of being – *Excuse me, I* am *a teenager!* – Olivia took her seat. From her pocket, she lifted out the crumpled paper; she'd practically been able to feel it burning a hole in her blazer, she was so aware of it. Throughout lunch-time when Henry asked her if she was feeling ill because she looked pale; when she'd attempted to distract herself in religious studies by replicating a revision page with the neatest handwriting she'd seen on a Studygram page; on her way home, as she'd waved off Tabby and Henry as they took the bus back to their part of town.

She slid it across the table to her mum. Olivia scanned her face for tell-tale signs, but she couldn't work out what Mum was thinking.

PARENT/GUARDIAN PERMISSION FORM

In order to implement new changes in the library, we now require students to receive permission from their parent/guardian regarding the books they take out. Please return this form as soon as possible, circling the appropriate response.

My child is allowed to withdraw books from the library: YES/NO

My child is allowed to withdraw books featuring LGBTQ+ characters from the library: YES/NO

Olivia didn't need to see the slip to know the precise words, the precise formatting. She didn't think she'd ever erase the image from her mind.

'Something that seems so simple will cause so much pain,' she said, before Mum could speak. 'There's your explanation: that's why I'm just fine.'

Mum got up, filled the kettle, and flicked it on.

'Well, this is *not on*,' she said over the bubbling of the boiling water.

The kettle clicked, fully boiled, and Mum got out two mugs. Olivia knew what she was doing: deadline time was always salabat time, the fresh ginger tea that was the cure-all for colds, coughs, sore throats or just general low moods. Ginger, lemon, honey and tea combined to create the best warm-hug feeling Olivia could imagine.

It was exactly what she needed right now and with this small gesture, Mum had communicated just how she felt: she knew what Olivia was going through, and she was on her side. It was an allied signal.

But it was too much for Olivia.

'Oh, Livvy, don't cry!' Mum rushed over, putting her arms around Olivia's shoulders and squeezing tight. Olivia felt the tears gush out before she could control them – hot tears, full of pain and frustration and confusion. Tears that blazed a trail down her cheeks until she could furiously wipe them away.

'I've tried to not get upset by it, Mum!' she cried. 'I've tried so hard all day, but I can't hold it back any longer! It's like someone has ripped my heart out and stamped all over it!'

'There, there,' Mum comforted.

'It's the warning part, that they've stuck on book covers, that I can't get over. It's such a specific word: warning. It's cautionary, threatening. This makes it seem like I should be hidden away, like my sexuality is forbidden. I'm sick of hiding when I don't want to!'

'And you shouldn't have to, Livvy. You are not something to be warned against, and you know that we have always supported you.'

Olivia was comfortable with who she was and knew

exactly how she identified: she was demisexual. Not attracted to anyone until she knew them really, really well. And even then it wasn't the kind of head-over-heels, madly in love, totally obsessed attraction that she heard everyone else talk about. It was something far less assuming.

But how was she supposed to feel comfortable with who she was when there were people actively trying to make her, and others like her, uncomfortable? And the thing that really got to her was that Mum was right, she had always had the support of her family; but what about students who didn't have the support of their parents, and needed refuge in these books to feel less alone? It broke Olivia's heart just thinking about the student whose parent had been so horrified. What an awful summer they must have had!

'Do you think the school should be doing this, Mum? Restricting access to books? You're an adult: is there a so-called "adult" reason for this? Because I can't see it if there is.'

'Sometimes people make decisions that mystify us. I'm sure that the complaining parent thought they were doing the right thing. We can't understand their logic, but we can question it. I see you, I see Kimberley, and I question what world you're growing up in, what world your father and I are raising you in. But all we want is for you to be happy and to do yourself proud, to act in a way that does justice to the wonderful young lady you are.'

'How can I be happy, truly happy, while I go to school and this is happening in the very same building?' Olivia wiped the tears from her eyes. 'How can I sit back and watch this happen under my very own nose, knowing that it might be okay for me – you'll fill out the permission slip – but other parents won't?'

'That's the million pound question,' Mum said, leaning across and wiping the last of Olivia's tears away. 'But it isn't like you to sit back and let something like this carry on. If you're angry about something, channel it into change. I know that when you believe in something, you see it through to the end.'

'Maybe I will,' she said, glaring down at her hands, tightened into fists.

'One thing, though: just don't let it get in the way of your studies. You've got an important year ahead of you. You do need to focus, if you can.' Olivia smiled weakly. Mum, never missing anything, continued, 'Sometimes, you've got to make your own light before you can find it. And if there's anyone I know who can conjure the light, it's you, Livvy.'

Olivia smiled. 'Thanks, Mum. Maybe you're right.'

Henry: She won't want to say anything but Olivia has been
    miserable all afternoon and not even showing her
    pictures from the TV series of *Pride and Prejudice* has
    been able to cheer her up

Tabby: I hate seeing you like this, Livs :(

Ed: OH NO, is everything all right?

Olivia: I'll fill you in when I see you, I just feel very emotional
    and raw right now and telling the whole story would
    warrant an entire essay and I do not have the energy for
    that

Henry: You are perfectly entitled to be feeling as you are.
    It's understandable

Cassie: how about if we're all free on saturday morning, we
    have a paper & hearts society meeting? that will make
    you feel better!

Ed: I'LL TAKE CHARGE! I have the BEST idea!

Olivia: Thanks, pals, that sounds like exactly the thing I
    need <3

Ed: Half ten at Brain Freeze in that case? Is it a plan?

Tabby: It's a plan!

Cassie: you okay??

Olivia: It's too difficult to explain over message! I don't know
    where to start! Do you want to come over to mine before
    we meet with the others??

Cassie: sounds good to me!

Cassie sent a gif.

Cassie: even though i am far too cool to be affected emotionally by a gif of two sea otters holding hands, i will make an exception for you

Olivia: So romantic! <3 <3

@TheIncredibleEd *Ready for today's PAPER & HEARTS MEETING with @WhatTabbyDid, @bookswithlivs, @cassie.artx and Henry which is going to be AWESOME*

@WhatTabbyDid *Can't wait to see you!*

@bookswithlivs *Yay! <3*

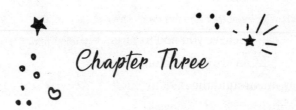

Chapter Three

'I can't believe you're making me do this!' Cassie said, the poo bag over her hand. She gagged the closer she got to the not-so-nice present Lizzie had left for them. 'I thought we were going for a relaxing walk! This is a *crap* situation.'

Olivia stifled another giggle, but it was too difficult to hold back; she doubled over as her stomach hurt so much from keeping it in. 'What about this isn't relaxing?!'

'Ha ha,' Cassie said, deadpan. 'You owe me one. Big time.'

Olivia leant over and gave her a peck on the cheek, grinning all the time. 'Does that count?'

'Only if you agree I can hold Lizzie the rest of the way, and you hold the dog-poo bag.'

'Deal!'

They were walking back from the park, where they'd taken Lizzie so she could run around to her heart's content. Unfortunately, having taken their eyes off her for a few seconds too long, Lizzie had discovered a pair of shoes belonging to a toddler and decided to run off with them.

'I can't believe you had to promise that mum you'd buy her child an ice lolly before it would stop crying. Lizzie only ran around the park five times – we were there barely twenty minutes,' Cassie said.

'You make it sound like I'm a pushover! What else was I supposed to do?!'

'Run away?' Cassie grinned.

It was nice to be out in the fresh air, just the two of them, Cassie looking way too glammed-up to be going on a dog walk in her flowery Dr Martens, dark red lipstick and ripped jeans; Olivia a little more practical in her sunflower-yellow pinafore dress, the front pocket overflowing with dog-poo bags and treats. It was a wonder all the dogs in the neighbourhood weren't running behind her, she had so many!

Cassie had barely got through the front door when Olivia had bombarded her with what had happened. Even though Olivia had been somewhat reluctant to tell Mum, there was no hesitation when it came to Cassie. As her girlfriend, but first and foremost her best friend, Olivia told her everything.

'Thank you so much for doing this for me,' Olivia said; the laughter had dissipated and sincerity filled the space between them. 'You didn't have to, and I appreciate it.

And it's nice to spend time with you! Being back to school is the *worst* when it comes to not seeing you.'

'You look better already,' Cassie said. 'And I knew you wouldn't pass up the chance for a Paper & Hearts Society meeting. Although now you mention it . . . maybe I should have organised it so it was just us two. Ed would never have known!'

'I don't think I could have dealt with Ed's wrath on top of the awful week I've had.'

And it had got worse: she'd spent the past few days watching as students were turned away from taking books out from the library, she'd had to have her braces tightened at the orthodontist and, to top it all off, she'd briefly lost her favourite copy of *Pride and Prejudice*.

DISASTER.

Cassie encouraged Lizzie to walk along. 'All because some parent wants to protect their darling child from reading a book with a queer character. Wow! Give them the Parent of the Year award because they're clearly an inspiration to all.' She rolled her eyes. 'Imagine how they would react if they found out their child wasn't straight or cisgender. That poor kid.'

'It doesn't bear thinking about,' Olivia replied. And it didn't. If *she* felt this way about it, how must that student feel?

As they followed the pavement up to where Olivia's house lay, she noticed a small black car pulling up outside the Santos home. Although she wasn't familiar with the car, she *was* familiar with the driver – Ed, dressed in a white T-shirt, big aviator glasses and a seasonally inappropriate Hufflepuff scarf.

The moment he saw Olivia and Cassie he honked his horn.

'All right, all right, we're coming!' Olivia called in response, and he wound down his window. 'What are you doing driving this?!'

'It was an early birthday present from my dad,' he said. 'Not that he's really that bothered about the eighteenth anniversary of my birth because he can't see me on my actual birthday, and then he had the audacity to explain that for *my* birthday, he'd bought my idiot of a brother a car, so I could have his old one. I mean, I'm *grateful*, but it makes no sense. Anyway, it doesn't matter.'

It was a sore spot, mentioning Ed's dad. It was an unspoken rule that they didn't unless they absolutely had to.

'Well, we'll have to make your eighteenth birthday extra special to make up for it,' Olivia said.

'With an amazing, fancy cake?!'

'Of course there'll be cake! I'll just put Lizzie in and grab my stuff, and then we'll be ready to go.'

'Don't be long!' Ed called. 'We've got a lot to pack in today!' but Olivia had already taken Lizzie from Cassie and was halfway up her front garden path.

Inside, she let Lizzie off her lead, which she hung back on its hook by the door, and grabbed her backpack.

'See you later! I'm off out with the Paper & Hearts Society!'

'Have a good time!' her dad called back from the living room.

She headed back to the car out front to find Cassie sending Ed evils from the pavement, where she had her arms crossed for full effect.

'I *have* to sit in the back or I'll get car sick,' Cassie said.

'You don't get car sick,' Ed said, 'or at least, you never have done before. You didn't the other day when I gave you a lift!'

'Oh, yeah. I lied. I just don't want to sit next to you, Ed. Sorry. Now let me sit in the back.'

Ed screwed his face up and pretended to wipe tears from his eyes. Olivia, with a shake of her head, let Cassie climb into the back while she took the front seat next to Ed. Olivia could hear Cassie's fingernails tapping away at her phone screen over the sound of the classical music CD Ed had chosen. He undid the hand brake and started up the engine, pulling off down the road.

'I heard it's good for road rage,' he explained, turning the volume up in response to Cassie rolling her eyes as the next instrumental melody played out.

'Didn't Henry and Tabby want a lift?' Olivia gripped hold of the door as Ed took a corner sharply, his signature driving move.

'Those lovebirds? Pah! They want all the time they can get together! They turned down a ride in the Edmobile and I feel very bitter about it.'

Olivia giggled. 'The "Edmobile"? Really?!'

Ed grinned. 'Brilliant, isn't it? I just came up with it on the spot, right then!'

'It's *very* original and very fitting. I love it!'

'I'm really looking forward to this,' Ed said. 'First of all: ice cream. Can the day get any better? Second of all: I think you'll be surprised at how *chill* my Paper & Hearts meeting is going to be. *Chill.* Get it? We're off to an ice cream parlour!'

Olivia snickered, despite herself. 'That's such a *cool* joke, Ed.'

'Actually,' Cassie said, 'it's left me feeling pretty cold.'

'Amazing!' Ed said. 'Maybe my meeting should consist entirely of ice-cream puns. Hey, wouldn't that be a great idea?'

Olivia knew where they were headed, but she still felt a rush of pleasure as they arrived.

'Brain Freeze!' Ed sang as he parked up. 'The one and only!'

Brain Freeze was a small ice-cream parlour in the town centre, complete with a vintage-style interior and more flavours than you could count. Their speciality was sundaes, although Olivia also had a soft spot for their ice-cream sandwiches: a sugary mess of ice cream stuck between thick layers of biscuit. She could rattle off the names of all the flavours – *Strawberry Sunshine, Chocolate Crush, Wondrous Watermelon* ... It was tradition to visit with her dad once a month on a Sunday, after waking up early, come rain or shine, heat-wave or snow-storm.

The bell over the door tinkled as they went inside, welcomed by a hubbub of noise and activity. There was a sweet smell in the air, fresh like the ice cream they were about to eat, tinged with nostalgia for all the happy memories Olivia had experienced here.

Ed went over to their usual booth by the window, putting the tote bag he had slung over his shoulder on top of the table. They slotted themselves into the seats – Olivia and Cassie on one side, Ed on the other.

'Do you think you can bring cats here?' he asked. 'Mrs Simpkins would *love* it. They should make ice cream for cats! Or maybe *I* should do that. I'd make a fortune and then people would come up to me and say, "How did you

32

make your first billion, Ed?" and I'd reply, "Cat ice cream is an extremely lucrative business." Amazing.'

'You're delusional,' Cassie told him.

The bell over the door tinkled again, and in walked Henry and Tabby, dropping hands as they crossed the threshold. Tabby's cheeks were flushed; Henry was wearing a red beanie hat pulled over his hair, an unusual colour choice.

He must be getting adventurous now he's got a girlfriend, Olivia mused.

She was glad for Tabby and Henry's arrival, so they could rescue her from more Mrs Simpkins chat; there were only so many times Olivia could stomach the story of Ed's cat Mrs Simpkins jumping into a freezer compartment when Ed had his back turned.

Oblivious to Olivia, Cassie and Ed watching him and Tabby, Henry pulled the hat off his head and his hair flew up in every direction, a messy mop, which set Tabby off into a fit of giggles. She tried to brush it down, but his hair wasn't having any of it. Then he turned and kissed her.

'I feel sick,' Ed mumbled, shielding his eyes. 'Somebody find me a paper bag, please.'

'Oh shut up, Ed,' Cassie snapped. 'God knows what you say about Olivia and me when our backs are turned, if this is the way you feel about Tabby and Henry.'

'It was just a joke,' he shot back. 'No need to get so shirty with me!'

But Olivia frowned. That was a good point. *What does he say about us when we're not around?*

Tabby and Henry spotted the others and, still grinning, came over.

'Hi!' Tabby said. 'I'm so excited! Can you believe I've never been here before?'

'A crime!' Ed called. 'You've never lived until you've been to Brain Freeze and tried every single flavour and every single combination of ice cream, sorbet and gelato. Trust me: I've done it. In one day.'

'I don't doubt you have. Tell me this, then: why haven't they banned you yet for eating too much ice cream?'

Ed scoffed. 'Because I'm their best customer, *obviously*.'

Cassie leant over to whisper to Olivia, 'He is so two-faced sometimes, I cannot believe it.'

'Let's go and choose,' Olivia said, 'before Ed starts another one of his Mrs Simpkins anecdotes.'

They headed to the ice-cream counter to order the sweetest treats in town. Olivia had her eye on a chocolate-brownie sundae, with vanilla and chocolate ice cream, sticky melted chocolate, big chunks of brownie, and whipped cream to top it off.

'I'll go first! Should I go for Peanut Butter Crunch or Blueberry Bliss?' Ed asked, scratching his chin. Olivia thought people only did that in films. 'Or no, actually, maybe something like Mango Menace would be better.'

On his one hundredth iteration of the same sentence, Henry patted him on the shoulder. 'Ed, maybe you should let somebody else go first if you're going to take so long. The queue will be out of the door if you don't hurry up.'

Ed ignored him. 'Or all three? Could I do that? Actually, that probably wouldn't taste very nice, would it?'

'Any guesses what I'm going for?' Cassie turned to Olivia.

There was only one flavour Cassie ever went for: mint chocolate chip. Every daytrip they'd ever been on, every time they visited Brain Freeze, she would always, always order a mint chocolate chip cone with a Flake and extra chocolate chips.

And, every time, Olivia would wrinkle her nose and say, 'I don't know how you like that stuff, it's like eating toothpaste,' just like she did now.

Cassie's mouth quirked up in a grin and she ran a hand through her short hair without catching her be-ringed fingers. 'Actually, I'm feeling extra adventurous today. I'm going to go for something new instead . . . chilli chocolate ice cream. Are you shocked?'

'Shocked?' Olivia said. 'I think I might fall over with the surprise! Are you sure you're my girlfriend and you haven't been replaced by a chilli-chocolate-loving alien?'

Cassie wrapped her arms around Olivia's shoulders, and Olivia felt herself blush. She wished they weren't in public.

'How are you feeling today, Livs?' Henry asked when they were back at the table. He was always so thoughtful; while Ed had probably completely forgotten about how she was feeling, there was no way Henry would ever forget.

She shrugged. 'In this moment? I feel much better, thanks to all of you. But, overall, I don't think I'm going to be able to shake off this despondence any time soon.'

'Okay, you need to fill me in,' Ed said. 'I'm the only one not in the loop here.'

So she did: she filled him in on every detail that had happened since she'd heard Mr Joyce talk about the slips on her first day back and how she wanted to make the school revert their decision. She injected true passion into her voice, let all the emotion she'd been bottling up fly out with each word.

'How is that allowed to happen?!' Ed exclaimed when she was finished. 'It was never like that in my time!'

His time being the year before last, not centuries ago.

'It strikes me that this is a very reactionary thing they're doing,' Henry said. 'They've had a complaint, so they've responded in an extreme way so they don't get further complaints, yet in doing so they're most definitely not doing the right thing. Whether they'll listen to reason, though, is another thing.'

'It's discrimination, plain and simple,' Cassie said. 'They'll have to listen.'

Olivia hung her head. 'I suppose it comes down to how important the words of students are over the adults who have complained. And I don't hold out much hope.'

'You can't give up, Livs,' Henry said. 'Your voice *is* important. Things will have to change.'

But the damage is already being done. I don't know if I can wait for change to just happen.

They dug in as soon as the waiter brought over their ice creams and sundaes and drinks; Cassie insisted on taking a picture for Instagram before she started eating.

As soon as the ice cream hit her tongue, Olivia knew she'd made the right decision. It was utter perfection: smooth and packed full of flavour with every mouthful, demanding to be savoured rather than gobbled up in one go. It was the best ice cream around, and she didn't think she'd ever taste better.

Ed overexaggerated the movement of licking his lips, whilst Tabby and Henry took dollops of their own orders to swap with each other. They were sitting close, their bodies pushed together as if severing the connection would tear them apart for ever.

'Are you sure you don't want to try any?' Cassie said, digging into the soft ice cream with her spoon and holding it out to Olivia. 'It's pretty mild, as chilli goes. Disappointing, really.'

'I'm okay, thanks,' Olivia said, taking another scoop of her own ice cream, mixed with chocolate brownie. 'I don't think the flavours would really go together!'

'Oh god, I love ice cream so, so, so, so, so much,' Ed said.

'We'd never have been able to tell!' Olivia joked.

Ed, taking another quick scoop, emptied his tote bag all over the table. Out burst felt-tip pens in packs, stickers and glitter pens, coloured card and scissors. It was like a craft shop had vomited everywhere.

'Ta-da!' He rummaged around the items until he found what he was looking for – a pack of cut-out white card in the shape of . . .

'Every Paper & Hearts Society member needs a Paper & Hearts Society bookmark, so that is exactly what we're going to make today. Bookish craft time!'

Olivia was impressed. It was always a risk putting Ed in charge of anything: he had a habit of not taking stuff seriously enough and was impossible to control. If he wanted to do something, he'd do it, regardless of the consequences.

So despite the fact that she was sure the Brain Freeze

table would be covered in glitter by the time they were finished, she was looking forward to this.

'I better win,' Cassie said, 'seeing as though I'm the only one with any art qualifications here.'

'I got an F for Fantastic in art!' Ed cried. 'Don't be so sure of yourself!'

'This is so cool!' Olivia said. 'But we're going to need to do this regularly because what will happen when I read more than one book? I'll *always* want to use a Paper & Hearts Society bookmark!'

'I take my hat off to you, Ed,' Henry said. 'I wasn't sure what to expect, but this is decent.'

'You're not wearing a hat any more,' Ed replied. He spread everything around the table to make sure they could all reach, and then set out the rules.

1. They had to take this seriously – although it was supposed to be fun, they also had to try to create the most impressive bookmark possible.
2. Once they were finished, the person to create the best bookmark would be crowned the champion, and everyone else would have to buy their ice cream for them when they next came to Brain Freeze.

'That's a ridiculous rule,' Cassie said. 'You can't expect us to do that.'

'I didn't make the rules,' he said, with a shrug.

'Um, yes, Ed, you did?' Tabby said. Olivia felt Ed's foot push past hers as he kicked Tabby under the table.

'Anyway,' Ed said, 'let's make a start. I can't contain my enthusiasm any longer or I'll burst!'

They set to work. Olivia decided to make hers as colourful as possible: at first, she lightly sketched THE PAPER & HEARTS SOCIETY in pencil, while blocking out areas to add glitter to, and then she moved on to precisely lining up the felt-tip pens she wanted to use in order to create her colour palette. *A rainbow effect would be best*, she thought, and slapped Ed's hand away when he tried to steal one of her pens, despite the fact the same colour was already sitting next to him.

She loved the fact that they were together, each working on their separate bookmark, lightly chatting but full of concentration. Cassie's mouth was pursed as she neatly drew on hers in a black fineliner she'd picked out of her bag; Henry kept sneaking glances at everyone else's creations, as if he wasn't sure of his own; Ed had covered his with his arm, like people did in tests to make sure nobody was looking or copying his ideas.

'How are you finding Ye Olde School?' Ed asked Tabby.

Tabby tilted her head to the side. 'Okay, I guess? It's just . . . I can't even put it into words. I'm so much happier already here than I ever was before I moved, but it's still difficult.' She stared down at the table. 'I had a panic attack when I got home on Thursday. I didn't want to mention it when it happened because I was trying not to think about it, but I said goodbye to Henry on the bus and then got off at my stop, and I barely got through Gran's door before I broke down.'

Olivia patted her hand. 'It's okay, you know. Having a panic attack isn't a step backwards for you, it's just part of the process of recovering.'

Tabby smiled humourlessly. 'I know, and I keep trying to tell myself that I'm not failing, that there will come a point when they're not a normal occurrence for me, but the process of getting to that point seems never-ending. I'm trying my best, but sometimes it feels like that's not enough.'

'It is enough,' Henry said. 'You've come such a long way already; you shouldn't beat yourself up over it.'

'Yeah,' Ed said, 'your best is *definitely* enough. Even half your best, or 0.001 per cent of your best would be enough.'

Olivia had seen Tabby's struggles with her mental health and anxiety over the summer, had noted the headway she'd been making in the past few weeks to understand herself better. This was new territory for Olivia, though: she'd never felt the rumblings of anxiety that Tabby experienced, had always felt comfortable and confident in her own skin, despite being aware of the differences between her and the majority of her peers, who never had to face life as immigrants to a strange, sometimes hostile country, as England could be. That was why she'd got on with Cassie so well, at first, because they both understood what it was like to live in a small English town, where everyone knew each other and difference wasn't easily accepted, where the default was white – and, as they would later determine, straight.

Ed cleared his throat. 'So I tried to get Felix to come to this meeting . . .'

There was silence. Felix had turned up at their final Paper & Hearts Society meeting of the summer after Ed had invited him, and was a renowned book snob. Olivia had grown up being forced into playdates with him and Ed, as he was Ed's next-door neighbour, and she would have screamed if he'd walked in today: his pretentiousness towards what was and wasn't considered literature was unbearable.

'Apparently he's far too busy from now up until Christmas, so won't be joining us. There may also have been some kind of reference to not being able to tolerate any discussion around books for young adults, and he tried to force me into reading *War and Peace* on his doorstep, which may be an excellent book, but there is a time and place for it. I'm sure you'll be very upset to hear that.'

Olivia breathed a huge sigh of relief.

'Heartbroken,' Cassie said. 'My heart is bleeding.'

Olivia swapped the red pen she was using for the orange one next in her row, and moved on to colouring the next block of rainbow.

'Ed, my man, please think about how much glitter you're getting everywhere and how you will be kicked out if you aren't careful.' Henry looked very concerned as he surveyed the mound of glitter surrounding Ed's bookmark.

'Me?! Kicked out? I keep this place going with all the ice cream I buy!'

Cassie rolled her eyes.

'Not that I can any more . . . I am completely broke and I'm having no success with job applications. Can you believe it? Nobody wants me!'

'What a surprise,' Cassie said with a raise of her eyebrows and a derisive grin.

'Can you not be mean for just five seconds, please? I feel very frustrated by this, Cassie, and I think you should be a little nicer to me.'

Olivia knew, though, that other than her, Ed was probably Cassie's favourite. It was a love-pretend-to-hate relationship and she would never be without him. He'd always been the same and so had she: Ed's silliness balanced out Cassie's reliance on sarcasm, and they were the best of friends. They'd just never admit it out loud. Or to each other.

Luckily, Ed had slowed down on the glitter and was trying to clear up the mess he'd made. In the process, though, he'd ended up with a big streak of it right down the middle of his nose.

Olivia, noticing this, burst out laughing and leant over the table to flick it away, which he protested wildly about.

'Wait! I should have taken a picture for posterity!' Tabby said with a disappointed groan.

This was ... good. Laughter and friendship and ice cream, bad arts and crafts and even more laughter. It was some way to healing. Not at the final destination, but one step closer.

They put the finishing touches to their bookmarks and were instructed by Ed to put them in the middle of the table for judging. From his bag, he took out a magnifying glass and a trophy so tiny it looked like it had been stolen from a child's doll's house.

'I am Sherlock Holmes, solving the crime of these terrible bookmarks! Listen up, peasants, for I shall declare the winner.'

'Ed, I don't think Sherlock Holmes would ever talk like that,' Henry acknowledged.

'Well, this Sherlock Holmes does! I am basically Benedict Cumberbatch. My Sherlock insists that you shut up while he investigates and makes up his mind as to the winner.'

'I've got this in the bag,' Cassie said to Olivia, and Olivia had to agree: she'd delicately drawn a grand bookcase with a sliding ladder in black ink, each individual book labelled in spidery writing, and it was a work of art. If she set her mind to it, Olivia thought she'd be able to sell copies, it was that good.

'And the winner is . . . Henry!' Ed declared, holding Henry's arm up in a champion's pose.

In a most un-Henry-like manner, Henry fist-bumped the air. 'I always knew I had it in me!'

Olivia had no clue how Ed had decided Henry was the winner, as he'd mostly chucked glitter – although less than Ed's – on his piece of card and written his name in the worst bubble writing the world has ever seen. 'Unbelievable.'

But Cassie laughed, rolling her eyes at the Frankenstein's monster of bookmarks.

'Free ice cream for a year, wasn't it?' Henry said, and he was still gloating when they left, proudly carrying his bookmark cradled in his arms like a baby. It was safe to say that the other members of The Paper & Hearts Society took great pleasure from poking fun at him, usually so serious.

'Group hug!' Ed cried, standing on the pavement outside Brain Freeze. He pulled Olivia in first, and then Tabby, then Henry, and finally Cassie. 'One for all and all for one! The Five Bookish Musketeers, saving Olivia's day!'

Olivia lost herself in the warmth of all their bodies, her friends, her life. It would never cease to amaze her how supportive they were.

'How do you feel now?' Tabby asked, squeezing Olivia round the shoulders before they parted.

'Better,' Olivia said, with a genuine smile on her face. 'Thanks to all of you, my Bookish Musketeers.'

And she meant it, too. Being able to escape her thoughts for a few hours was exactly what she'd needed.

As winner of today's Paper & Hearts Society bookmark design competition, Olivia has tasked me, Henry, with creating the entry for our scrapbook. While I can't say I understand Ed's decision, I will not refute it because it is one of the proudest moments of my life, even greater than the time I saved Ed's life when he ran out into the road to pet a cat and was nearly hit by a double-decker bus. Which sounds very morbid now I'm writing it down, but I promise at the time he laughed and I'm glad to say no Eds or cats were harmed in the process. Also, it wasn't really a double-decker bus, but more a minibus full of old-aged pensioners. Ed, however, has sworn ever since that it was a red bus like the ones that drive around London.

My top tips for making the perfect bookmark

1) Think about what you love most in the world and throw all your passion into the little piece of card in front of you.

2) The reason it's your perfect bookmark is because YOU have made it – in moments of doubt, remember that only you have your artistic talent, and nobody else could replicate your pièce de résistance.

3) Find some kind of Washi tape or other material that will de-sharpen the edges. The last thing you want is a paper cut.

4) When your friends try to make fun of you for your bookmark masterpiece, ignore them. The only thing that matters is if you love it.

5) Glitter. (But not as much glitter as Ed prefers.)

Chapter Four

There was nothing worse than being forced to do PE in the rain when you knew you still had hours of school left. Olivia's dark hair was flattened to her head in clumps, she was chilled to the bone, and her skin felt raw from the pelting droplets falling on her. She wrapped her blazer tighter to her body, feeling her teeth chatter together, as she headed to her locker with her PE bag in tow.

To top it off, her team had lost the end-of-lesson netball match and her voice was hoarse where she'd shouted instructions at Ife, who was playing goal defence. She hoped Ife would have forgiven the shouting by the time they had English later that afternoon, or it might be awkward.

'Have you done the physics homework for tomorrow?' Lara from her science group asked, as she pulled on her locker door – it always stuck, it was that old – and put her PE bag inside.

'Yep,' Olivia responded and took out a breakfast bar. 'I didn't *love* those equations, but I thought they were okay once I got the hang of them.'

'Can I borrow the answer to question five from you?'

She thought about it for a split second: her parents had always encouraged her to work hard, to seek her own answers in life, but she also didn't want to be mean.

She shrugged. 'Sure, I'll message it to you later.'

'Thanks, Olivia, I really appreciate it.'

'No worries!' she called as she left the changing room and headed to the library to find more books to read over the weekend. For fun, and to help with her English homework too, which required researching Shakespearean sonnets.

The sonnets, it turned out, were relatively easy to find, but the bigger and more important decision was what she would read this weekend.

There was no point choosing a seven-hundred-page tome because she'd want to finish it all and she knew her dad would be looking over her shoulder at every opportunity, asking if she'd done her homework yet. And there was no point choosing something she wasn't sure she would like because she'd get bored and spend all weekend on social media, prompting even more annoying questions from her dad, who wished his two girls would spend more time in the real world than online.

So it would have to be something familiar, yet new. A favourite author; a favourite genre; something cosy and snug for the approaching autumnal days. The possibilities were endless.

'OW!'

Olivia felt the impact smack against her skull as she rounded the corner; she was sure that if she were a cartoon character, she would have stars floating around her head right now. OUCH!

'Can't you watch what you're doing?' the girl said blearily, clutching her head.

'I'm sorry! Oh my goodness, I'm so, so sorry!' Olivia flapped about, one hand over her mouth in shock. 'Are you okay? I really am so sorry. You're right: I should have been paying better attention! I'm so, so sorry!'

'It's fine,' the girl said, rubbing her temple one last time and moving to pick up the books she'd dropped, which Olivia now rushed to help her with. 'I'll just have a massive egg, won't I? Maybe bigger than my actual head, or maybe a cool bruise. I'll just tell everyone I got it fighting zombies or something. Don't sweat it, honestly.'

Olivia smiled, relieved that she wasn't being shouted at. She handed over the books she'd collected. She spied *Everything Leads to You* by Nina LaCour and *Out of the*

Blue by Sophie Cameron, two books she'd already read and loved. You could tell a lot about someone from the books they took out of the library.

'Zombie-fighting is certainly an interesting hobby, but I'm glad you're okay. And if anyone asks, I'll help corroborate your zombie story. Oh, wait!'

Recognition kicked in. 'Wait a second, we were in here the other day together, you were also complaining to Miss Carter about the ridiculous new library policy.'

'Right, that's me,' she replied. 'I'm Nell. As in Nell Gwynn. Or maybe Nelly Dean from *Wuthering Heights*? My mum never could figure out which she chose it from. And you're Olivia, right?'

Olivia nodded. She liked the way Nell spoke: with enthusiasm and warmth, accompanied by a smile that created creases below her eyes.

Nell smiled, but then her face dropped as she looked down at the book on top of the pile she was holding. 'It's no use,' she huffed, 'my mum didn't pay enough attention when she filled out my permission slip. She was too busy running around after my two sisters. So she only ticked the first box, letting me take books out of the library. Means I can't take a single one out with one of these ridiculous labels on – I don't know why I tried. Miss Carter can't do anything about it.'

'This gets more and more unbelievable!' Olivia spluttered.

'Tell me about it. My friend Rocky is coming to the library every lunch to read because their dad refused to sign the permission slip altogether. Says he won't allow any child of his to read about, and I quote, "unsavoury subjects". Rocky was right upset about it.'

The sensation of the blood boiling in Olivia's veins was returning.

'We have to do something.' Olivia had grabbed Nell's arm; she looked into her eyes. 'Where's Rocky now? I think I've got a solution. Hand me your books and I'll see if we can work around it.'

'I'll go and get them,' Nell said.

After a while, Nell returned with her friend. 'This is Rocky!' she said, and Rocky, with their short chestnut-brown hair and a lazy grin, greeted Olivia with a wave.

Olivia filled Nell and Rocky in on the plan.

'As a Year Eleven student, the library allows me to take five books out at a time, for two weeks. I don't have any books on loan at the moment. I need to take the Shakespeare sonnets book out, but I'll forfeit the rest. My mum's signed my permission slip in full.'

'Are you sure?' Rocky asked. 'It would be amazing, but no pressure!'

'Whatever happens today, you are walking out of this library with your books. It's time to evade the system!'

'I won't be walking,' Rocky said, 'I'll be skipping out with my books in one hand and my middle finger raised, cursing the system.'

'I'm with you on that one,' Nell said.

'Maybe we need a battle cry,' Olivia suggested. 'Fighting against injustice, one book at a time! Wish me luck.'

'Hello, Olivia,' Miss Carter said, when Olivia got to the front of the desk and took the books from her. She glanced over the WARNING stickers on the front, checked her computer, presumably for Olivia's permissions, before scanning the ISBNs on the back. 'How are you?'

'I'll be honest with you, Miss Carter,' Olivia said, standing up straight, 'I've been better. And I think other students in this library have too.'

Miss Carter sighed. 'I'm working on it, I promise. Don't think I'm idly sitting by, having a good time. Because I'm not.'

She didn't say anything else – she silently handed Olivia back her books, and gave a small, reluctant smile.

'Well, don't think I'm sitting by doing nothing, either.' Olivia puffed her shoulders.

'Olivia . . .' Miss Carter warned. Olivia could see the worry in her eyes. 'Don't do anything that will get you into trouble. It's an important year to play by the rules.'

'Would I ever break the rules?' Olivia replied sweetly.

'That's what worries me. When it comes to books, I don't know what you'll do.'

Olivia shook her head, clutching the books in her hands tightly, as if Miss Carter would see past her exterior and know what she was up to.

It was only a small rebellion, but it made her feel powerful. Strong. Capable of anything. It was a start. Rebellions only needed to be small to make a difference.

She held her head high as she spun on her heel and retraced her steps.

'Let's go, before she can figure out what we're up to,' she said to Nell and Rocky as she passed them. With a nod to each other, they did as Olivia requested and the three of them left the library.

Once outside, Olivia handed over the books.

'You don't know what this means to us,' Nell said, hugging the books to her chest.

'I'm glad I could help,' Olivia said. 'Hey . . . there's still plenty of time left before the bell. Why don't we go find somewhere to sit so we can chat?'

'Sounds great. Shall we head to the canteen?' Rocky asked.

'Perfect!'

Nell commanded the way and they each seized the opportunity of getting a – albeit lukewarm – hot chocolate, which they took over to a corner table out of the way of the energetic canteen.

The books sat between them and Olivia felt comforted by their presence. They were a reminder of everything the students would lose, a token of everything she hoped they'd be able to gain.

If we join together, that is.

'What I don't understand,' Rocky said, 'is why you're doing this for us. You don't know us and we don't know you. You've got no reason to help us.'

She did a quick risk assessment in her head: 1) Rocky and Nell were both eager to take books featuring characters on the LGBTQ+ spectrum out of the library, so they probably weren't evil and prejudiced and wouldn't pounce on her, and 2) they both seemed nice and friendly. It would be safe.

She cleared her throat. *Don't be nervous now. It will be okay.* She still looked around, though, to check if anyone else was listening. 'I know how much books like this helped me,' she began. Deep breath. 'When I first came out, I looked for every book I could find, I searched high and low for characters who were like me. Who I could understand.'

'I told you she was one of us!' Nell exclaimed, touching Rocky on the shoulder and grinning into their face. 'I told you!'

Olivia giggled. 'You too?'

There were happy butterflies fluttering in her chest and a dizziness in her head. The nerves dissipated, and she felt a new openness that she hadn't felt at school yet; she'd always felt the need to keep that part of herself – her sexuality – tight under wraps, not talking about it unless prompted. It wasn't hiding – it was being protective.

She knew Cassie, *obviously*, but it was amazing to meet more young people who were in the same position as her. At school, surrounded by people who were either straight and cis or too afraid to come out. And was it any wonder people were too afraid to come out, when 'gay' was still slung about as an insult and the mere suggestion of someone being queer was enough to cause the library to go into lockdown?

'I've always known I wasn't straight,' Nell said. 'People always give the argument that reading books or watching TV and film with queer characters will cause a gaypocalypse but being constantly bombarded with straight couples has never turned me straight. I can't remember a time when I didn't know it. S'why I feel so affronted by all this.'

'And I'm non-binary,' Rocky explained. 'For me, it means that I don't identify as either gender – I don't feel masculine or feminine and, for me, gender isn't either/or. I go by the pronouns they and them, rather than he or she.'

'I'm so happy our paths crossed, but I wish we hadn't been brought together under such awful circumstances. It doesn't seem fair. Something needs to be done and I don't think I can do it by myself. At least, not as effectively as with multiple people, and I know we've only just properly met but—'

Rocky clutched a hand to their chest, their mouth dropping open in surprise. 'Olivia, is this a *proposal*? How sweet!'

It took Olivia a moment, and then she burst into laughter. 'Yes, it is! Sorry there's no ring; do the books count?'

'You know, I think they might just. What do you say, Nelly-bobs? Are you in?'

Nell flicked her hair over her shoulders. 'Let's show 'em what we're made of. What do you have in mind, Olivia?'

'So I've had this idea . . .' she began. 'I've seen it on the internet, these book drops. People take their unwanted books and leave them for other people to find to spread the love of sharing stories. With the current situation at school, we already know from personal experience that it's going to be so much harder for LGBTQ+ students to access books from the library.'

'Yeah,' Rocky agreed. 'Suddenly, they – *we* – feel like there's something to feel ashamed of because you're confronted by a big warning sticker every time you go to pick up a book.'

'Exactly. So I'm suggesting that I take my very favourite books featuring queer characters off my shelves, and we leave them around school in places where hopefully they'll be picked up and lovingly looked after.'

'Makes sense,' Nell said. 'I like it.'

'Hey, I think that could work!' Rocky said.

'As long as you're happy to do that with your books,' said Nell. 'We'll do our fair share of work, pull our weight. We're in this together.'

'I don't mind!' Olivia said. 'My books are precious to me, but even I'm happy to make this kind of bookish sacrifice for such an important cause. There's no point complaining, is there, if all we do is sit idly by without making our opinions known?'

'We won't have to ... out ourselves, will we?' In a voice that instantly diminished any confidence they may have appeared to have, Rocky spoke. 'Because as much as I want to help, I don't want to have to do that before I'm ready.'

Olivia's eyes widened. 'Oh no, no, no, of course you won't! I promise you now, I won't make you do or say anything that you aren't one hundred and ten per cent comfortable with. I can't say it will be easy – we might not get anywhere – but that's my one guarantee. I promise.'

They finished off their hot chocolates, Rocky pensive but nodding away as Olivia went into more detail about the book drops she'd seen and the books she thought they'd be able to use.

'The main thing is that we get these books into the hands of those who need them most. After that, if you're still both willing, we can see what else we can do.'

Nell ran a frustrated hand through her fine hair. 'We'll be willing, trust me. I'd do anything to stop them carrying on with this. Anything. I'll chain myself to the library door and refuse to move. That's how dreadful I think this is.'

Rocky must have recognised the eager look on Olivia's face because they shook their head. 'I'm not sure if that's reeeeaaally a viable option here.'

Olivia curtly nodded. 'Hm, I think you might be right! I do get carried away with these things! You'll have to rein me in. My friends are always telling me I take on too much. But I can't help myself!'

'So you'll let us know when we're ready to go, yeah? We'll be right there, ready to do everything we can,' Rocky said.

'We'll be the dream team!' Olivia grinned. 'Woo hoo!!!'

She punched the air, drawing the attention of the students around her, but she couldn't care less. They'd actually agreed!! THIS WAS MOMENTOUS! *That's my good deed for the day done*, Olivia thought. *And with*

Rocky and Nell, a little bit of my faith in humanity has been restored.

She'd forgotten all about the cold she'd felt before lunch – it had been replaced by a warmth deeper than the toastiest fireplace on a snowy day.

I think I might have just taken the first step to making a difference.

And it felt amazing.

Cassie: can i come round to yours tonight? i need to get
away for a bit x

Olivia: Of COURSE! I'd love love love to see you!!

Chapter Five

Olivia's bedroom was a shrine to books: they lined three of the four sides of the room in floor-to-ceiling bookcases, only giving way when you got to her canopy bed, tucked into the space by the bay window. Her desk was neatly arranged with stacks of books she was currently reading or wanted to read soon, and even the back of her door was adorned with a *Pride and Prejudice* poster.

But the usually organised bookish landscape had been thrown into chaos; there were piles of books all over her floor and, for once, Olivia didn't even care.

That one will be great for the book drop, it's bound to be picked up ... Hm, I'm not convinced this one will be effective but ... YES! That's perfect! So that's one ... two ... three ... six ... nine ...

'Why are you taking all of the books down?' Cassie asked from her position on the bed, underneath the stick-on illuminated stars on the ceiling. Tonight she wore her dark brown bobbed hair pulled into tiny French plaits at the back of her head, and her lack of lipstick – which she usually always wore – made her face look a little barer than Olivia had seen in a while.

'Huh?'

'My question was: why are you making it look like an earthquake has hit your room?'

Olivia dropped herself on to her fluffy cream carpet.

'Well ...' she began, but her vision caught on Cassie's open sketchbook, which she'd been doodling in. At least, Olivia had thought she'd been doodling in it but now she could see that the doodles were really harsh, deep lines etched into the page. Etched into Cassie's precious notebook, which she always protected with her life.

She suddenly felt bad that she'd barely paid Cassie any attention since she got here.

'Do you like it?' Cassie said contemptuously, turning her sketchbook around to show Olivia properly, who struggled to keep the horror from her face at the wounded page.

She held one side of the sketch so that both her and Cassie were holding on to it at the same time. Their eyes met. 'You know you only doodle like this when something's on your mind, don't you?'

Cassie rolled her eyes. 'I'm fine. It's just a harmless doodle.'

'Really? It doesn't look harmless to me.'

Olivia watched as Cassie closed her eyes, trying to imagine what was floating through her mind. She thought it would be so much easier if she could unlock Cassie's head with a little key and gaze in, her thoughts floating freely when they could be let out into the open.

'I didn't go to college today,' Cassie said, eyes still shut tight against the world. 'I got ready, was about to head out, but Mum was in such a state. There was no way I could leave her; I checked and she hadn't taken her medication and was refusing to eat. How could I walk out the door and live with myself all day, knowing she was alone at home?

'I feel so lost . . .' Cassie's voice became so soft it was almost impossible to hear. 'The summer is over and now it feels like reality has set in. I don't know who I am any more. Everything feels so empty inside of me. I live every day for Mum, every single breath I take seems to be for her, and I've got nothing left to give. I can't see a way for it to get better.'

Olivia let Cassie talk, not interrupting her flow, but as soon as Cassie had rounded off, opening her eyes again to stare up at the stars, Olivia moved closer, lying down next to her.

'It will get better,' she said, but she wasn't sure herself. *Would* it get better for Cassie?

But like she could read Olivia's mind, Cassie said, her voice turning colder, more bitter, 'You can't promise that and I wouldn't let you promise that. Things are bound to get worse the closer the anniversary gets. I haven't even had time to grieve. I don't feel like Cassie any more.'

'You're still Cassie,' Olivia said. 'You're still *my* Cassie, the Cassie who is smart and funny and way too sarcastic sometimes but who we love for it. I know you think you have to be strong, but you already *are* strong. Stronger than you even know. And you're not alone in this. This doesn't have to be just your burden. You've got me, too. You've got Henry and Ed and Tabby. You have all of us, and we're here for you.'

Cassie reached out and squeezed Olivia's hand. 'I know, and I really appreciate it, I swear. I wouldn't be able to do this without all of you.'

'You would.' Olivia squeezed back. 'You'd find a way. But you don't have to do this without us.'

Cassie turned her head to the side, smiled. Olivia did the same.

'Thank you,' Cassie said.

Anticipation built in Olivia's body, buzzed around her brain, as they both leant in, both knew what was coming. Their lips softly met; they lost themselves in the kiss.

It's like the first time, Olivia thought. In Bath, when they'd both finally admitted to each other how they felt and Olivia thought she was going to sprout wings and burst into the sky because she was so happy. Every time was like that first time, reminding her of how much Cassie meant to her and how that was only growing and growing.

They may not be surrounded by grand buildings or caught up in the eagerness, hope, of that first time, but to Olivia, every kiss was special. It made her feel more alive than ever before.

Later on, filled up on food they'd eaten downstairs with the rest of the family – Olivia's mum had always loved Cassie and welcomed her like one of their own – they snuggled down on Olivia's bed to watch a film on her laptop, her warm throw blanket over their legs. Olivia leant her head against Cassie's shoulder. If she focused her mind, she could hear Cassie's heart beating, and her own beating in her ears too.

Surprisingly, Cassie's favourite film was *Grease*, and she knew every single lyric to every single song. A most un-Cassielike choice. Olivia smiled as she thought about how great it was that you could still discover things about a person even if you'd been friends for years.

Halfway through the film, Lizzie battered her head against the door and Cassie pressed pause while Olivia got up to let her in, whereby the little dog promptly jumped up on to the bed and made her own little nest to curl up into.

Olivia smiled at the view before she got back to her place. Cassie had lost some of the tension that had marked her features and looked happy as she scratched Lizzie behind the ears. It melted her heart, the two of them looking like perfect pals, Lizzie gazing with pure adoration at Cassie. She could see the appeal.

She took her place back on the bed and Cassie pressed play on the paused film.

Olivia was so relaxed, she thought she could fall . . . asleep . . .

BEEP!

You have 1 new message request.

Nell: Hey Olivia do you mind if I add you to a group chat with me and Rocky in it?

'Who's that?' Cassie asked as Olivia picked up her phone.

I can't burden her. I can't. She clearly has too much on her plate at the moment to be getting involved with my agenda!

'Just a girl from my religious studies class asking for the homework information we got today.'

Cassie nodded and turned her gaze back to the screen. 'This is my favourite scene,' she said, nudging Olivia's arm to get her attention. 'Ha! Watch this, watch this . . . Amazing!'

'Amazing,' Olivia echoed, but her gaze had gone back to her phone.

Olivia: Hello! That would be so great!!

By the time the credits rolled and Cassie was getting ready to leave, Olivia had been added to Nell and Rocky's group chat and was sneaking glances at her phone every two minutes. Cassie shouldn't mind – she was always checking her Instagram when she should be doing other stuff.

'It will be okay, you know,' Olivia said, just as she left.

'Thanks, Livs. I hope you're right.'

Olivia reached up to leave a kiss on her forehead.

'I'm always right, silly,' she said, injecting cheer into her voice. 'Trust me!'

Olivia: My mind has been ALIVE with the book drop! We'll
have to sort out a time to meet this week so we can start
putting things in place!

Rocky: Are we actually going to be dropping books on
people's heads?

Olivia: Hahaha, that might make them listen to us!

Rocky: The art room is free on Wednesday at lunch – want
to meet in there?

Olivia: That sounds perfect! We can't use the library for
OBVIOUS reasons so this seems like a very practical
solution! I love it!

Nell: Gotta love a good practical solution. Wednesday it
is. :)

Olivia: Have you read much of your books yet?!

Nell: Yep, I'm reading *Out of the Blue* by Sophie Cameron
and it is basically my dream book. In love!

Olivia: Ooh I love that one too! SUCH a good choice! I'll see
if I can think of anything else similar that you'll love just
as much!

Nell: Thanks! I'd love that :)

Henry: Do you all want to come round at 11 on Saturday
morning for the next meeting? Ed, will you be awake by
then?

Ed: I will wake up early at 10:58 just for you and then I will
teleport to your house

Henry: Great, sounds totally realistic and not past the
bounds of human possibility

Ed: Knew you'd understand!

Tabby: Can I get in on this teleportation business please?

Ed: Just imagine . . . THE PAPER & HEARTS SOCIETY:
TELEPORTATION EXPERTS

Tabby: I think it could catch on!

Cassie: for god's sake, don't encourage him tabby, he'll
never stop talking about it now

Ed: Or maybe I should get a JET PACK

<u>Physics topics to revise before Tuesday's exam:</u>

Energy equations

~~Particles – solids, liquids and gases~~

Renewable energy

Atomic structure

Electricity

~~Equations~~

Chapter Six

From the years Cassie had spent tucked away in there, Olivia could find her way to the art classrooms with her eyes closed. She'd always visited Cassie here when she wanted some quiet during lunch-times and Cassie had stayed behind to do extra artwork. Olivia hadn't been back since she'd dropped art before GCSE and Cassie had left, taking her ginormous portfolio with her. So it was with a feeling of nostalgia that she walked in now, laden down by a tote bag full of books that she'd had stuffed in her locker all day.

The art block was the most colourful part of the entire school. There was no need for paint on the walls – every single possible space was filled up with displays of past students' artwork, colour charts, and examples of the work they hoped their students would achieve, although Olivia wasn't quite sure that anyone would fully replicate a Monet or van Gogh's *The Starry Night* while they were here. The sides were covered with clay statues, containers of brushes, pots for water and paint, boxes of pencils and pens, and the tiles on the floor were spattered with dried paint and ink.

Without a book in sight, it wasn't Olivia's idea of heaven, but she knew it had been Cassie's, and wished she was here now.

Olivia was the first to arrive and she started by taking the books out of her tote bag and piling them up on the table in three stacks: one for each person. It was a wrench getting rid of them, taking them off their shelves, leaving only a dusty imprint behind, but it only made her want to succeed more because she knew she couldn't give the books away in vain.

If we can bring joy to even one person, that will be enough.

There were more books waiting for her at home that she'd sorted out, but she hadn't wanted to bring them all in one go, just in case the project wasn't very popular; it would minimise waste and, bonus, was less to carry. It was no easy feat bringing all these books in! Her shoulders ached just thinking about it.

She turned round as the door squeaked open before her, and smiled warmly – trying to contain any excitement – as Rocky entered. They grinned back.

'Hi!'

'Hey, Olivia! You're eager!' Rocky pulled out one of the stools opposite her and sat down. Olivia hated the stools because her short legs were always left hanging, and they also pushed your thighs into the wood of the table if you didn't angle yourself correctly – not ideal when you were trying to concentrate and couldn't get comfy.

'We come here to finish off photography projects sometimes so I thought it would offer us enough privacy to work. Everyone else is always off doing lunch-time revision sessions on Wednesday.'

'Do you do photography?' Olivia asked.

'Yeah! I love it. That's what I want to do, I think, become a photographer.' They shrugged. 'I'm not sure if I'm any good, though.'

'I'm sure you are! I always think that if you *love* doing something, you're good at it no matter what. It's the enjoyment that counts. You should have more faith in yourself! I'd love to see some of your photos some time.'

Rocky looked down at the table, a slight blush rising to their cheeks.

'Well . . . I do have a secret Instagram page where I post my pictures. But, like I said, I don't think it's any good.'

Olivia squealed. 'Show me, show me, please!! I'm sure you're *amazing*!'

Rocky rolled their eyes, but did take out their phone from their inside blazer pocket. Tapping away, the phone was then slid across the table. Rocky shielded their eyes, as if they couldn't bear to look at Olivia's reaction.

Her eyes immediately caught on the bright, vibrant pictures of the town they both lived in: a brilliant-red postbox, the town hall, the vistas of the hills and fields surrounding them. The images made Olivia think about her hometown in a way she hadn't quite known before.

'Rocky! I knew they'd be good, but these . . .! These are out of this world!'

Rocky blushed. 'Oh, you flatter me,' they said, waving in protest.

When Nell came in a few moments later, Olivia could see Rocky's relief, but she knew that she'd have to bring it up another time, just so Rocky could see how talented they were. To capture the life of an environment through the lens of a camera – that was special.

'Hey,' Nell said, taking the stool next to Rocky, 'I am ready to take on the world today. Let's do this.'

'That's what we like to hear!' Olivia placed her hands on the book piles. 'I've collected together lots of books from my own bookshelves, ones I think people might like and wouldn't be able to access in the library if they haven't had their permission slip signed. We can put little labels in each one, perhaps, asking students to make a stand against the new library rules? Do you think that would work?'

Nell frowned while she thought about it. Olivia watched her face intently, seeking the approval she was hoping for.

But was it too chancy? Maybe that was too much of a stand.

'It would have to be small and tucked in the pages,' Nell suggested. 'Because if a teacher was to get hold of a big leaflet, that might be too risky. My mum would go ballistic if she found out what we were doing. I do not need that hassle. No, we need something the reader is going to find, and only the reader.'

'So we'll have to *rely on fate*,' Rocky said in an ominous tone and, not for the first time, Olivia thought they sounded just like Ed. He'd have said exactly the same thing.

'Or not,' Nell said. 'How about we write personal messages on Post-it notes and put them in? Tokens of our love and appreciation. There are bound to be people who are feeling disheartened.'

'I *love* that!' Olivia said. This is why she needed Rocky and Nell: she would never have thought of that on her own. Three minds were better than her one.

'Here you go, a pile of books each. And I've got Post-its in my pencil case, hold on.'

'Who carries around Post-it notes?!' Rocky laughed.

'Clearly someone who wants to change the world, Rocks,' Nell said, shoving them in the arm.

'Point taken,' Rocky said, and took a Post-it note from Olivia's pile.

'So what kind of tone do you think we should set with the messages?' Olivia turned to Nell. She had her own ideas, but she didn't want to go overboard too soon. It had been Nell's idea, after all.

'You seen those things online where people leave messages on mirrors or wherever, that say things like "You are amazing" and "You are loved"? We could do that in some, and in others more book-related messages. I don't think it has to be particularly deep. Just something nice to make someone smile when they open it up. Memorable.'

'Now that I can do!' Olivia exclaimed.

They set to work; Olivia bit the top of her pen as she stared down at the Post-it note and wondered what message she should leave. No, it didn't have to be deep, but she wanted it to be something that wouldn't be discarded, chucked in a bin to be forgotten for ever. What would she like to read if she stumbled across a book that had been left to be found?

I hope this book will mean as much to you as it has done to me. x

Yes. That was exactly it. Exactly how she felt.

'I hope you don't mind me being nosy, but who's in your profile picture with you?' Nell asked.

It was her and Cassie, taken in the last days of the summer holidays, when it had just been the two of them, away from The Paper & Hearts Society, laid out on a picnic blanket in the park. They were both grinning from ear to ear, Cassie with her sunglasses sitting on top of her head, and Olivia with a starriness to her expression that foretold of the love she was feeling.

Nell must have seen it when they were messaging back and forth, and the thought of the picture made Olivia smile.

'Oh, that's my girlfriend,' Olivia said, her cheeks rising to a blush.

'Girlfriend!' Nell said. 'Awwww, that's so cute!'

'How long have you been together?' Rocky asked.

'Well, she's been my best friend for years, but we got together over the summer. I still can't believe it sometimes!' She opened a book and stuck her Post-it inside.

'Very romantic,' Nell said. 'Had you liked her for a long time . . . like that?'

Olivia twisted her head to the side. 'Yes? And no? It took me by surprise at first: because I'm demisexual, I never really have crushes. I have to know someone well before I might even have a sense that my feelings might be a little more, and I'd been friends with Cassie for so long that it was unexpected.'

'Unlike me, then,' Nell said with a small laugh. 'I always end up having hopeless crushes!'

'So when was the moment you realised?' Rocky asked, moving on to their next Post-it note. 'When was the moment that it hit you?'

Remembering brought back all the giddy, bubbling emotions and recollections that she treasured most. 'It was about two years ago,' she began, tracing a heart carved into the wooden table with her finger. 'I was with my other friends and we were visiting a literary festival. Ed and Henry – the other two – had gone off to search for some food, which left Cassie and me. Suddenly, she turned to me and grabbed my hand and said she had a surprise, and she'd booked a ticket to an event with my favourite author at the time. She'd made sure that Ed and Henry were entertained, and it was just the two of us, and as I looked up at her and realised how thoughtful she'd been and had always been, I knew there wouldn't be anyone else in the world for me.'

'Rocky,' Nell said, fanning herself with her hand, 'I think I might be hyperventilating from all the unbelievable cuteness I have just heard. Love is real!'

'Wow, who'd've thought it?'

'Oh, don't be silly,' Olivia said, brushing them away. 'It's just . . . how it is!'

'For you, maybe!' Nell said. 'Some of us aren't that lucky.'

Olivia noticed that Nell was doodling love hearts on her Post-it absentmindedly. 'That doesn't mean you'll never find it,' she said, reassuringly.

'So how should we split the books?' Olivia continued. 'Do you mind which ones you take or where you go?'

'I'm happy with whichever books. I have biology next period,' Rocky said.

'And I have French in the languages corridor on the other side of the building,' Olivia said. She could stash them on top of the lockers; she knew just the place.

'And I have PE,' Nell finished. 'Perfect for leaving in the changing rooms when we're all finished. Bound to be someone in there for an after-school club later.'

'I couldn't have planned things better myself!' Olivia exclaimed. 'We'll take three books each and leave them on our way to lessons, and then they'll be brilliantly distributed around the school. We'll need to leave them in places people can't easily find, but also won't ignore them or, worst case scenario, do something stupid like destroy them. Sometimes we have to assume the worst of our fellow humans.' She laughed, if only to distract herself from the thought that her precious books might actually be ruined.

'We can keep an eye on things to make sure that doesn't happen,' Rocky said, clearly noticing Olivia's anguish. 'I have awesome powers of distraction and attack!'

Nell snorted. 'You like to think you do.'

'I am offended, Nellington, that you assume I don't.'

'I don't assume. I know for a fact you don't. Need I remind you of the time my little sister took you on in an arm wrestle and she won? She was three!'

Rocky shook their head. 'I let her win,' they grumbled.

Olivia grinned. The more she got to know them both, the more she liked what she saw. They were like a double act, bouncing off each other and complementing each other's nature.

That's what it must be like when other people see The Paper & Hearts Society together.

'Imagine if other people wanted to join and make a group to inspire even bigger change,' Rocky said. They were putting the finishing artsy touches to their final Post-it note. 'Wouldn't that be awesome?'

Olivia blinked. 'Awesome? It would be all my hopes and dreams, achieved!' But she shook her head. 'I doubt it will happen.'

'You told me to have more faith in myself earlier, so now it's your turn.'

'I do have faith in myself,' Olivia counterpointed, 'but I don't want to end up disappointed. If I'm not careful, I'll start thinking thoughts that are too big for my brain to cope with and all my ambitions will spin out of control, and that is *dangerous*.'

'You'll have to rein yourself in, you mean?' Nell said.

'Exactly! Because if I don't, you'll find me standing in the middle of the main corridor, screaming at everyone to join our library gang and people will assume I've lost my marbles completely.'

'Hey, I think that might just work,' Rocky teased.

'Oh, I meant to say, Olivia. It's my birthday on Saturday and I'm having a party at my house with some friends from my year and a few other people I know from school. Rocky will be there. Want to come?' Nell asked.

Oh, she loved parties! The excitement and mingling, the music and laughter.

'I'd love to!'

Nell beamed. 'I'll message you the details in our group chat later, in that case. It'll be fun!'

She didn't doubt it would be. And she was touched that Nell would think to include her; she didn't have to. They barely knew each other, yet Olivia felt like she'd known her and Rocky for far longer than lots of people she'd known for years – Paper & Hearts Society excluded, of course.

And with that they each took their books and went their separate ways.

Olivia found Tabby waiting outside the French classroom not speaking to anyone, lined up behind another group of their fellow French students. On her way past, she took one of the books and reached up high to slide it on top of one of the lockers.

First one: done!

On her way out, she'd tackle the lockers on the other side.

'Livs!' Tabby called when she spotted her, and Olivia smiled and waved. 'Where've you been? Henry and I were looking for you!'

Olivia tapped the side of her nose. 'Elementary, my dear Tabby. I have donned my superhero cape and have been saving the world!'

Tabby laughed. 'I won't pretend to know what you're talking about but it definitely doesn't sound French.'

'*Non, mon amie!*'

Before they were called in, Olivia cast a glance at the hidden book peeking out from the top of the lockers. She had only to hope that it would be taken before the week was out.

Ed: I am soooooooooooooo excited for Friday night!!!! Livs, do you want a lift??

Olivia: I'm excited too! I'm fine, but thank you! I'll see you at Henry's!

Henry: Can I have a lift please Ed?

Tabby: Henry . . . it's at your house

Cassie: (think that might have been a terrible joke on henry's behalf, tabby)

Ed: You will regret saying that because now when I see you I'm going to pick you up and throw you over my shoulder

Henry: Please don't

Cassie: please do

Henry: Cassie, whose side are you on?!

Cassie: my own, obviously

Chapter Seven

LATE, LATE, LATE, LATE, LATE! Olivia screamed at herself, rushing about her room to pick up everything she needed for today's Paper & Hearts Society meeting. She'd told Henry she'd be there early to help him set up, but she should have left twenty minutes ago and she was still no closer to leaving the house.

She had been deep in her thoughts, getting ready and putting the finishing touches to her make-up, when she'd looked down at the time and nearly jumped out of her skin.

I've got to get going! What did I do with the Paper & Hearts Society scrapbook? I swear I put it in my backpack last night! But as she ripped the zip open to look, it was to find no scrapbook in sight. *Great, Olivia, you had ONE JOB! One job!!!*

Cassie: where are you? want me to come and meet you? x

If Cassie was messaging to see where she was, she should definitely get a move on. Cassie was usually the late one.

The one time I told Ed not to pick me up. The one time I told him I could manage! Typical!

The scrapbook would have to be left. She'd have to make some excuse because there was no way she'd be able to find it *and* not turn up five hours late.

She swung her backpack over her shoulder, noticing how light it felt without the scrapbook, like something much larger was missing.

'I'm going!' she called into the kitchen on her way down the stairs, pulling her shoes on faster than lightning and slamming the front door quickly behind her before Lizzie could follow.

Olivia: I'm on my way!!!!! I PROMISE I'LL BE THERE AS SOON AS I CAN! I. AM. ON. MY. WAY!!!!!!

When the bus finally turned up, she urged the driver on with her mind but, of course, it was Friday evening and the bus was full, each passenger painstakingly pressing the button to get off at every stop.

Finally! When the bus doors creaked open and spat her out, Olivia panted up the street towards Henry's house. She didn't have to wait long before the door swung open and Cassie stood on the threshold, grinning in the way Olivia only ever saw Cassie grin at her.

'Hi,' Olivia said, in the soft voice that always made itself known around Cassie. The only time she ever felt close to shy.

They headed inside, close together, and were met by warmth and laughter, the sound of giggles and exclamations. The sound of friendship.

'We're in the conservatory,' Cassie said, leading the way to the back of Henry's house. With each step Olivia took, the noise became louder, until it reached its height as they passed out through the kitchen and into the open brightness of the conservatory. She sat down in the remaining armchair.

'You'll never guess what, Livs?' Tabby said instead of hello, her strawberry-blonde hair fanning around her face and glasses. She was sitting next to Henry on the sofa, and fiddling with a pink hairband around her pale wrist. 'You know that art class I went to with Gran this morning, the one recommended for people recovering from illness?'

'Yeah.' She remembered Tabby mentioning it when they'd walked part of the way home from school together.

'Well, it wasn't just any old art class. Gran got the time mixed up, so we got there for the earlier class.'

'Wait until you hear this!' Ed said. He'd positioned himself in a green deckchair and was pushed right back, practically lying down, looking very pleased with himself.

'So I walk in,' Tabby said, 'Gran's holding my arm, we take a seat and start talking to some of the other ladies there. I was the youngest by about fifty-five years, but that was fine. I'm used to it at Zumba. It was all going to be great and Gran was really looking forward to it. So then we're sitting around, getting our easels set up, and this man walks in and goes over to a podium in the middle of all our easels, which are in a circle. And then, wait for it . . . he starts taking all his clothes off! He just strips completely naked, and all the other women are loving it! Gran practically drowned in a puddle of her own drool, and I'm there totally confused, wondering if I've died and woken up in an alternate reality. It was a life-drawing class! And Gran just sat there, like she was supposed to be there! I didn't know what to do!'

Ed laughed and didn't stop laughing, and it caught and they were all laughing.

'And are you sure she didn't plan this all along?' Henry said, wiping tears from his eyes.

'She swears she didn't, but she must have done! There's no way she couldn't have, the cheeky so and so! She stayed for the art class afterwards, too. It was nice to see the glint back in her eyes.'

'I love that so much,' Olivia giggled. 'I wouldn't have known how to react!'

'I would have paid good money to see your face, Tabby,' Cassie said.

'Ha ha. Come to the next class and see for yourself, Cassie, she's booked us in next week! Sometimes, I'm sure she's an alien from another planet. I will miss her, though, when we move out at the end of the year.'

'I think I could be a life model,' Ed said. 'I have the physique and rugged good looks for it. Maybe I'll sign up for the life-drawing class Tabby is going to.'

Tabby almost spat out her tea.

'Eewwww!' Olivia said, covering her eyes with her hands, more to block out the mental image than anything else. 'I do not want to picture that, Ed! Why did you have to go there?!'

'Yes, quite. On that note,' Henry said, 'I think it's time to get started on today's meeting. This is officially the first Paper & Hearts Society meeting I've hosted, which is a huge honour and I know I have big shoes to fill, but I hope you'll enjoy it, nonetheless. And I hope you won't be *too* silly, Ed.'

'I make no promises,' Ed said. 'Except that I'll keep my clothes on.'

'Thank god for that.' Cassie rolled her eyes.

'Very good, Ed,' Henry said. 'Right then! Today, The Paper & Hearts Society are having our very own Book

Olympics, where we compete to become gold-medal readers. We'll be split into two teams – unfortunately, slightly uneven teams – and will complete a range of different activities, which will be added up, and the winners will receive . . .' He reached into the pocket of his trousers and came away with three gold medals.

'Shiny!!' Ed cried.

Olivia had to give it to Henry: this was a fantastic idea.

'Right,' said Henry. 'I've got five wooden sticks. Three are painted blue, two are red. Each of you will draw a stick to determine which team you'll be on.' He walked over to Ed's deckchair. 'Ed, close your eyes and pick a stick, please.'

Ed darted a hand out, managing to tug on multiple sticks, causing Henry to bat his hand away.

'Just one, Ed!'

'How am I supposed to see if I have my eyes closed? This is flawed.'

Eventually he came away with blue. Tabby came away with red, and then it was Olivia's turn. As she shut her eyes, she waved her hands over them, like she was feeling for magic. She knew the result she wanted, though. It would be best if she wasn't on Ed's team because there was no way he'd take it seriously.

She made a grab for one of the sticks, feeling the rough wood in her hand. She opened her eyes.

Blue.

Typical. I'll have to make the most of it and hope he's in a determined mood.

Next, Cassie took red, which left Henry with the final blue.

'We've got Olivia!' Ed cried, grabbing her hand and spinning her around. She giggled, spinning him right back. She felt guilty, then, for not wanting to be on his team: when he was like this, unintentionally funny and carefree, he was impossible not to love. 'We've got Olivia!! And you, Henry.'

'You make me feel so special,' Henry said as he watched on, but he was smiling, hands in his pockets. 'We need team names, so confer, please.'

Ed pulled Olivia and Henry into one corner of the conservatory, lowering his voice to a deep whisper.

'Something Shakespeare-related!' Ed beamed.

'Fine,' Olivia conceded. 'It can be Shakespeare-related, if it must. But still sensible.'

I can't seem like a spoilsport.

They threw ideas around between the three of them, until Ed finally landed on the perfect name. He actually jumped up in the air, shouting, 'GOT IT!'

Olivia braced herself.

'*Blessed by Shakespeare*,' Ed said, excited. 'Because Shakespeare will bless us as competitors and make sure we win! Shakespeare will always be with us that way.'

Henry and Olivia exchanged a glance. Were they really going to let him have this? It was tempting to say no, but they both knew that it was easier to let Ed have his way and make him happy.

'Fine,' Henry said. 'But Shakespeare better bless us.'

'I know he will,' Ed said. 'I spoke to him beforehand and sorted it all out. We're good mates. Did you know he's a pro at using Snapchat?'

The other team called themselves the Ultimate Bookish Champions to End All Champions, although Tabby said it was close between that name and Better Than Ed.

Ed, of course, spluttered in protest and claimed it was never possible to be better than him.

Henry explained their first task: a book relay. He would sit out to be the adjudicator. Each team was handed a copy of the same book – in this case, *Great Expectations* by Charles Dickens – and had to turn to the same page. They numbered themselves one and two, and whoever was first had to read their two selected pages; once done, they would pass the book to their teammate, who would then read the following two pages. The winning team would be the one who read their four pages out loud the quickest and shouted their team name at the end.

'Remember: cheaters only cheat themselves,' Tabby said, 'and yes, I'm looking at you, Ed.'

'I feel very victimised right now,' he retorted.

Olivia and Ed sat opposite each other, wearing their best game-faces. Ed said, 'I'll go first because I'm the slowest reader here. Olivia, you're the fastest so if you go last, you can pick up our slack if I get us way behind.' He cracked his knuckles.

Olivia heard her phone beep. She took it out of her pocket.

Nell: Just keep thinking of whether anyone might be reading
   the books we put out this weekend
Olivia: Me too!!! They might be reading something THIS
   second or THIS second
Rocky: Or even THIS second?
Olivia: Exactly!!!

'Earth to OLIVIA.'

'Huh? What? Yeah, that's fine, Ed.' She barely knew what she was agreeing to.

'In five ... four ... three ... two ... one ... READ!' Henry shouted, and Olivia saw Ed race to get started, while she sensed Cassie next to her doing the same.

Quicker than she'd expected, Ed read his pages and passed the book to her. Anticipation bashed against her chest; she wanted to jump up and down on the spot to let some of her energy out, but instead let the buzz take over her. She had to read faster than she ever had in her life.

All the books she'd read, all the speed-reading she'd done in hastily found minutes between classes or waiting for the bus or whilst reading a good book and being so engrossed that she couldn't tear herself away, came down to this.

She let her eyes soar along each line, barred the pictures the words created from igniting her imagination, and focused purely upon the words and their mechanics – an adjective here, an adverb there, a long monologue that she wished would hurry up so that she could read faster and faster and faster and faster and . . .

'ULTIMATE BOOKISH CHAMPIONS TO END ALL CHAMPIONS!' shouted Tabby, jumping up and down in glee. Cassie joined in, exultant.

'My contact lenses nearly burst out of my eyes doing that,' Cassie said. 'That would have been gruesome.'

'Is it normal to feel out of breath?' Tabby asked.

'Well done,' Olivia said weakly to the other team. She turned to Ed and Henry. 'We'll just have to make sure we win the next one. We can't afford to lose that, too – we'll be too far behind otherwise.'

'Too right we'll win,' Ed said, pouting. 'Shakespeare is depending on us.'

Henry gave her a funny look. 'Are you all right, Livs? You seem to be taking this very seriously.'

She cracked her knuckles. 'You have to take these things seriously, Henry. It's a life or death matter.'

'That's the spirit!' Ed said, thumping her on the back.

Rocky: Do you think we should put more books out, if we
see on Monday that they've all gone?

Nell: Think it would be nice to! :)

Nell: Olivia, have you got any more book recommendations
for me? I finished *Out of the Blue* last night and now I
don't know what to read. I need you to work your book
magic!

'. . . Livs?'

'Huh?!' She snapped her attention away from her phone, to find Ed behind her, loudly munching on a ginger biscuit.

'Ooh, who are Rocky and Nell?!'

'No one,' she snapped. 'Just some people from school. You don't have to read my messages, you know, Edward.'

Ed looked genuinely upset. 'Are you starting a rival book club?' he joked, a squeak in his voice. 'This seems suspiciously like cheating on us from my bookish perspective. You're not going to abandon us, are you?!'

She slammed her phone down on the worktop. 'No, Ed, I am *not* going to abandon you. I'm allowed other friends, *okay*? I'm trying to make a difference in the world; you might not care about that, but I do.'

'You've never mentioned them?' Cassie said. Was it Olivia's imagination, or did she see hurt flash across Cassie's eyes?

'Oh, didn't I? I thought I had! We're trying to do something about the library. It's not a secret! We're getting a campaign going.'

After that, she pretended to be very absorbed in a painting on the wall, happy when Henry declared, 'Anyway, on to the next challenge!'

As he explained, the next challenge would go like this: a nominated person from each team had to name as many book titles as possible within the space of one minute. No hesitations allowed, and each book title could only be said once. They would be in separate rooms so no cheating could take place, and the remaining people (or person) from the other team would adjudicate.

'This is my chance,' Olivia said to Henry and Ed; they were huddled together, talking tactics. 'I know I've got this in the bag.'

'We've got to win,' Ed said. 'I hate losing.'

'*You* hate losing?' Henry said. 'If Tabby wins, she'll never let me hear the end of it.'

'I *will* win,' Olivia said, confidence shooting through her. 'There's no other possible outcome. I either win or die trying.'

She was only half-joking.

'You're going down, Livs,' Cassie said with a grin, flicking her hair over one shoulder.

'Oh, I am, am I? I wouldn't be so sure about that, if I were you. Your team will be in tears on the floor by the end of this.'

'Wow, I've never heard you be so mean before,' Tabby said.

Olivia grinned. 'Trust me, this is friendly.'

Tabby left to go with Henry and Ed; Olivia and Cassie were alone.

'Are you ready?' Cassie said, deadly serious, her finger hovering over the stopwatch on her phone. She winked at the last second.

Olivia nodded her head. Just once. 'I'm ready.'

She heard Cassie count down, but she'd turned away from her: Cassie was too much of a distraction. A tile on the floor was far more interesting and kept Olivia's concentration as sharp as it could be. Quicker than she thought five seconds felt, the timer had started and it was go, go, go, go.

First, the obvious place: Jane Austen. '*Pride and Prejudice*,' she said, frantic, counting on her fingers without registering how many titles she was saying, '*Persuasion, Sense and Sensibility, Northanger Abbey* . . .'

Where next? The first thing that popped into her head, '*Harry Potter and the Philosopher's Stone, Harry Potter and the Chamber of Secrets* . . .'

Her mouth felt dry by the time she'd got to the end of all the Harry Potter books, but still she had to keep going. The seconds were drifting through her fingers like hourglass sand.

What had she read for school recently? Oh! Shakespeare! '*Much Ado About Nothing, Romeo and Juliet, Macbeth, Hamlet* . . .' She stalled. Her mind had gone blank!!!

Feeling more frantic than ever, wondering how much time she had left, there was only one thing she could do and that was to push on.

She was sure she was blinking more than was humanly possible, trying to rack her brain for as many book titles as she could think of. A new tactic: imagine a shelf from her bookcases back home and say the titles as quickly as she could.

She was off again, racing and racing and racing, reeling off book titles like there was no tomorrow.

'Time!' Cassie called, hitting stop on her stopwatch. Olivia crumpled on to the floor, burying her head in her hands.

'Don't tell me!' she said. 'I don't think I can bear it!'

'You were born for this, Livs,' Cassie reassured her. 'You basically went at the speed of light.'

I hope so!

'We're ready for you!' Cassie called through the closed door, which burst open, Ed on the threshold, his arms in a jubilant pose.

'Wow, Tabby was seriously, seriously good!' he said, marching into the room, Henry and Tabby following behind. 'I mean ... our team will have done better, of course. I must be loyal. I bet you've done spectacular, Livs!'

Henry nodded towards Tabby. 'I've got to say, you did very well. I'm proud.'

'As a competitor,' Cassie said, 'I should say something about how Olivia may have been good, but I hope our team was even more awesome. But as a girlfriend? Woah. That was *intense.*'

The adrenaline rush was beginning to wear thin and the nerves had kicked in. Had she done well enough? In her mind, everything seemed slow, yet maybe that was just the pressure.

'We'll say the results at the same time,' Henry said. 'Ed, Cassie – will you do the honours?'

Once again that day, Blessed by Shakespeare lined up to face the Ultimate Bookish Champions to End All Champions. Ed and Cassie stared into each other's eyes; Olivia was facing Tabby.

Tabby grinned and some of the tension from the air around Olivia crackled and dissipated.

It's just a silly game and doesn't mean anything, it's just a silly game and doesn't mean anything, it's just a silly game and doesn't mean—

Ed and Cassie opened their mouths. 'Seventeen,' Ed said, reading Tabby's result, at the same time as Cassie said, 'Twenty-eight.'

The wind was knocked out of Olivia's lungs as she felt Ed lift her from the ground and bounce her up and down and, despite herself, she giggled, caught up in his glee.

The decider was a competition to reconstruct a poem cut up into individual lines. Henry had assured them that he'd asked his dad to select and dismantle the poem, ensuring he was as clueless as they were, and it was the task of both teams to accurately piece the poem back together again.

The poem in question was 'The Raven' by Edgar Allan Poe, which seemed to go on for yonks. Olivia wasn't averse to an excellent poem, but when the pressure was on, she couldn't concentrate at all on how good it was.

Henry, however, was practically drooling. She was sure he was going to pull a magnifying glass out of his pocket in a minute and go full-on Sherlock Holmes. 'No, Ed, that can't go there, look at the metre,' he said. 'Every stanza ends in "more", "evermore" or "Nevermore". Look at the pattern!'

His tortoiseshell glasses slipped down his nose and he pushed them back up, running a hand through his hair. Watching Henry for long enough, Olivia kept noticing him look up and over at Tabby, and she wondered if Cassie ever did the same with her. Just the thought was enough to make her blush.

The timer was ticking down – they had twenty minutes to piece together as much of the poem as they could and stick it down to a piece of A3 paper.

Ed was covering one of his hands in Pritt Stick and peeling the dried glue off. 'This is so much better,' he said, 'with PVA. Hey, don't look at me like that. I'm meaningfully contributing to this task.'

Olivia, Henry and Ed shrieked with delight when it was revealed that their reconstructed poem was the closest to the original.

'I did it! I did it! I did it!' Ed cried, earning him a playful whack on the arm from Henry.

'That means . . . WE DID IT!' Olivia cried. 'We won!'

'WHAAAAAATTTT!' Ed screamed, lifting his shirt over his head and running around the room. 'WHAT! WE WON. WHAT! WHAAAATTTT!!'

He then made a dive for Henry, who hadn't realised what Ed was going to do until it was too late.

'Put me down!' Henry yelped, batting at Ed's back. One leg intermittently touched the floor, his long legs no match for Ed, and once he'd been lowered clumsily back to earth, he scruffed Ed's curly blond hair until it looked like a bird's nest.

They all crashed down on to the sofas, laughing and celebrating.

'I need to make a winning speech!' Ed said.

'No need to rub it in,' Tabby said, but she pushed him up so that he was standing in front of them all.

It was clear Ed was a natural dramatist. 'My dear bookish friends, it is my greatest pleasure to be standing here in front of you today, you who I have so much respect and gratitude for. It wasn't an easy journey to get to this point – it's taken many years of hard work, dedication and, most importantly, chocolate cake in all the reading breaks. I knew we could do it, though. We truly were Blessed by Shakespeare. I know I should thank both of my teammates, but the person I really want to thank is our Graceful Host, Henry.'

'I think it's supposed to be "gracious", Ed,' Henry said.

'Whatever. I think you're graceful too. Like a ballerina! And we wouldn't have been able to win if it weren't for your awesome games. A toast to Henry, and to Shakespeare, please! I know we don't have anything to toast with but you can all pretend. Use your imaginations!'

Olivia was still buzzing from the winning energy as she departed Henry's house later that afternoon.

'Do you want to come into town with me?' Cassie asked as they walked side by side down the street away from Henry's. Ed had had to get off ASAP and Tabby was staying because Henry's little sister, Belle, was returning home soon and Tabby wanted to see her. 'There's still time to stop and get a hot chocolate somewhere before it gets dark.'

That left the two of them.

Olivia groaned. 'I've got so much work to do, Cassie, I've got to get back. Next time, though?'

Cassie looked down at the ground and nodded; Olivia hated the awkward disappointment that filled the gap between them. 'Next time, definitely.'

They split ways and Olivia struggled to see where she was going as she stared down at her phone walking along, caught up in the new group chat. She did touch her lips, though, as she felt the ghost of her and Cassie's parting kiss sitting sweetly against her skin.

Rocky: Recommendations sound good, I'd love some too because I don't know what I should read next

Olivia: I'm just on my way home then I shall raid my mind for book recommendations for both of you! My favourite challenge!!! Revision can totally wait . . .

Nell: Revision can ALWAYS wait :D

Cassie: are you free tomorrow evening? it was so nice to
see you at the paper & hearts meeting earlier, but i feel
like i haven't seen much of you on your own and i miss
you :(

Olivia: Yes! How about 7?! I miss you TOO! <3

Cassie: amaaazzzinnggg! i'll bring snacks with me and we
can watch a film or something?

Olivia: At mine? That sounds brilliant!

Nell sent you a link.

Nell: Hi Olivia! Messaging you as the proper invite to my
party I mentioned the other day. Saturday (eek it's
tomorrow!) at 6:45. Hope you can make it :) By the way,
the theme is glitter!

Olivia: tomorrow?

Nell: Yes!

Olivia: ~~I can't tomorrow after all, I'm so sorry! But HAPPY~~
~~BIRTHDAY!~~

Olivia: I'll be there!! I'll make sure I get my sparkles out of
my wardrobe especially!

Nell: Great! I'm sure you'll know a few people from school at
least. It should be fun!

Olivia: You know it!

Cassie: i'm so excited, livs x

Olivia: Me too! But can we make it a bit later? My mum has someone coming round and they won't leave until then. Come over for 9pm? Is that too late for you?

Cassie: anytime is good for me! okay!

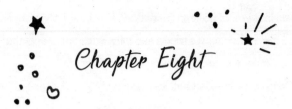

Chapter Eight

I'll only stay for an hour or so and then I'll be home in plenty of time to get back for Cassie. It will all work itself out; it's nothing to worry about!

Olivia had curled the tips of her hair so that it fell in waves over her shoulder blades, and had put on more make-up than the basics she usually wore at school: more mascara, some highlighter, liquid lipstick.

Wearing her favourite dungarees – the ones embroidered with a bright yellow sunflower – a glittery bronze jumper underneath, and sturdy black boots with a little heel, Olivia followed the map on her phone as she tried to work out how to get to Nell's.

This would be her first party of the school year and she loved the anticipation – no nerves, just delight at what was to come. She wouldn't know many people – only Rocky and Nell – but that only added to her excitement because there was nothing like meeting new people.

Turn left on to . . . There, up ahead, she could see other people streaming to a house a little way up the road. She crossed over into Nell's garden, where an apple tree was holding court in the centre, to find Rocky waiting by the door.

'Olivia!' they cried on seeing her, ushering her in. 'Nell's inside, herding everyone away from where they're not allowed. Go on in. I'm just waiting for the last guests. I'll follow you in soon!'

'Thanks, Rocky – so, so, so great to see you!' she said, entering the large hallway. There was a collection of mismatched coats hanging over the stair bannisters and enough people hanging around that she had to squeeze between them. There was a study to the right of the entrance, where a group had already begun to form, then the next room to the right was the bathroom, and then the hallway led down to the kitchen.

The layout of Nell's house was perfect for a party: whereas Ed's favoured everyone being squashed together, Nell's allowed for enough room to spread out between the spacious kitchen, living room and the back garden.

Most of the guests were in the year below and while she knew them by sight, she didn't know any of them by name and didn't think she'd get the chance to ask them over Ariana Grande's *Thank U Next* playing on a speaker. Olivia headed to the kitchen table filled with snacks and drinks, knowing there wouldn't be time to feel uncomfortable about not knowing anyone in the room if she had something to do. And there was always something to do, if you looked hard enough. She popped a handful of cheese savouries into her mouth, one by one.

'You made it!' She felt a tap on her shoulder and turned around to find Nell, dressed in a black glittery dress, grinning. In greeting, she gave Olivia a little hug. 'Glad you could be here!'

Me too, but I can't stay long, Olivia was about to say, but before she could, Nell cut through her words. 'Had anything to eat yet? There's plenty, just help yourself. Rocky's out front, you must have seen them on your way in, but they'll be in soon. Not many more people to arrive!'

'Yes, thanks! Great snack selection! It's a good turnout!' Olivia shouted over the music.

'Shut the door when you come inside!' Nell swung round to shout at the three people who had just come indoors from the garden. 'Sorry about that, it's mayhem around here when you're trying to watch everything. What were we saying?'

'A good turnout!' Olivia repeated.

'I know! *So* happy with that! You always worry that nobody will turn up, right?! But most of all, so glad you could be here. I feel like we've known each other for ages.'

She felt the same – it was like Rocky and Nell had been a part of her life for much longer than just the start of the school year. They had turned a horrible situation into something positive. Meeting them being the largest positive.

They stood around chatting by the food table, Nell pointing out who people were and scoffing her face with Party Ring biscuits. 'My favourite,' she explained, putting one on each thumb. 'Wait. Hold on. What are they doing out there in the garden? That's not for sitting on!' Before Olivia could so much as blink, Nell was racing outside.

'Olivia, there's someone I've got to introduce you to!' Rocky had come in, clearly done manning the door, and had brought someone with them: a boy with a short Afro and a bedazzled shirt. She remembered him from an assembly held a few years ago: he'd spoken with confidence about his parents who were immigrants, and what it was like to be black in a school consisting mainly of students who were white and didn't have to think about anybody else's experiences unless confronted with the truth.

'This is Alf,' Rocky said, 'he's in mine and Nell's year. Alf – this is Olivia! You'll never guess what, Liv? Can I call you that? Anyway, Alf found one of our books! He has the note with him to prove it.'

'Livs, Livvy, Liv – I don't mind what I'm called! That's so cool you found one of the books!'

Alf pulled a crumpled blue Post-it note from his jeans and opened it up.

A BOOK JUST FOR YOU, YOU GORGEOUS HUMAN BEING

'I recognised Nell's handwriting because we sit next to each other in English,' Alf chuckled. 'I did appreciate being called a gorgeous human being after I'd been covered in mud during rugby that afternoon.'

'I bet you did!' Olivia laughed. 'What book did you find?'

'Hmm, *The Art of Normal*, or something like that?'

'*The Art of Being Normal*! You were close! I love that book so much!' Olivia said. 'I hope you enjoy it.'

'I want to study English at uni and I'm trying to read all I can, so thanks. It will come in handy.'

'I might steal that off you after you've done with it,' Rocky said, taking a bite from their sausage roll.

'Be my guest, I never have anyone to share books with and nobody ever wants to talk about them.'

Olivia and Rocky exchanged glances, a look that said, *Are you thinking what I'm thinking?*

'You don't want to join our group of rebels taking on the library and their stupid permission slips do you, Alf?' Rocky smirked. 'Channel all that smart book information in your brain into something great?'

Alf tutted. 'Don't even mention those permission slips to me. It's discrimination, pure and simple. I don't know how the school can get away with it.'

'That's what we think!' Olivia cried. Shared outrage was the best outrage. 'We're trying to do something about it.'

'Well, let me know what I can do and I'm in,' Alf said. 'I'm lucky that my parents signed mine, but there's a couple of people I know who haven't been so fortunate.'

'We need to stick together,' Rocky said, 'and we can do with all the help we can get.'

Nell came zipping past then. 'I think Delia and Chris have gone upstairs into my mum's bedroom!' she hissed, grabbing hold of Rocky's sleeve. 'Come on, we have to stop them! Nobody's allowed in there!'

'Sometimes I wish I could sit and read in the corner at these things,' Alf said, leaning down close so that Olivia could hear his words over the music and shouting and laughter. 'I love socialising, but I also love not socialising, if you know what I mean.'

'How does that work?!' Olivia replied. 'Although I do see the appeal of a reading party, combining the two!'

Alf laughed. 'I think I must be an ambivert, when you're neither introvert nor extrovert. It makes it pretty weird in situations like this.'

She could only tell the extrovert part: whenever someone passed them, to head out the sliding doors to the garden or to walk back through the hallway, they nodded or raised a hand to Alf. He looked relaxed as he leant against the worktop, backlit by the lights underneath the kitchen cabinets.

'It's good of you to offer to help us,' she said, on a more serious note. 'It's nice to know it's not just us who are concerned about what's going on.'

Alf nodded and took a slurp of his drink. 'I try not to worry about these things because otherwise I'd just worry constantly,' he said, 'but you can't help but think that if they can do this, what else might they do?'

The thought had crossed her mind too. It was a slippery slope, the game the school were playing. One they shouldn't be getting away with.

She liked him already, his easiness and charm. Everything was careful and considered, intelligent. He reminded her of Henry, definitely trustworthy and kind.

'False alarm!' Nell called to Olivia and Alf, coming into the kitchen with Rocky. 'Nobody panic, it was all fine.'

Nell led the four of them into the living room, where the furniture had been pushed out of the way in place of a DIY dance floor, and insisted that they all did the Macarena, which Rocky had put especially on the playlist.

Alf laughed. 'I'm pretty sure this isn't played any more, for good reason . . .'

'Watch and learn, Alf, watch and learn,' Rocky boasted. 'These moves were made for me.'

Always keen for a good dance, Olivia let the silliness of the music take her away and ended up outdoing Rocky at every move, while more guests had come in from the garden and joined in.

Olivia, Rocky and Alf couldn't stop laughing as the song finally drew to a close; Alf was laughing the loudest – his extroverted side coming out even more.

She heard a phone ring, faintly, from somewhere close.

'Is that your phone?' Olivia asked Alf, wiping the sweat from her face unglamorously.

He took his out of his pocket and shook his head. 'Nope, not me.'

She took her own out.

CASSIE.

A voicemail was waiting.

'Hey Livs, where are you? I'm outside your house but nobody's in. I'm a bit early, but I figured your mum wouldn't mind if I joined you and your family friend. Have you all gone out for dinner? Let me know where you are and I'll join you. You haven't been sleeping, have you?'

Without thinking, Olivia called Cassie straight back. 'Hey Livs, thanks for calling. Wow, that music is loud! Where are you?'

'Oh, I'm out!' she shouted into the receiver. 'Don't worry, I'll be back in time, like we agreed!'

'Did you just hear what I said? Have you seen the time? I'm outside yours and it's nine on the dot.'

'What?!' *This really isn't working.*

'I said, I'm outside your house! At the agreed time! Olivia, are you okay?'

'I'm fine! Hold on! I'll go somewhere I can hear you properly!'

She put an apologetic hand up to Nell, Rocky and Alf and weaved her way to the front door and outside. Cassie was still on the line, and when Olivia got out into the quiet, she could hear Cassie's huffy breathing.

'Can you hear me now?' she asked.

'Yeah,' Cassie said. *Ah, she sounds annoyed.*

'Can you repeat what you said?! I didn't quite get it!'

'I SAID, I'M OUTSIDE YOUR HOUSE, WAITING FOR YOU!'

Olivia quickly pulled her phone away from her ear and winced. She caught the time as she did. **20:57,** it read. *How did I get so carried away?*

'There's no need to shout! Look, I'm sorry, Cass, I lost track of time and my parents have gone out to the cinema; their family friend cancelled, there's nobody at home. I can leave now and I'll be there in twenty minutes, max.'

Cassie huffed. 'I didn't have to come out to see you tonight, Livs, but I did. I wanted to hang out, the two of us.'

'I want that too, I really do, but things are tricky right now. I've got so much on at school and I'm trying.'

'At a party?' Cassie said sarcastically. 'You didn't even message me to tell me your plans had changed. You know what, Olivia,' and Cassie's breath came out heavy down the phone, 'just forget it. We can do this another time.'

The phone line went dead and Olivia slowly moved it from her ear; she stared at the blank screen.

She stood in the now-empty garden feeling horrible at the thought of Cassie walking home alone in the dark, disappointed and upset.

'Olivia, what are you doing out here?!' It was Rocky, coming up behind her and turning her round so she was facing the house. 'Come on in! Nell wants us to take a selfie!'

She felt pulled in two directions: maybe if she hurried, she'd be able to catch up with Cassie, put things right. But then again, Nell had invited her, and she didn't want to be rude by bowing out early.

I'll stay for fifteen more minutes and then I'll head home.

'What was that about a selfie?' She put her party smile back in place, and let Rocky link arms as they returned inside.

But even as she smiled into the camera lens for their group selfie, as she stayed an extra five minutes, then ten, then twenty, she couldn't shake the image of Cassie walking home on her own, probably feeling more abandoned than ever.

Why does it feel, all of a sudden, like I'm losing a grip on everything that's important to me? It's like I'm a juggler and people keep throwing more and more juggling balls at me.

She'd message Cassie in the morning and make it up to her. She'd make amends.

I don't want her to feel like she's lost me. And I can't lose her.

Olivia: Look Cassie, I'm so sorry about last night, I don't know what got into me. I'll make it up to you, I promise. <3

Cassie: it's fine, let's just forget about it. i don't want to argue with you

Olivia: <3 <3

@Nell: *Thank you to everyone who came to my party last night! This lot love a selfie with a glitter cannon! Clean up duty this morning definitely not so fun. @bookswithlivs #Glitterybirthday #themacarena* 😃 😂 🧜

Chapter Nine

What was the equation again? Olivia thought, flicking back and forth between the notes she was making and her physics revision guide. No matter how much she read through everything, she couldn't get it saved in her memory. It was the bane of her life at the moment – committing everything to memory for her mock exam. Which was tomorrow. She sat back violently in her desk chair, throwing her head up at the ceiling in frustration, groaning.

I HATE PHYSICS! I HATE IT WITH ALL MY BEING! YES, IN PRACTICE I MAY LIKE GRAVITY AND ENERGY AND ALL THAT STUFF, BUT I HATE LEARNING ABOUT IT!!!!!

She was beginning to curse Isaac Newton as if he'd personally attacked her. It wasn't helped by how tired she was feeling after Nell's party – it had been late by the time she'd got home and settled down enough to sleep, and she was paying for it today.

Her phone lit up from its place on her desk, and she paused the timer she'd been using to measure how long she'd been studying for. Which was far less time than it felt.

Tabby: Right everyone, listen to me please! Our very own Edward Eastfield is turning 18 very very soon and it's down to us to throw him a party to remember!

Cassie: is it ed's birthday? i caught him shouting about it as i walked past the drama studio earlier and so i haven't quite understood whether it's his birthday or not

Henry: Never! That sounds most unlike Ed, shouting about his birthday.

Tabby: I'm still getting used to the area, so where do you think the best place to go would be? It will also be my first time hosting a P&HS meeting and I am feeling the pressure!!

Cassie: i'll go wherever i'm told to go as always, i don't really care

Tabby: Olivia, what do you think?

I have no clue what I think because my brain is being weighed down by the gravity of revision. She opened up the other messages waiting for her. She could return to Tabby later.

Rocky: Are you both happy for me to add Alf? He seems
keen to be involved!

Olivia: YES!

Nell: Double yes with bells on!

Rocky added Alf to the group chat.

Nell: Welcome, Alfred!

Olivia: Shall we meet up again to chat properly?

Alf: I like the sound of that. It will be good to speak without
the loud music this time.

Nell: Name the place and I'll be there :)

Rocky: Ready and waiting!

Rocky: Not literally obviously because I'm actually currently
hibernating in bed watching my fifth hour of BTS
interviews

Nell: You and your K-pop obsession, honestly

Rocky: I am extremely dedicated

Olivia: Let's meet in the library – we can work without being
overheard but it also seems apt to chat in the place we
are trying to save!

Alf: See you all there tomorrow!

Olivia: I've got a mock tomorrow morning, but lunch-time
sounds good.

Alf: Okay let's stop bothering you, you must be busy revising!

I wish! Olivia thought. *It's far easier to procrastinate than
to revise.*

She contemplated going downstairs and grabbing some food, just for something else to do, but Kimberley was down there practising her clarinet and she couldn't risk taking off her noise-cancelling headphones – not if she didn't want earache. Her heart went out to her poor neighbours who had to put up with the sound bleeding through the walls.

Her finger drifted to the Instagram button and she couldn't help but scroll through her feed, the occasional study-related picture making her guilt disappear slightly. She scrolled through stories, reacting with laughing faces at pictures and videos she hadn't so much as cracked a smile at; staring at a picture of Ed's cat, Mrs Simpkins, for far too long, until she looked like a big blob of fur rather than a living, breathing animal; longingly admiring other people's bookshelves and book stacks and 'currently reading' posts.

This is no good either. Why can't I just press a button and all the information I need will automatically jump into my brain?

Tabby: Hi Livs! Thought I'd message you separately. I'm trying to firm together plans for Ed's birthday and wanted to know if there's anything in particular you'd like to do?

Olivia: I'm happy to do whatever you need me to do!

Tabby: I'm feeling really anxious about it to be honest because I just want to get everything right for Ed. I know

he won't be upset if something goes wrong, but it does
feel like a lot to think about!

What could she offer to do that would be a help to Tabby
and be nice for Ed, too?

> Olivia: I can make the cake?!
> Tabby: Would you? That would be amazing! I'm going to
>   bring some snacks and treats but a homemade cake
>   would be so much nicer than a shop-bought one and Ed
>   would love that!
> Olivia: Ed's favourite is Victoria sponge, so I'll make sure I
>   make a delicious one. It will be fun!!
> Tabby: Thank you, Livs!

She locked her phone screen and turned back to the
revision guide, but even the bright pictures and diagrams
were sending her to sleep. It helped to trace a finger over
the words, to repeat them over in her head once she'd
finished a sentence, to bullet-point everything on to a
revision card when she'd completed a paragraph.
Eventually, the information would have to worm itself into
her brain. Right?

By this point, she'd expected her pile of revision cards
to be . . . Well, more impressive than the meagre few that
littered the top of her desk.

'Arrgggggghhhhhh!' she groaned, and chucked her pen down with as much force as she could muster.

It would be so easy to take a notebook out and write all my bookish ideas down . . . So easy! And so much nicer!

No.

Not an option.

Unless . . .

'Stop,' she told herself forcefully. 'Stop it, Olivia. Just concentrate.'

But it came as a justifiable relief when the next message flashed up on her phone. *Does no one else have any revision to do?! No work?!* she wondered. *I'm the only one who seems to be doing anything today!*

Cassie: want to facetime?

Olivia's breath caught in her throat. She hadn't spoken to Cassie since the messages they'd sent each other after the party, and in her revision gloom, it was easy to let guilt creep back in.

That wasn't good of me.

Putting a thumbs up in reply, she accepted Cassie's request and smiled as she appeared on screen.

'Hey, Livs,' Cassie said, emotion muted. She was talking quietly, as she only ever did when she was speaking to Olivia from home. Tucked into a corner of her small bedroom, the curtains behind her closed and making the camera grainy from the lack of light, Cassie was bare-faced, wrapped in a blanket that draped over her shoulders.

'Hey,' Olivia responded.

'What are you up to?'

'Oh, not much.' She waved a revision card at the lens. 'Just revising.'

'Cool.'

Are you annoyed with me? Olivia wanted to say, even though she already knew the answer. *Even though you said it was fine. Because it's okay if you are. I understand.*

'I am sorry, you know. I shouldn't have let you down like that.'

Cassie raised a single eyebrow and smirked. 'No, you're right. You shouldn't have. But you know I'll forgive you, so I suppose we can just forget about it.'

'Okay,' but there was no relief in saying it – she didn't think Cassie would forget. Would let her forget. When she'd been slighted, Cassie let it show until you felt as much remorse as it was possible to feel.

Olivia almost smiled as she thought back to young Cassie – she must have been ten at the time, Olivia eight – not speaking to Ed for almost a month because he'd criticised a drawing she'd spent days on. Ed had tried all of the tactics under the sun to get her to talk to him again, even going so far as making her a pop-up card that had little stick figures of the both of them, but it wasn't until he'd properly apologised, from the heart, that she'd forgiven him.

Olivia stopped herself from smiling, though, because she wanted to show Cassie that she was taking this seriously. That she was serious about *them*.

'So who were you with?' Cassie asked. Olivia could see straight through her act of indifference, noting the way her eyes couldn't hold on to the lens for long before she broke her gaze, and her sudden interest in the condition of her nails.

I've got to be honest. It's the only way we can repair this situation. 'I was invited to Nell's party – she's part of our campaign group – and I thought I'd be back in time . . .' She trailed off. Not sure where to go next, she weakly repeated, 'I am sorry.'

A second passed. When Cassie spoke, the hardness had gone from her voice, leaving an emptiness that took Olivia aback. Speaking softly, she said, 'Every second I'm away, all I can think about is what my mum might be doing, whether she's okay, whether it's safe for me to leave her. Every minute I'm away could make a difference. Our time together is precious to me, Livs. I thought – out of everyone – you might have understood that.'

'Cassie . . .' *I've been so stupid.*

Cassie shook her head. 'How's all of that going? This campaign? You hardly ever mention it to me, which is fine – you don't have to share it with me if you don't want to – but sometimes it would be nice to hear about what's going on with you.'

The hardness was back. Impenetrable. To Olivia, it felt like a moment of opportunity had vanished into thin air.

'I think it's going well.' She shrugged. 'But it's only a start – I don't know how we'll ever get the school to overturn their decision. It's just nice to meet other people who feel the same, I suppose, and to feel like we all understand each other.'

'It's nice to feel understood,' Cassie said, with a little huff. 'Anyway, I'd better leave you to your revision, I guess.'

Find some neutral ground, don't end the call on a bad note.

Olivia groaned. 'This revision is the *worst*! Please don't leave me to it or I might chuck my revision cards out of the window and watch as they get run over by a car. None of it will go in!'

'What is it?' Cassie asked.

'Physics.' She rolled her eyes. 'I'm fine with chemistry and biology, but physics makes absolutely no sense to me and I don't know if it ever will.'

'I'd offer to help,' Cassie said, 'but there is a reason I stopped doing science as soon as I left school. And it's not because I'm so good they thought I'd show everyone else up, just saying.'

Olivia grinned. 'Are you sure about that?'

It was a relief to hear Cassie laugh. 'Absolutely positive. You'll be fine, Livs. I'm sure you're overthinking it and once you sit down, all that knowledge tucked away in your busy brain will come pouring out.'

'I hope you're right,' Olivia said with a sigh.

By the time they'd hung up, it was dark out and Olivia felt a little better about things between them. There was still a slight tension, but at least they were talking and could make jokes, which always improved things.

And I'll do better next time. No. There won't even be *a next time. I'll make sure there isn't.*

She returned to her revision guide, pushing the cards away to purely read. Everything else took up way too much time! If she was going to get to the end of the section she needed to know for the test, she'd have to be speedy about it.

Gravity . . . apples . . . Argh, this is making me hungry.

With every page she turned, her eyes began to burn and blur more, until she had to blink every few words just to be able to see. There was an aching in her temples, a dryness in her throat, and a rising panic that flickered like a burning candle.

'Aren't you going to get into bed?' Olivia was startled by Mum coming in, her hand hovering over the light switch. 'Livvy! It's great to see you working so hard on your revision, but you need to look after yourself, too. Come on! Bed for you.'

Mum came over and rested her hands gently on Olivia's shoulders.

'You know me,' she said. 'I just wanted to get all my revision done for tomorrow!'

'Good for you – but make sure you turn your light off soon. Or at least read to wind down. You've been so busy lately, you must be exhausted with all the revision. I think your exam will go very well indeed. Night, night,' Mum said, closing the door behind her.

Olivia looked down at the revision guide, her eyes fluttering under the sudden wave of exam nerves that overcame her.

A few more pages. And then I can sleep.

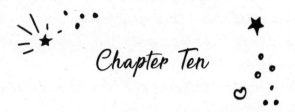

Chapter Ten

Sitting by the window in the physics classroom, Olivia felt that if the wind blustered any more aggressively, she would be blown away.

The walls had been covered with large sheets of paper to cover displays containing giveaway information, and there was to be absolutely no talking. The school was taking this very seriously. She was at a table of her own, everyone spread out around the room to mimic test conditions.

And Olivia felt sick.

The test papers were handed out, the start and end times were written on the wipe board at the front and then it was time to begin, with just a scientific calculator and her clear pencil case for company.

Deep breath, Olivia. Gather your thoughts. You can do this! It's only physics – it's not impossible.

With some trepidation, Olivia turned over the first sheet to reveal the first question. She stared down at it. And stared. And stared some more.

A diagram of solid particles glared back, and the first questions were easy – things she'd learnt a long time ago and had barely had to revise for. But as she turned the page again, her pen froze.

No answers to the posed questions would come, and she read the words back over and over in the hope that new light would be shed on what was being asked.

I'll come back to it, she told herself, and turned the page, but it was much of the same: some questions she knew half the answer to, others that seemed to be written in a foreign language she'd never been taught before.

She looked around her at her fellow students, all scribbling away with their heads practically touching their desks. She looked at their teacher, answering emails at his desk, only periodically looking up to check that everyone was working as they should be.

She had to put a new strategy in place: *Write down anything you can remember and hope that at least part of it is right, or by the end, you can come back to it and can correct anything you think is wrong.*

But even when she went to do that, she found that her knowledge was far less than she'd expected it to be. She had to settle on splurging her thoughts down, taking up way too much room with stuff that didn't make any sense, in the hope that it would at least seem like she'd tried.

'Ten minutes left!' the teacher was suddenly saying, and Olivia frantically flicked through the test paper to see all the gaps that were still left unfilled – so many gaps!

This is a disaster of epic proportions and I've never felt so awful about a test in my life.

She felt sweat dripping down her neck, heat rising up her throat and dizzying her brain. Her jaw was cramped from all the tension she'd been keeping in her body and she cut into the palms of her hands with her nails to stop herself from crying, to bring her back round to the moment where she had to write for her life and get the last answers finished.

I know I've failed, she thought, and she meant it. She was one of those people who knew if they'd done well or done badly on a test, not someone who always assumed they'd done badly, only to get a good result and be surprised.

I'll have to go home and pretend to Mum like it went okay.

'Put your pens down, please, and close your papers! I'll come round and collect them now. And no talking until the last paper is in!'

That wasn't a problem: Olivia didn't think she could talk if she tried, and she never thought she'd see that day!

She thought of her unheeded revision schedule, lying discarded under a pile of papers on her desk. *I would have done badly anyway, even if I'd revised every second of every day.* But she knew that wasn't necessarily true.

She needed to calm down. Dismissed from class, she headed to the girls' loos, bombarded, on walking in, by the sickly scent of over-sprayed, mixed perfumes.

Olivia raised her eyes to the mirror. As she looked up, she shocked even herself: her eyes were wide, her hair was sticking limply to her head, and she looked like she'd seen a ghost. A physics ghost. She immediately wanted to splash cool water on her face, even if only to prove that she was still in existence.

'Ugh,' she said aloud, scraping her hair back and rubbing her bloodshot eyes.

At that second, a door of one of the toilet cubicles burst open and a younger girl came out, her face blotchy, tears in her eyes. Making herself as tiny as she could, she stood in front of the mirror next to Olivia and dabbed at her face while pulling back her coily hair.

'Are you okay?' Olivia asked. She was tempted to put a hand out to rest on the girl's arm, but Olivia didn't know her and didn't want to scare her away.

The main door opened and the girl shrank back even more, but it was only someone going into one of the cubicles.

'It's nothing,' she said, but her bottom lip began to quiver and a fresh round of tears sprung to her eyes. 'It's – I just – I had a terrible lesson and it was all too much!'

Olivia put a comforting hand on her shoulder. 'Why don't we go somewhere a bit – well, a bit more hygienic? I happen to know where there's a good bench that's hardly ever taken. Or I could find a friend for you?'

'I don't have any friends,' the girl whispered, and Olivia felt part of her heart crack at the pain in her voice.

'What's your name?' Olivia asked gently.

'Saffy,' she said, doe-eyed as she gave in to Olivia's coaxing.

Olivia sheltered Saffy from the view of the other students milling about the wide, open corridor as she led her to the spot she'd picked out. Olivia had spent a lot of time here last year after Cassie had left to go to college – she'd had to adjust to it just being her and Henry, and reading was the perfect companion, staving off most of the newfound loneliness.

The stairs leading from the history corridor to maths upstairs had a little bench tucked underneath it, left there a long time ago and never moved. Most people used the main stairs, close by, so it offered the peace and quiet Olivia knew was necessary. They sat down next to each other.

'Would you like to tell me about it? I know you don't know me, but you can talk to me. I'm happy to listen and help as best as I can. I hate to see anyone upset!'

Saffy tucked her head down, gripping the edge of the bench with clenched fists. Her curly hair covered her face and her shoulders were tense, up to her ears. 'We had to choose teammates in PE and I was the last to be picked for netball *again*. It happens every single week and nothing I do will help! I try to talk to the other girls outside of PE lessons and they don't seem to want to know, and I try to act like it doesn't bother me when I'm not picked, but I can't help it.' Saffy shrugged. 'I don't know why nobody likes me.'

'Ugh, PE lessons are the *worst* for that,' Olivia said, 'and I commiserate greatly, but I guarantee it's not anything you're doing wrong. Is there no one you get along with, even just a little bit?'

She sighed and shook her head. 'Most people make fun of me.'

'Okay, tell me this: who do you feel the happiest around? For me, when I'm around my friends, I feel like I've been enveloped in the warmest hug or like I'm wearing a really snuggly winter jumper. So, when do you feel like that?'

She sat up slightly but didn't say anything for a while. Until, 'I don't know. I want to feel like that, but I look at everyone else, and it's like they *are* feeling like that, so why can't I? I feel like I shouldn't be there, like I'm too young or too silly or too bad at all of this. They . . . can't accept me.'

'Never let anyone tell you you're "too much" of something – usually they just say that because they feel bad about themselves. They don't think they're enough, so they say you're too much.'

'Are you Kimberley Santos's sister?' Saffy asked.

Olivia nodded. 'Yep, that's me.'

'I've heard Kimberley talk about you. She's in my geography class.'

'Is she?'

'Is it true you have a girlfriend?'

Olivia wanted to roll her eyes – what had Kimberley been saying?! – but she managed to stop herself at the last second. 'Yes, I do.' She smiled reassuringly.

'I made the mistake of telling someone about . . . about me, in Year Seven. I thought they were my friend, but they weren't. I had to come out before I was ready, and nobody understood me. They still don't. They either laughed or made fun of me or said I was making it up for attention. But why would I make something like this up?'

'I had no clue at your age,' Olivia said, 'so, if anything, it's a testament to you that you know yourself and your mind so well. No decent, honest person should ever make you feel that way about yourself. They're not a true friend if they do.'

But Olivia knew, in her heart of hearts, that it was easy enough for her to say: she'd been able to come out in her own time, when she was ready, to people she knew would be accepting. She was one of the lucky ones.

'Everyone seems confident but me.'

Olivia shrugged. 'It might seem like it, but I haven't always been this way, this confident. When I tried to come out to my friends, I had to write them a letter instead of telling them in person, even though they're the most welcoming bunch of all. I tried telling them to their faces but I completely blanked!' Olivia shook her head as she thought back to the memory. 'I couldn't do it, even if I wanted to. So even when you have the very best of friends, sometimes that's not enough.'

'So it's okay that I don't find this easy?' Saffy said.

Olivia smiled. 'You'll find friends who get you wholeheartedly one day, too. It might not be yet – school isn't the best years of everyone's life – but it will happen. And when you do, remember this moment?'

'I will,' Saffy said. She seemed to perk up, then. 'Or, I'll try to.'

Olivia hoped, if nothing else happened, that she'd made a difference. Because it was those small steps, the small connections made between people, that orchestrated change.

A flash of an idea hit her with force. 'You don't want to come with me now and meet some friends of mine, do you? I know it sounds weird – but I think you'll love them.'

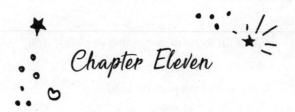

Chapter Eleven

A nook in the corner of the library proved the best place for the meeting point. The little alcove, shielded by a bookcase from the rest of the room, was perhaps the most popular area of the library, and was also now the reason Olivia was so out of breath.

Task achieved – table secured – she cracked open the new notebook she'd brought just for the occasion, and turned to Saffy, who no longer seemed upset – more nervous than anything.

Olivia had given her the rundown on what they were doing and had found in Saffy a willing, albeit anxious, helper.

'Are you sure they'll want me here?'

'I'm sure,' Olivia said. 'They'll be more understanding than you think. You haven't got anything to worry about.'

Saffy audibly exhaled. 'Okay, thank you. If you're sure.'

'H-hi.'

Olivia looked up at the new voice, and into the rounded face of a boy with dull brown hair and a worry line between his brows. He hovered by the table, one hand barely touching the seat opposite her.

She'd not seen him around before.

'Hello,' she said, a little confused.

In response, he took his other hand out from behind his back and in it, she saw a book. Not just any book: a book with an illustrated pink cover, one she would have recognised from anywhere.

'Oh, you're reading *Heartstopper*!'

He blushed. 'Oh yes. I love it so much. I've been almost constantly reading it since I found it. Have you read it?'

It's always a good sign when you find someone reading one of your favourite books, Olivia thought. That's how you knew you were in good company.

'It's one of my favourites! I've read volume two too and all the web comic so far. I look forward to every instalment!'

Alice Oseman, the author and illustrator of *Heartstopper*, had started by sharing the story, about teenage boys Nick and Charlie who fall in love, as a web comic, and it had since been turned into a series of graphic novels, which Olivia adored. She never missed an update.

'Wait . . .' she said. 'Did you say you found it?'

He didn't say anything for a few seconds too long and Olivia felt an awkwardness creep in. But it was gone as soon as he said, 'I found it on the top of my locker in the languages corridor after school last week.'

'Oh, that is the best, best, *best*!' Olivia exclaimed, and then clapped her hands over her mouth because even if Miss Carter didn't mind the library being chatty, Olivia's outburst certainly was a little too loud. Quieter, she said, 'I put it there!'

'I know,' he said.

'You know?' How could he have known? Had he seen her?!

'Miss Carter told me.'

'Miss Carter?!' Oh no. If Miss Carter had told him . . . *She must know! She must have found out!*

Seeing Olivia's worry, he continued, 'I came into the library because I found a note inside the book, but I still wasn't sure if it was mine to take. So I spoke to Miss Carter, she took one look, and said she assumed it was you. I only came in here to get a revision guide but then Miss pointed you out. I wanted to say hi and thanks for the book.'

Olivia looked in Miss Carter's direction and she couldn't be sure but it seemed she had a sneaky smile on her face.

'I'm so glad you did! Sit down, sit down,' Olivia said, gesturing to the seat. 'What did you say your name was?

I'm Olivia. I'm sure you'd be interested in speaking to some of my friends who will be here in a minute. Ah, I'm so happy that it was you who found *Heartstopper*!'

It wasn't long before they were joined by Rocky. 'I'm here, I'm here!' they cried, hurtling round the corner of the bookcase at a speed too high for inside. They only just managed not to crash into the table. 'Sorry! I had food tech and nearly had charred scones. So I've had to rush!'

They were carrying a large baking tin with a Christmas motif wrapped around it. They lifted the lid. The smell of fresh baking wafted out, and revealed inside, like peering into a treasure chest, was a dozen scones, tightly packed in.

'Don't say I'm not thoughtful,' Rocky said. 'I know how much you love a sweet treat . . . Oscar! What are you doing here?'

'Oh . . . I . . . Um . . .' was Oscar's reply.

'We have IT together,' Rocky explained to a clueless Olivia. 'Oscar's always copying off me when he doesn't think I'm looking.'

They shoved Oscar playfully.

At the sight of Rocky, the embarrassed air that had clung to Oscar since his arrival disappeared.

'I found one of Olivia's books,' he said, 'and now I've ended up here and it seems like it might have been fate.'

Rocky snapped the lid of the scone tin shut when they saw Oscar peering in. 'Not yet! We've got to wait until the rest are here. I'm sure it will be a difficult wait, so ponder on this: did I really use sugar, or did I accidentally put double helpings of salt in? A very important question. You'll soon find out.'

Olivia couldn't help but feel a little put off at that.

'Okay?' she whispered to Saffy, who nodded.

'I'm just trying to take everything in,' she whispered back, offering a smile.

When Nell arrived she, too, was surprised to see Oscar, who was also in her year.

'Oscar!' she said, taking off her tote bag and sitting down next to Olivia. 'You here to join us rebels?'

'Rebels?' Oscar said, and he shrunk back in his chair, only to sit up again a second later. Someone else had turned up, but it wasn't Alf as Olivia had expected, come to complete their group.

'Hey Morgan,' Oscar said to the new person approaching, just as Rocky said, 'We're trying to fight against these ridiculous new library rules. We're rebelling.'

'You are?' the newcomer, Morgan said, brown eyes wide.

'Yeah!' Rocky said.

Morgan's shoulders relaxed. 'That is such a relief to hear. I've been wanting to do something, but I haven't known what.'

'That's what we're doing now!' Olivia said, and she felt a tingle of excitement at how everything was coming together.

'Where do we sign up?' Morgan said. 'We're in, aren't we, Oscar?'

'I, uh, I guess,' Oscar said. 'But . . . I . . . Well, yes.'

Alf was last to arrive, finishing their little – but ever-increasing – group. He looked polished and put-together in his uniform, just as he had the other night at the party.

As he sat down next to Oscar, Olivia noticed the blush rise further up Oscar's cheeks, so that even his eyelids seemed to be painted in a dusky red.

'Hey Oscar,' Alf said.

'H-hi,' Oscar stuttered, and Alf grinned in response.

'You don't mind if I sit here, do you?'

'No, no, not really – I mean, not at all.'

Olivia thought Oscar looked secretly pleased. Well, maybe not *secretly* pleased. It wasn't so hard to tell.

'We're a team of vigilantes,' Rocky said, leaning forward, 'brought together by our collective queerness, ready to take on the world one rainbow at a time.'

Nell cocked her head to the side. 'Well, I wasn't going to put it quite like that, but I won't lie: it does work.'

'And I feel comfortable,' Rocky said to Olivia, 'because I know Oscar and trust him, and I know he trusts Morgan, so we're okay.'

Saffy cleared her throat. 'I've got a question,' she said. 'Isn't . . . isn't "queer" a bad word? An insult?'

Olivia was pleased to hear her speak up, and Oscar's sentiment replayed itself in her head. Was it fate that had led them all here?

Rocky, first pondering the question, answered, 'That's a good question. To some people it might still be because historically it was used as an insult against LGBTQ+ people, but now people are trying to reclaim it so that it's not negative any more – so that doesn't have all the bad associations and is something you can be proud of. So you can choose to use it if you like – or if you'd rather not, that's fine too.'

Saffy nodded and sat back, satisfied with Rocky's answer.

Olivia recognised the same energy in Rocky as she had herself when she was speaking about something she was extremely passionate about, and it only made her love her new friend more.

'Why don't we introduce ourselves properly?' Nell said. 'Olivia, you go first. Tell everyone a bit about yourself. Then we can decide where to go next.'

Okay, here goes. Unlike Tabby on her first day, Olivia loved a good introduction. 'I'm Olivia,' she said, 'and I'm demisexual. I suppose I'm out, but maybe not completely openly. My family know, as do my friends, and I have a girlfriend, Cassie, but I always feel that even if I did come out, people don't get what it means to be demisexual. I've heard all sorts, things like, "Why do you have to put so many labels on stuff?" and "Oh, you just haven't met the right person yet." But I know how I feel, I know how I identify, and I find it tiring to have to explain myself so often. That's why it's so important to me that the library isn't seen as a place of discrimination.'

She blinked. Had she really just said all that? As she was talking, she'd felt an unexpected pressure in her chest, pushing down, making her force out her words more than she ever had to.

And there was a pressure behind her eyes, too, like she was going to cry.

'I get the same,' Rocky said, voice gritty with emotion. 'I'm only out to my friends, not at all at home or in the scary world outside, and I find it so tiring. You have to hide your true self constantly. And even if I did come out, what then? You don't just come out once – it's a constant process. Even when you do come out, like you said, Olivia, they don't always understand.' They laughed sarcastically. 'You wouldn't believe the amount of fuss people create using correct pronouns. Is it so confusing that I go by "they" and "them"? Those two little words sure do scare a lot of people.'

'Can I go next?' It was Alf who'd spoken. He raised a hand. 'I'm Alf, I'm in Year Ten – which is how I know Nell,

Oscar and Rocky – and I'm bisexual. I suppose I wanted to go next because what you just said, Rocky and Olivia, really spoke to me; I feel like when people hear the word "bisexual", they have this stereotypical image in their heads. They say you're greedy, that you can't make your mind up, that you haven't been with the right person yet. If you go out with a girl, they think you're straight; if you go out with a boy, they think you're gay. If you haven't gone out with anyone yet, they question how you know you're bisexual. It feels like I have to constantly prove myself.'

As she was listening to Alf speak, Olivia felt a peculiar feeling come over her. Some kind of warm, tingly sensation in her veins, flowing to her heart.

Because I finally feel like they get me. I finally feel like I've found . . . acceptance from everyone around me.

'I get that too,' Nell added. 'I've never had a girlfriend, and I'm out pretty much to everyone, but I keep being hard on myself because it's like straight is the default. And I think we're all made to feel different, especially if we know we're queer when we're young. "It's just a phase" or, "You'll grow out of it." And then I doubt myself, and I don't *want* to doubt myself. I know who I am. I don't want to be made to feel like I don't.'

'The doubt is *real*!' Olivia exclaimed.

Time for the next introduction . . . She felt like she was part of some speed-dating activity but instead of dating, the outcome would be their friendship – and comradeship. Or, she hoped that would be the outcome. She did *not* want to be dumped.

'Hey, I'm Morgan,' Morgan said, with an awkward little wave, 'I'm . . . Sorry, I still find it really difficult to talk about. I'm . . . I'm trans. I feel like I've always known, but it's not until recently that I kind of realised I could actually do this, actually transition. I've always known I'm a girl, but . . . Well, I'm not out at school yet. Only at home, and to Oscar. I've felt quite alone at school.'

'You've got us now, if you'll have us,' Nell said, 'mainly because we never leave each other alone.'

'I'd like that,' Morgan said, and her smile lit up her whole face. 'I'd like that a lot.'

'Oscar, you next?' Nell said.

Oscar took a deep breath in; as he spoke, he averted his gaze from the faces watching him, choosing instead to fix his sight on the table. 'Oscar,' he said and then, realising he'd just blurted out his name, corrected himself. 'I mean – I mean, I *am* Oscar and you've probably already noticed but I really, really hate everyone to be focused on me so I'm going to get this over with really quickly and tell you that—'

There was a moment of silence as he stopped dead. And then he laughed. A bright yet hearty laugh, ringing out and filling the gap in conversation he'd left. 'I forgot what I was going to say!' he said. 'I had it all completely planned out . . . and now I can't remember.'

Alf said quietly, 'Take your time. There's no rush.'

But it was as if Oscar hadn't heard him, even though Olivia was sure he had.

'I feel a bit nervous because . . . because it was my mum who complained to the school.'

Silence.

Hushed silence.

'It was your mum?' Olivia tried not to whisper, but she had to. She couldn't push the volume into her words.

Oscar nodded. 'She doesn't know I'm gay. She just picked up a book I'd taken home and started reading it and was horrified.' He hung his head. 'She was horrified . . . at me. She just didn't know it.'

'Oh, Oscar,' Rocky said breathily, 'you didn't say!'

Oscar shrugged. 'How could I? It's not the kind of thing you can mention when we're sat there doing binary code.'

Rocky pointed at Oscar, smirking, 'Was that a non-binary joke you just made?'

He shook his head with a laugh. 'It was unintentional!'

'We won't be upset if you don't want to help us with this, knowing how personal it is to you,' Olivia said to Oscar. 'We'll fully understand.'

'One hundred per cent,' Alf echoed.

'No,' Oscar said, 'this has got to be my fight too. I feel guilty; I want to be able to channel that somewhere.'

'Okay, but please don't feel guilty. None of this is your fault,' Olivia said.

'I want to be involved, too,' Morgan said. 'I don't really like reading, but I can still see how important it is. And I want to get one up on Oscar's mum. That's my main motivation. She would never let Oscar come over to mine when we were younger because I had a giant snail as a pet, so she thought I was a bad influence.'

'Michelle was amazing,' Oscar said. 'I really missed out there.'

'Well, you've come to the right place. Olivia's a book expert and she's really helped pull everything together,' Nell said, and she explained everything they'd done so far: the book drop, the conversations they'd had, and what their aims were.

'Let's go around and say what we like reading. That way we can get to know each other better and I can gauge what we're working with. And it's fine if you don't *love* reading! Maybe tell me about the last book you read that made an impact on you?' Olivia said.

'I can go first,' Alf offered. 'As I told you at Nell's, Olivia, I've been trying to read as much as possible recently because I want to go to university one day to study English, and the further ahead I get now, the better prepared I'll feel. My favourite book, though, is *Maurice* by E. M. Forster. When I read it – well. There was no other book in the world for me. I felt complete.'

'Oh, good choice!' Olivia said. She was sitting up dead straight now, attentive and excited, trying not to act *too* over the top. *Rein it in, Livs. You've only just met them; you don't want to scare them away with your squealing!* 'I've been meaning to read that. I'm so happy you mentioned it!'

'You put me to shame. I still haven't finished reading *Every Day*,' Rocky said. 'I keep trying but I can never find the tiiimmeeee.'

'Because you spend all your time listening to K-pop,' Nell pointed out. 'You'd get way more reading done if you weren't so involved in the fandom.'

'But the fandom is *life*. I can't function without it – you've got to realise that by now.'

Olivia giggled. 'Books can be life too! Are you at least enjoying it?'

Rocky tilted their head to the side. 'Yes? It's brilliant but I'm reluctant to say I'd want to read it, or something similar to it, all of the time. It's nice to recognise parts of yourself in books, but at the same time I want to escape too. I like reading about characters who don't have the issue of having to get a part-time job just to afford a decent binder because they can't tell their parents they're non-binary; sometimes I want to read about characters who don't experience dysphoria. I feel so stuck in my head that I have to get away from all the feelings, all the thoughts.'

'Tell me about it.' It was Oscar who had spoken, quiet but firm. 'Yes, sometimes you want to read something sad and cathartic, but I don't want to read about pain *constantly*. We at least need the option.'

Olivia knew there was something incredibly special about reading a book and seeing yourself in it, in a way that you haven't seen before. The book ceased being just a book – it began to be a pathway into understanding yourself and, ultimately, accepting that *who you are is who you are and you shouldn't have to change yourself for anyone.*

The safe feeling overcame her again. 'Do you find,' she said, looking around at each of them, 'that when you read books with characters like you, characters who aren't stereotypical or completely wrong, who get how you feel and you know won't judge you, that it feels like a piece of your heart is healing?'

That was how she'd felt when she'd read about a demisexual character for the first time – like a part of her heart, the part that wondered why she didn't have crushes like any of the other girls she was friends with or didn't get why they were so enthusiastic about boys and impressing them, was mending. Because, for the first time, there was somebody else out there like her, who went on their own journey and came out the other side.

'I have to be so careful, though,' Nell said. 'I'd be rich if I had a penny for every time I was promised good lesbian representation and then a TV programme or film chucked the "bury your gays" trope in at the end. We can have happy endings too!'

It was one of the oldest – and worst – tropes in the book when it came to queer representation: have everything going really well for your queer couple, and then right at the end kill one or both of them off.

'At least you can watch stuff like that,' Oscar said. 'My mum screens everything I watch and read. All of you can read with pride; I feel ashamed if I read anything she won't approve of.'

'What did you say?!' Olivia cried, and he jumped out of his seat so far she must have surprised him with her outburst.

'At least you can watch stuff like that?'

'No, the other bit!'

'About reading with pride?'

'Yes! Reading with pride! That's amazing! It's perfect!'

'Read with Pride,' Alf said, with a nod. 'That would make a great name.'

'And every group of bookish superheroes taking on the world needs a good name,' Rocky said.

'Does this mean I'm going to have to like reading now? I like the pride bit, I'm just not convinced about the books,' Morgan said.

Olivia understood that not everyone liked reading and even though books were her entire reason for being, she accepted it. 'By the end of this, we might have you tolerating books, Morgan,' she said. 'Who knows?!'

'Stranger things have happened,' Morgan replied.

'Right. Read with Pride, now that we've met, why don't we meet up next weekend? The book drop has evidently worked its magic – so I think we should go away and have a think and then have a proper catch up. Morgan, Oscar, Saffy – are you all happy to be added to our group chat?'

'Yes!' they said in unison.

Olivia clapped her hands together in glee. 'Eeek! I know this isn't something I should be *excited* about but, honestly, my heart feels so full right now! We are going to show the school – and the world – what we are made of.'

'It's a plan,' Oscar said. 'Time to read with pride.'

'Read with Pride!' Nell said, punching the air.

Going home that evening, Olivia realised that despite her horrendous mock exam, it had been the most fun day of the school year so far. It wasn't just meeting people that Olivia loved, but meeting people who shared a passion and had different knowledge and experiences to the friends she already had, who she would hopefully be able to learn more and more about as time went on. In particular, she loved the moment when it all clicked: when you finally got someone, felt like you knew them inside and out. And, in the meantime, there was all the exciting work as you led up to that point. Asking questions, listening intently, being involved in many different situations. Sharing parts of yourself.

It was all so scintillating. It made her world far brighter.

Ed: It's my birthday tomorrow tomorrow tomorrow!!

Ed: And I'm celebrating early with a job rejection because I have been deemed incapable of working in a supermarket

Tabby: Tomorrow!! Yay!

Cassie: to be fair, they made the right decision there because you're too clumsy for stacking shelves

Ed: You can't be rude like that to the birthday boy!

Cassie: i can do what i want, it isn't your birthday yet

Olivia: Cassie, are you coming round to mine so Ed can collect us here?!

Cassie: sounds good to me

Ed: Shall I do an hourly birthday countdown?! Or a minute countdown?!

Henry: Please god no, save us

Olivia added Oscar, Morgan and Saffy to the group chat.

Olivia changed the group chat name to 'Read with Pride'.

Olivia: Introducing . . . READ WITH PRIDE!!

Rocky: Woo woo wooooo!!

Nell: Hi Oscar and Morgan :)

Oscar: thx for inviting me

Rocky: Oh yeah, a word of warning: OSCAR STILL USES TEXT SPEECH WHEN HE WANTS TO ANNOY ME

Oscar: its easier, i dunno y u make fun of me

Rocky: lol

Oscar: . . .

Morgan: He does the same to me!

Oscar: is it 2 l8 to leave?

Rocky: NOOOOOOOOOOOOOOOOOO

Olivia: Now, Rocky, I have to put my foot down and insist
that you leave poor Oscar alone, I think it's very
endearing of him to use text speech!

Oscar: lmao

Rocky: HE IS DOING THIS ON PURPOSE TO ANNOY ME

Olivia: My notifications are going to go crazy if this is always
like this!!

Chapter Twelve

There had been no possibility of reading that morning. There was far too much to do: so many Read with Pride messages it was impossible to count, two pieces of homework that had been forgotten, and Ed's birthday party to get ready for.

It was safe to say that Olivia was stressed out. Even after she'd got everything done.

'You look fine,' Cassie said, applying her signature deep-red lipstick in the mirror hanging in Olivia's hallway. As usual, she was chilled and unbothered by Olivia's stress.

'But I haven't washed my hair for four days and I've had to scrape it back in this awful way and I think it might smell!'

'Nah, it doesn't. Just use some dry shampoo.'

'Good thinking,' Olivia said, running back upstairs.

'It's the rest of you that smells,' Cassie teased when Olivia came back, can in hand.

'Cassie!!' Olivia whined, but Cassie just laughed.

The honking of a car horn sounded from outside, and Cassie moved away from the mirror to peek through the glass of the front door.

'That'll be Ed,' Olivia said. 'You'll have to go out and tell him we'll be ready soon because he'll keep honking and get more and more impatient and I'll get dry shampoo everywhere if I'm rushing and you know what he's like, he'll just stress me out more and I cannot, cannot, *cannot* handle any more stress.'

'Livs,' Cassie said gently, drawing closer and reaching out for her shoulders. Olivia baulked at the touch. 'Relax. It'll be okay. There's no need to stress: Tabby will have everything under control.'

That's true. If I'm feeling like this, I wonder how Tabby is feeling!

'Thanks.' Olivia relaxed, then once she was used to it, felt her shoulders dip and the muscles in her neck relax. Until—'I don't think I finished wrapping Ed's present!'

'Okay, Olivia, listen to me now: you didn't have to wrap Ed's present because we bought him a collective present this year, so you really don't need to stress.'

In that case, they were ready. Olivia pushed her shoes on and locked the front door behind her. She wished she was an octopus, able to juggle everything with eight hands, rather than her measly two. It would make life so much easier.

'Are you okay?' Cassie asked before they descended the path. 'Livs, you look . . . Well, you look great, but you do seem a bit out of it at the moment.'

'What do you mean?' Olivia said, honestly puzzled. 'I'm fine! I've just got a lot on. It's nothing to worry about.'

'Look, I'll say it and then we can forget about it: I know that you've been worried about the school library, I know that's been on your mind, and I'll support you no matter what. But I worry that you're spreading yourself too thin.'

'Spreading myself too thin,' Olivia echoed, pooh-poohing the sentiment. 'Really, Cassie, I think you're making it all up.'

As soon as she said it, she regretted it. She wanted to take it back, fall on her knees and beg for Cassie's forgiveness.

'Fine,' Cassie said, and blinked the comment away. 'Maybe I am.'

And then the moment for apologising was over and Cassie had sped up; she felt miles away, rather than just a few steps ahead.

Ed was waiting out the front, Tabby and Henry already in the back of the car. He must have left early to pick them up and doubled back to collect Olivia and Cassie.

'Happy day of your birth!' Olivia trilled, opening the side door. Henry looked like he'd been flattened into the back – the top of his head was touching the ceiling and his knees were tight to his body to make enough room.

'Welcome to your ride, ladies and gentleHenry! Buckle up because you're in for a treat!' He started the engine. 'Happy birthday, me!'

Cassie took the final place in the back and Olivia took the front seat. They set off down the road, out of town and down the country lanes to the lake where they'd held their *Hunger Games* re-enactment for a previous Paper & Hearts Society meeting. It seemed like a lifetime ago to Olivia.

'I've just had a thought: no balloons,' Ed said in the middle of changing gear. 'It's my birthday. There's no balloons! It can't be a birthday without birthday balloons! Cassie, you had one job!'

'Shut up,' Cassie said from the back. 'Some of us are concerned with saving the environment.'

He hit his hand against the steering wheel. 'But you specifically signed up to organise the balloons. You said you didn't want any other role.'

'Exactly. It was tactical. Now concentrate on where you're going or you'll miss the turning.' Cassie turned back to the graphic novel she had open on her lap – *Giant Days*, which she'd already explained to Olivia was about a group of friends who meet in their first year of university – and flicked the page over extra noisily.

Ed was still grumbling about the lack of balloons as he pulled into the glorified car park, which was more of a sandy, dirty field than an actual car park.

'Do you think I should give the car a name, by the way? What is a fitting name for a bashed-up machine that resembles a black hole, if a black hole were covered in scratches and looked like it would break down at any time?'

Tabby, Henry and Cassie piled out of the back of the car, and Ed opened the boot up.

'I thought you'd named it the EdMobile?' Olivia had liked that one.

'Nah, I changed my mind. I don't think it fits well enough.'

'I think you should name it after your favourite friend,' Tabby said, bumping his shoulder with hers.

'That's a fab idea,' he said. 'Hey, Cassie, do you mind if I use your name?'

'Don't talk to me.'

To help Tabby out with hosting her first meeting, Olivia thought it would be a good idea to prevent Ed and Cassie from having a full-blown fight. She tactfully changed the subject. 'What does it feel like to be super-old?' she asked. 'Eighteen is basically the same as eighty these days.'

'Which I don't think anybody would thank you for saying,' Henry said, 'especially if they're over the age of eighteen.'

Olivia laughed.

'I feel like a new human,' Ed proclaimed, opening his arms wide to the sky. 'I woke up this morning and instantly felt my brain become weighed down by all the new knowledge and wisdom I have. I've said it many a time, but now I know for sure I am far superior to all of you.'

'Until I catch you up,' Cassie said, ruffling his hair in a way Olivia was sure was supposed to be affectionate but in fact looked rather rough. 'Anyway, where are we going with all this stuff?'

'Please, please, please, pretty please, can we go down by the lake?' Ed asked. 'You know how much I love that little spot where the geese and ducks come up.'

'Yeah,' Henry said. 'We may as well make the most of the actual lake, while we're here.'

'No way am I sitting there,' Cassie said. 'You know I'm scared of swans. They're evil.'

'They are *not* evil,' Ed said. 'Stop victimising the defenceless swans, they've done nothing to you!'

'Not that you know of,' Cassie muttered.

'Sorry, Cassie, but I'm afraid I've got to agree with Ed on this one.' Olivia nodded towards him. 'It is his birthday, after all!'

Cassie folded her arms across her chest. 'Fine, but if some kind of moving creature even dares to look at me, I am leaving right away. And I shall hold you responsible for ruining my life.'

They trudged down to the lake, weighed down by the items they were carrying, where there was an ideal picnicking spot by a sort of beached area. The chill autumnal air clung to them, the crunch of the first falling leaves a companion noise. It was one of the first days Olivia had needed to wear a semi-warm coat, and she'd wanted to draw it closer to her on a number of occasions when her old foe the cold sent a shiver down her spine.

'I can see ducks,' Cassie hissed at Olivia, 'and lots of them.'

'Don't worry,' Olivia giggled, 'I'll protect you from the big, scary ducks and their ginormous teeth.'

'Ginormous teeth? Nobody said anything about ginormous teeth.'

Olivia giggled again, shaking her head. 'Just joking! I don't think they have any teeth. Can you imagine if they had human-sized teeth?!'

When they'd picked out their spot – clear of bird droppings and far enough away from the water that Cassie would go near it – Tabby set them to work: the picnic blanket needed arranging; the food had to be set out on the reusable plastic plates she'd packed; Henry had been tasked with procuring the party details, such as the party hats and streamers; and Ed tried not to make too much of a nuisance of himself.

'Can we eat already?' Cassie said from the edge of the picnic blanket furthest from the lake. 'The longer we spend here, the more nervous I'm getting. It's not fun.'

'I promise we won't let swans go anywhere near you,' Henry said. 'So you can relax.'

'Don't make promises you can't keep.'

Ed dived on to the blanket, followed by Henry who was definitely too tall to dive, and Olivia was the last to take her place.

There was one more bag to empty of its contents; Tabby's life flashed before her eyes as Ed raised it above his head.

'Careful, that's fragile!' Tabby cried, right before Ed slammed it to the floor. She put her hands together in prayer.

'That sounded like china,' Ed said, peering into the bag.

'It *is* china!' She swatted his hand away. 'Don't you dare touch it! Hands off!'

'I think you might want to leave that alone, Ed,' Cassie said.

Tabby carefully took a teapot out of the bag and out of its protective layer of newspaper.

'A teapot?' Henry asked.

'Tabby only drinks her tea with lots of milk,' Ed said, 'and I think that's a disgusting habit. How are we friends really?'

'I ask myself the same thing all the time,' Tabby said, rolling her eyes at him affectionately.

'So what's going on then?' Ed asked, picking a china cup and saucer out of the same bag and unwrapping them. 'These look like something my grandma would have! She loves all this floral china stuff.'

'If you'll be quiet for two seconds, Ed, I can explain myself! And I'm choosing to ignore the grandma comment.

'I thought,' Tabby began, her hands waving about as she got more eager to tell them, 'that to celebrate our darling Ed's birthday – and to ensure a memorable Paper & Hearts Society meeting, we would have a tea party! But not just any tea party: an *Alice in Wonderland*-style picnic. I brought little china cups for us and a teapot, and there are tea-themed biscuits and cake and *all* the sweet treats.'

Trepidation and silence as they waited for Ed's reaction . . .

'YOU GUYS!' he cried, opening his arms wide. 'Please hug me. I feel overcome by emotion!'

'Mind the teapot!' Henry warned, only just managing to save it from rolling off the picnic blanket.

Olivia burst with happiness and satisfaction as Ed gathered them all in for a group hug. She really did love them and never wanted to be without them and their magical friendship.

'You're squashing me,' Cassie grumped, but Olivia also felt her squeeze tighter into the hug.

This was what it was all about: being surrounded by friends you loved more than anything, who understood you better than anyone else in the world.

'Is it time to tuck into the food yet?' Cassie asked.

'Food, food, food, food!' Ed chanted. 'Foooooodddd!'

'Would you do the honours, Henry, and pour the tea from the flask in the bag behind you into the teapot, and then into the cups?' Tabby asked.

They wolfed down their sandwiches and sweet treats, drinking their tea – 'Definitely not enough milk,' Tabby complained – and popping on their party hats. Ed used his party hat like a unicorn horn, poking Tabby's shoulder with the point and laughing as she swatted him away.

She had decorated the little finger-sized biscuits with playing cards and white rabbits to match the *Alice in Wonderland* theme.

Olivia brushed the crumbs off her hands, amazed by Tabby's handiwork. For her first Paper & Hearts Society meeting, she had certainly done a wonderful job.

'The only thing that would make this better was if Mrs Simpkins was here dressed as the Cheshire Cat,' Ed said, helping himself to a second biscuit.

'Damn, why didn't I think of that!'

'Because, Tabby, we have to have some ambitions for next year. Or maybe even Halloween – you can come round and we can dress her up and go trick or treating. She'd love it!'

'Speaking of Mrs Simpkins . . . Olivia, do you have the cake?'

. . .

The cake.

The cake.

THE CAKE.

IT WAS MY JOB TO MAKE THE CAKE!

'Mrs Simpkins in a cake?!' Ed exclaimed and he looked so hopeful that Olivia wanted to cry.

'Uh . . .' she said. Or she didn't really say – it wasn't words that came out of her mouth, more like a jumbled mess of incoherent sounds. 'Unghhgh . . .'

'Did you leave it in the car?' Tabby asked. 'I can go back and get it! It's no problem.'

'Well, um . . . Well, about the cake . . .' She thought she might have stopped breathing. Everything felt tight, restricted, hot and clammy.

'I didn't see you put anything in the car,' Cassie said. 'You were in such a flap, you must have left it at home.'

They were all looking at her. She'd have to come clean. She'd have to tell them.

She'd have to tell them that, until that point, she'd forgotten all about the cake she was supposed to be in charge of. She'd forgotten how she was supposed to decorate it with a cat stencil that Tabby had bought specially, and how she was going to make it out of Ed's favourite Victoria sponge recipe.

She'd forgotten. How had she forgotten?!

'There is no cake,' she managed to say.

'No cake?' Tabby asked.

'No cake.' They were the only two words she remembered how to say. 'N-no cake.'

'It's fine, Livs, I don't like cake that much anyway. Don't worry about it.' Ed, reading the situation, brushed it off.

But that made it worse: cake was Ed's favourite thing in the world! The obvious lie made her feel awful.

'How did you forget the cake?' Cassie asked.

'It doesn't matter,' Ed said, 'these biscuits are good enough for me!'

'Well, anyway, we have got you a card,' Cassie said, and at the same time Henry took out the present they'd all chipped in towards.

Handing them over, Ed held both in his hands as if they were made from gold, before ripping open the envelope of the card first. He gasped as he saw the front.

There, adorning the cover, was an illustration that Cassie had spent every spare moment working on for the past few weeks: a detailed colour drawing of the five of them. In the middle, wearing a birthday party hat, was Ed with Mrs Simpkins at his feet, and on either side stood Henry and Cassie, and then Tabby and Olivia.

Cassie had captured them perfectly: their expressions and poses, their clothing and style.

Ed wiped a tear from the corner of his eye. 'This is . . . I'd ask for another group hug but I don't think I could contain my emotions if I did! And I've still got to get through this present!'

He tore into the paper and squealed with delight as he unwrapped the decorated box with the picture of Mrs Simpkins printed on top, with a speech bubble coming from her mouth reading 'HAPPY BIRTHDAY, ED!' He opened the lid, and gave another gasp.

'You shouldn't have!' he said, taking out the paper and carefully reading the words written on it. They had all put money in for him to go for a reading retreat at Woolf and Wilde: he'd get to buy himself three books, get a complimentary hot chocolate in the café and attend an exclusive reading evening after the shop was shut.

'It's perfect! Thank you, thank you, thank you, bestest friends in the entire world who I love with all my being!'

Seeing how happy he was made a heavy ball of guilt place itself next to Olivia's heart.

He would have been even happier if you'd remembered to make the cake.

A huge mute swan had glided over to their side of the water and was clambering up the bank, far less graceful when not swimming. It waddled to the blanket, drops of water sliding down its white feathers.

'Look!!' Ed squealed. 'I wonder if it wants a biscuit!'

'Ed, I don't think that's a good—' Henry started, but he stopped mid-sentence to stare horrified as Ed grabbed a cupcake from the blanket and held it out to the swan.

It went okay for the first few seconds. At one point, it did look like the swan might actually take the cake and ask for a cup of tea to go with it. But then an almighty hissing started up, and Ed shrieked, stumbling back. The swan beat its wings and as Ed stumbled further back, it followed him.

'Leave me alone,' he told it, 'go on, go back to the water. Just leave! Me! Be!'

He backed away, slowly at first, and then picking up the pace as the swan, too, picked up its pace. And then he was off like a dart, wailing louder than a banshee as the swan chased after him, thrashing its wings madly. Olivia was sure she'd seen an evil glint in its eyes.

'HELP!!!! HELP ME!'

'Drop the cake!' Tabby cried, whilst Henry stood up and looked as if he was unsure if he should go after him or not.

Cassie had composed herself now the swan had gone in the other direction, and had her phone out. 'This could go viral,' she said, following Ed with the camera lens.

'Should we rescue him?' Olivia was rather concerned that getting eaten by a swan on his birthday might not be the best present. 'How do you rescue someone from a swan attack?!'

'It's slowing down, he should be okay now,' Henry said. He was cupping the sun from his eyes with a hand as he watched on. He called out, 'Calm down, Ed, and walk slowly back this way. It will give up its cause if it doesn't see you as a threat!'

'Are you sure it's stopping?!?!' Ed called back.

'Yes,' Tabby said, 'I think it's safe!'

Not tearing his gaze from the swan, which had indeed ceased its chasing, Ed cautiously skirted far around it.

'Told you I was scared of birds,' Cassie said, raising an eyebrow. She patted Ed on the back. 'Pure evil, the lot of them.'

'Let's go home,' Ed panted. 'We can eat the Pringles in the car. I'm not staying here a minute longer.'

So they trekked all the way back to the car, lighter now that they'd eaten all the food, singing 'Happy Birthday' as they went. Ed pretended to be a conductor; Henry and Tabby tried to outdo each other with who could be the loudest.

'It's not like you to forget something like the cake,' Cassie said. She dropped Olivia's hand from hers, and Olivia mourned its absence.

She had no excuse; she knew Cassie was right.

Cassie continued, 'If there's something wrong, Livs, you can tell me. I'd rather you were honest with me than keeping something back.'

Olivia came to a stop and Cassie paused next to her. 'I'm not keeping anything back, Cassie. It was a genuine mistake. What reason would I have to hold something back?'

Cassie shrugged. 'I don't know, Livs, but you're just acting weird lately and this is the latest in a long line of things that makes me think there's something up.'

'Cassie,' she breathed.

'Come on, slowpokes!' Ed called down the hill. 'We've got birthday karaoke when we get back to the car!'

'Coming!' Cassie called back, leaving Olivia with only her guilty thoughts.

@bookswithlivs: *HAPPY BIRTHDAY, EDWARD EASTFIELD aka @TheIncredibleEd! We love you more than ANYTHING and hope you've had the best, best, best, BEST day celebrating! As well as our glorious selfie from today, I'm also attaching this wonderful picture of you aged 9 dressed up as The Very Hungry Caterpillar because the entire world deserves to see it. Only 365 days to go until your birthday! <3*

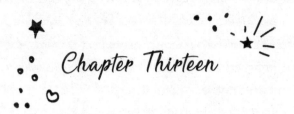

Chapter Thirteen

Her hands trembling with the sense of trepidation sitting heavy in her bones, Olivia watched as her physics teacher, Mr Wells, wrote up the grade boundaries, the wipe-board pen squeaking against the surface and filling the quiet of the science classroom.

If she could just scrape a Grade 4 . . . Was that too much to ask for? She knew the test hadn't gone well, but that didn't mean that she wouldn't have passed – any lower, and it would be a fail.

Even a small pass is a pass. That will be fine.

She didn't quite believe that, though – although there was no shame in it, or shouldn't be, she knew she wanted to do well. She knew it was expected of her to do well. She was hard-working and attentive to her studies, and this was her final year! If she wasn't taking it seriously now and doing well, what was the point of all the effort she'd put into her previous years at school?

It all came down to this.

It felt like an age passed as the tests were handed back one by one. Opposite her table, Olivia watched as Lara took one look at the scribbled grade at the top of the page and punched the air. 'Yes!' she hissed, and showed her friend next to her, grinning.

Olivia felt a shiver go through her. *It will be okay*, she told herself. *It will all be fine. There's no need to worry.*

She wished she had someone with her – Tabby, maybe, or Henry, who would be able to calm her and convince her that she was being silly. But she was alone in a room full of people, all of them with their own concerns, paying no attention to her.

'Disappointing, Olivia.' She jumped as Mr Wells slammed the exam paper down in front of her, then she wondered if she'd heard correctly. 'I'd expected better of you.'

Her eyes drifted down to the front page where, emblazoned on the top in glaring red pen, was: **GRADE 2**. She choked back a cry, sure she'd pinch herself and wake up from the nightmare she was in. Grade 2?!?! That was ... that was impossible. She'd never got a 2 before! That was a massive fail.

Heat rose up her body, flushing her cheeks.

'I'll do better next time,' she managed to push out, as Mr Wells walked away.

But will I?

He never replied – just carried on to the next student, his hard-lined mouth transforming into an open smile.

Maybe I'm just a failure now. I'll never get to where I want to be in life. I don't work hard enough. I've let everyone around me down.

She pushed the tears away as far as she could, but her tear ducts were overflowing wells, stinging under the pressure.

'Your exams are only a few months away,' Mr Wells said, standing back at the front, 'and there are some of you who really need to start taking this seriously. At this point in the year, I should not be seeing some of the marks I am. If we don't start seeing improvements, you'll be put in intervention and I'm sure that's something none of you want.' There was a pause and then, pointedly, 'Well done to the *rest* of you, who I can see are putting lots of effort in.'

But I put effort in! I tried my best, but apparently that was nowhere near adequate. How could I have let this happen?

She could hear her heart beating rapidly in her ears, blocking out the droning of Mr Wells's voice as he talked through the paper; blocking out the excited chatter as her fellow students compared notes.

In this moment, the only two things that existed were her shame and her exam paper, which she stared down at as if it would disappear if only she looked at it for long enough.

So far, it had not disappeared. It only grew bigger in her imagination, morphing until it felt like a paper monster, ready to engulf her in a cloud of failure.

How am I going to tell my parents? They'll be furious! They'll be wondering what I've been doing all this time!

Maybe they'd stop her being involved with Read with Pride and The Paper & Hearts Society.

I can't even think about that!! It would be unbearable!

It was a relief when the bell went to mark the end of the school day.

She walked home in a fog, not sure how she managed to get to her front door because she could barely remember putting one foot in front of the other. As she shoved the door open and crossed the threshold, she felt any sense of composure she had left give way. It rippled through her, the pain and disappointment – a crushing feeling that had her clutching her throat to hold back the sickness that was rolling through her.

She had the house to herself and ran upstairs to her bedroom, where she proceeded to throw herself down on her bed, burying her head in the cushions.

I'm going to fail all my GCSEs! I'll never amount to anything! One bad grade and that's it! I haven't been working hard enough, I should have put more time in, I can't have been pushing myself enough. I've never not done well before!

She only moved to stop her mascara from leaking down her cheeks and on to her fresh bedding. Assuming the foetal position, her stomach aching from the sobs wracking her body, Olivia felt the crushing shame that came with knowing you'd done something wrong. With knowing you'd let the people around you down.

My parents have done everything they can for us. Everything, even when it meant them going without. All they've asked for in return is for us to try our best – and I know this isn't my best. It's not even a little bit close.

Somewhere in the back of her head, though, a little voice whispered: *It's not your parents you're thinking about, it's* you. *You feel like you've let yourself down.*

She'd have to do better. She'd have to revise more, push herself, make sure she was doing everything in her power to succeed. She couldn't—

'Livvy?! What's going on?!' Kimberley. Olivia heard the squeak of her bedroom door, felt her younger sister come closer, then reach her arm out tentatively to touch Olivia's shoulder.

'I'm a failure!' Olivia wailed. Her eyes were shut, as if them being so would banish Kimberley. She was perfectly happy wallowing here in her own misery, without her sister poking around.

'A failure?'

'A failure!'

'Right . . .'

'I'm a failure!'

'Yes, we've established that – but why?'

Olivia shook her head – although she felt childish, she didn't want to put into words *why* she was a failure. But maybe she was scaring her sister.

Indeed, when she looked up, Kimberley looked horrified. Which only served to make Olivia wail again: the two sisters were so similar physically that Kimberley's horror looked just like a mirror reflection, and that only multiplied the shame she felt.

'I failed a *stupid physics test*,' she managed to say and, for full effect, punched the pillow next to her. 'Stupid, stupid, ridiculous physics test and I feel so bad about it that I never want to think about physics ever again and banish it from existence.'

Kimberley cleared her throat. 'If you did that, we'd all be floating around wondering if someone could turn the gravity switch back on.'

'Don't try to make jokes out of my misery,' Olivia said, throwing a scowl in Kimberley's direction.

'But I have *solid* physics jokes,' Kimberley said. 'Except when they're liquids or gases.'

'That's terrible,' Olivia complained, but she did feel the corner of her mouth twitch involuntarily with a smile.

She brushed the wetness from her eyes on her sleeve,

the skin tender and sore from the tsunami of tears she'd given in to. Kimberley sat down on the edge of the bed and stroked her shoulder, and there was no one Olivia would rather be with in the moment than her.

'Don't tell Mum or Dad,' Olivia said, sniffing. 'Not yet. I'll tell them in my own time.'

Kimberley nodded. 'I won't. Want me to put the kettle on?'

Olivia grunted a yes. 'And I'm going to need you to go out to the shop and buy me the biggest bar of chocolate you can find.'

'Seriously,' Kimberley huffed, but she got up. 'Fine. But you owe me. Big time!'

Once Kimberley had left the room, Olivia closed her eyes again, darkness pressing in, the fog and the gloom weighing her down.

A failure. I'm a failure.

Olivia: I'm not coming into school today, I must have caught
    some virus and I'm feeling rough
Tabby: Get well soon, Livs! <3

Day two of despair. Olivia had spent the entire time staring up at the ceiling in her room, hoping the numbness would disappear from her brain and let her feel . . . something. Anything. Convincing Mum she had a migraine and needed leaving alone had been easy – every muscle in her face was tense, dark circles appearing like purpling bruises under her eyes, and all she could think about was lying in bed and giving in to sleep's oblivion.

She'd had to stop her dad from fussing because, no matter how much she clutched her head and batted him away, he wouldn't stop pestering her with questions – How are you feeling? Is Cassie coming round this weekend? Did you manage to take Lizzie out earlier? That would have done you good, wouldn't it, some fresh air?

That was the downside of your parents working from home: at times like this, when all you wanted to do was stay in bed and mope, they were always there. At least she had Lizzie, who was taking advantage of the bodily warmth under her duvet and had created her own nest, nuzzling into Olivia to comfort her. But Lizzie was the only one who could be tolerated.

It was late on Friday afternoon, the streetlights beginning to flicker on outside her window, when Olivia heard the doorbell ring. She could see in her mind's eye the route her mum was taking at that second: from her place at the kitchen table, hunched over her laptop, she'd look up hazily, thrown out of her journalistic world, then proceed slowly, only just realising once she got to the door between the kitchen and the hallway that she should probably hurry in case the caller decides nobody is in. There was just enough time after that to fling the front door open, if nobody else had beaten her to it – that was usually Olivia and Kimberley's favourite game.

The low murmur of conversation floated up the stairs. If she strained her ears enough, Olivia could catch part of it. 'Hold on and I'll see how she is,' she heard in her mum's voice.

Footsteps on the stairs. The slow creak of her bedroom door. 'Olivia?' Softly, so as not to wake her. Little did she know Olivia was already awake. 'Livvy?'

'Mmm?'

'Oh, you are awake. It's Henry. He says he's got some homework to give you. Are you up for seeing him?'

Slowly, she peeled herself away from her duvet and got up, smoothing her hair down. 'I'll come down now,' she said, and let her mum get back to Henry.

She wrapped her pink fluffy dressing gown tight around her body, kicked on her slippers, and smoothed down her bed-hair in the mirror. She wasn't really up for seeing any one right now, but for Henry, she'd make an exception.

. . . *And I need that homework or things will only get worse.* I'll *only get worse.*

When Mum saw her come down the stairs, she scarpered back to the kitchen table, and Olivia led Henry into the living room. She didn't worry about what she looked like as Henry had known her long enough not to care and, honestly, she was too tired – despite all the sleeping she'd done – to think about it for more than five seconds.

He was still in his school uniform, blazer sleeves rolled up, with some papers tucked under his arm – the dreaded homework, she assumed. The lenses of his glasses were dirty, and his tie was hanging loosely from his neck, relaxed.

'I thought we'd have to send round a petition to persuade you to come back to school,' Henry joked, sitting down on one sofa, while Olivia took the other. 'It's not like you to be off so long – I thought you'd need convincing.'

'A petition?' Olivia smiled. 'I doubt you'd find enough people to sign it.'

'I don't know about that. Tabby and I have been beside ourselves,' he said. 'How are you feeling?'

She sat back into the sofa, giving it a second while she decided how to answer. 'You know what migraines are like. Plain evil, that's what.'

Don't cry, don't cry, don't cry. She bit her lip to stop herself, but only managed to draw Henry's attention.

'Oh, Livs!' he said, and jumped to put his arm around her. 'What is it?'

'I failed,' she whispered. 'I failed my physics test – really badly – and I feel so awful about it and just can't get it out of my head and I don't know what to do, Henry, it seems like the biggest deal in the world!'

'Why didn't you say anything?' Henry said, squeezing her tight. 'It's nothing to be ashamed of: you wouldn't be human if you did well at *everything*.'

'But it is,' she said, glad she didn't have to look him in the eye. 'Because exams are only a few months away and if I'm not getting it now, if I still don't understand it, how will I ever do well? And if I fail physics, I might fail something else, and then I might not get the grades I need and then who knows what will happen!'

Henry drew back so he was facing her. She hated the look he was giving her, as if he couldn't believe what he was hearing. 'Olivia,' he said, 'one test is not going to ruin your life. Trust me, in three years' time you won't remember any of your GCSE grades, let alone this grade that doesn't even count. Relax, okay? You have plenty of time.'

'But exams are important!'

'Not at the expense of your mental health, they're not,' he said, firm, 'not if it means you're working yourself into a state over all of this. You are not your exam results. An exam paper can't tell if you're kind or

184

caring or funny or passionate. It's just a mark. It's not your entire worth.'

Olivia huffed. 'Can you not leave me to my pit of despair in peace? You're speaking far too sensibly for my brain right now and I don't like it.'

Henry grinned. 'Isn't that why we're friends, so I can talk you down from your crises? Now, is there anything else bothering you, while I'm here? I can be your unofficial therapist.'

Bother wasn't so much the right word – even though she'd basically made up having a migraine, she was experiencing a weird brain ache every time she thought about everything she had to do, everything that was going on.

'Nothing you can solve easily, unless you have any sway with the school. I don't know why I even try.' She wiped at her face to stop herself from tearing up again, although she thought that maybe she was all dried out. 'I'll have to spend all my time revising now so I'll never do all the Read with Pride work I want to do, and if I don't do the Read with Pride work, I'll let everyone down, but if I don't revise, I'll let myself down and, in the process, still let everyone else down. So I can't win, can I? I've basically lost already! What is the *point*?!' She tried to keep her voice down because she didn't want her parents overhearing in the next room, but it was impossible for it not to rise as she got to the end of her impassioned monologue. 'I'll just have to tell everyone tomorrow that I quit.'

Apparently, the tears weren't all dried out. She turned her face so Henry wouldn't see – but it was no use. Nothing escaped his attention.

'What's happening tomorrow?' he asked, and put his arm back around her shoulder, rubbing gently with his thumb.

She sighed. 'I'm meeting the Read with Pride group at Woolf and Wilde. And no, before you say it, I'm *not* replacing The Paper & Hearts Society, because I know you're all thinking it.'

'We are *not* all thinking it,' he corrected. 'We're all in awe of what you're doing and think it's amazing. But there's no need for you to go there tomorrow and quit. I swear I overheard someone today say they found a book around school with a note in it and were loving it. That was you, wasn't it? Would you really want to stop all the good you're doing?'

She shrugged but was secretly pleased to hear another story of it working.

'The best way you can cheer yourself up is by having a great time tomorrow in your favourite bookshop, making the world a better place,' Henry said.

He's always right, she admitted. *Even though that will mean kicking Lizzie out of my bed, which she'll hate.*

'Thank you, Henry,' she said as he made his way out, wrapping her arms round his middle to give him her best squeezy hug.

'That's what best friends are for. I'm not a bookish musketeer for nothing, am I?'

Henry: How are you doing now you've had time to recover, Livs?

Olivia: A lot less rotten than I felt before you came. Thank you for being so lovely to me <3

Nell: Can't wait to see you all at Woolf and Wilde!

Morgan: I can't believe you're making me set foot in a bookshop, this is against my principles

Alf: Don't worry, we'll protect you from the scary books, Morgan. We won't let them come anywhere near you.

Oscar: nice try in a bkshp

Rocky: BKSHP. NO. OSCAR. MY EYES.

Saffy: are you okay olivia I haven't seen you around for a few days

Olivia: I'm getting there, thank you, Saffy! I'm looking forward to seeing you all tomorrow!

Chapter Fourteen

Pushing the door open to Woolf and Wilde, stepping from the damp street into the comfortable warmth, Olivia didn't feel like she was entering a bookshop: she was Lucy Pevensie, pushing through the wardrobe for the first time into Narnia. She was entering a magical world. One where there were hopefully fewer White Witches. Just the thought made her nose tickle with the sickly-sweet smell of Turkish delight.

I am in HEAVEN.

The first time she'd passed through the tinkling entryway of Woolf and Wilde, she was six years old, excitable and awestruck; she'd held on to her dad's hand, twisting her head this way and that to take in all of the books, surrounding her on each side in the most magnificent bookcases she'd ever caught sight of. She'd grown up in the children's section, attending all their weekend read-alongs, where as many kids as possible would pack into the colourful, adventure-themed corner and be read to by a bookseller. Then she'd progressed on to the teen section, saving up all her pocket money to be able to choose the books she wanted for her collection at home. To her, Woolf and Wilde was like a second home.

Henry had been right: this was what she needed to make herself feel better. Getting ready this morning, the excitement building, and even managing to fit in a tiny piece of homework, had restored her spirits and put her back on the right track.

She headed to the café, snaking her way past the non-fiction shelves and staff picks, past this week's bestsellers selection, until she was opposite the till and could head left through the arch into the huge café. It was modelled on the Mad Hatter's Tea Party from *Alice's Adventures in Wonderland*, which made Olivia smile with the remembrance of Ed's birthday and everything Tabby had organised. As well as a pang of guilt: there may have been cake in the counters here, but there certainly hadn't been cake in Ed's stomach at the festivity.

It was a simple mistake. A lapse of judgement on my part. It won't happen again.

After ordering herself one of Woolf and Wilde's famous hot chocolates, she took a seat at one of the large booths at the back, sipping away while she read through the scribbled notes she'd made in preparation – when she should have been sleeping last night. She yawned.

I really think this could work. This could turn the tide in our favour: we have to make a big statement. A statement that will reach far further than any of us. There has to be a movement.

It was ambitious. It would be hard work. But she had to try.

Her hot chocolate was gone by the time she'd finished reading back through all her notes, the thick, creamy drink having warmed her up from the inside out. She still wasn't sure if the way forward was clear, but she was hoping they'd be able to work that out together.

It's going to be so nice to sit down with Read with Pride and throw around ideas. This is what I love most!

But when she looked up, it was to find Ed bustling over to her, his cheeks flushed red from the cold. He took off his scarf and scooted into the booth, facing opposite Olivia.

'Hey, Livs! I've been here ages!' he said. 'I've been upstairs, trying to resist the temptation of buying all the books. At one point, I thought I'd got lost because I spent so long staring at one case of books that I couldn't remember how to get back downstairs again. That's what I call good book-shopping!'

'Ed, what are you doing here?!'

This was not part of the plan.

'I was looking for a book on how to train cats, but they

didn't have any for mine and Mrs Simpkins's skill set. Advanced, by the way.'

Olivia shook her head in disbelief. 'You know, for a moment there, I thought we were having a sincere moment, Ed. Turns out, I was wrong. How do you somehow work cats into every topic of conversation?'

'I was blessed by the Cat Overlord at birth. It's just a talent I have.'

'Seriously, what are you doing here?'

He mimed zipping his lips shut and didn't say anything, even when Olivia wheedled him, until Rocky arrived.

Which was not what she'd hoped for. What if Read with Pride weren't comfortable with Ed being around? He'd make too many cat jokes and she didn't want to be ashamed of him because she wasn't, but she didn't want to put them off; they might prefer dogs – or, in Morgan's case, giant snails. There was only so many references to the Cat Overlord that anyone could take.

Rocky was wrapped up in a snuggly jacket with a faux fur collar and pulled off a hat with a pom-pom on top as they came over.

'Hey, I'm Ed!' Ed said, as soon as Rocky was at the table. 'It's nice to meet you! I'm Olivia's best friend. I'm sure she's mentioned me loads.'

Rocky grinned and shook Ed's outstretched hand. 'Actually, she hasn't at all.'

'I'm wounded, Olivia! Wounded! I will never get over this injustice! How could you treat your best friend like this?'

'Ed! Seriously – look, I'm sorry, Rocky, he's going now.'

'No, I'm not, I'm only just getting settled.'

Next to arrive was Saffy, who was far shyer of Ed and his outlandish behaviour, along with Alf, who Olivia was sure would get along with anyone without really trying.

But that didn't matter: Ed was still an interloper and she had no idea how to get rid of him without hurting his feelings.

Saffy looked a little confused, but once she'd introduced herself shyly to Ed she was more comfortable, and slotted in easily next to Alf.

Out of the corner of her eye, Olivia caught a familiar movement. Two familiar movements. One that she would know anywhere, knew better than her own self sometimes.

Cassie. The casual way she walked in her Dr Martens, the easy style of her clothes that only she could pull off, the little smirk that always played on her lips. Here, in Woolf and Wilde. Where she, like Ed, was not supposed to be.

Next to her, the third intruder: Tabby, carrying two hot chocolates and concentrating all her attention on not spilling them.

'My dearest companions! The other parts of my soul!'
Ed cried out on seeing them, and Olivia tried not to look
embarrassed. Rocky was loving it, though, and even shy
Saffy seemed amused.

'Ed, if you open your mouth to make one more
ridiculous comment, I will pour my hot chocolate all over
your head,' Cassie warned. 'I am not your dearest
companion.'

'Sorry we're late!' Morgan and Oscar looked confused
as Cassie ushered them into the booth, but they did as
they were told.

Olivia didn't have the headspace to explain to them
who Cassie, Tabby or Ed were – she hoped it would
become self-explanatory after a while, or someone else
would do the job for her.

She thought she might faint.

Even more so when she saw the last pieces of the puzzle
slide into place as Henry turned up, flanked by Nell.

'Hey, Olivia!' Nell grinned.

'Am I the only one who doesn't know what's going on
here?' Olivia said, her mouth hanging wide open. Why
did everyone else seem so chill about it?!

'Yep,' Nell said. 'No need to make introductions: I'm
already acquainted with your lovely friends.'

'But . . . how?!' she spluttered.

'I saw how upset you were, how overwhelmed, and

thought that you could do with some help. So I had a chat with The Paper & Hearts Society and we all agreed that we'd do anything we can to assist,' Henry said.

'It was a surprise,' Nell said, carrying on the story, 'when Henry messaged me to ask how they could be of service to us, but there's no way we could turn it down – I feel like we're just getting started! We all agreed that Read with Pride would be much stronger and more formidable with the help of your book club.'

Olivia clutched her cheeks, which were hurting from the growing grin she couldn't get rid of. 'Read with Pride featuring The Paper & Hearts Society?! REALLY?!'

'Really!' Henry said with a chuckle.

Olivia breathed a sigh of relief as everyone squeezed around the table. She had to hold back the tears that could easily spill if she let them, her friends from different circles coming together for her! It made her feel so full she could burst.

Olivia noticed that Oscar and Saffy, in particular, looked a little nervous, flicking their gazes back and forth between the people they knew and felt comfortable with, and The Paper & Hearts Society, who were completely new and therefore unpredictable.

'We're all here!' she said, unable to resist a small squeal that turned into a joyful laugh. 'My two worlds have completely collided! Wow!'

'I may have been bribed with cake and hot chocolate, but I am ready,' Ed said, taking a long sip of said hot chocolate.

'Hey, why wasn't I bribed?' Rocky protested. 'I'm missing out here.'

'We'll just have to find another reason to give you hot chocolate,' Olivia said amiably. 'Right then … Are you ready to hear the idea I have for what we can do next? I really hope this all makes sense – it might be totally wild, but just hear me out, okay? Okay! Right!'

This was it, her grand idea, the plan that was hopefully going to change everything for them.

'It was Henry who gave me the idea, actually.'

'Me?'

She nodded. 'When I saw you yesterday, you mentioned a petition and that's when it clicked into place: the book drops we've been doing have been great, and have clearly worked, but we need to go bigger and send a clear message to the school. We can start an online petition and get students to sign it. If we get enough signatures, they'll have to listen!'

'But do we know how to get enough people to sign a petition?' Tabby asked, looking round at the group. 'You'd need a lot to make it worthwhile. In theory, it works. But in practice? I'm not so sure.'

'That's not the spirit!' Olivia thought she might burst out of her seat with the passion she was feeling. 'If we all thought like that, nothing would ever change! We'd live the same day over and over again, annoyed but doing nothing about it. Yes, we might not know *now*, but that's the point! We keep going until we do know! We'll figure it out as we go along!'

'Good luck with that one,' Cassie said. 'The school will keep doing what they want, petition or not. What makes you think they'll listen to a word a bunch of kids are saying? You're being way too optimistic.'

Olivia was taken aback. Why wasn't Cassie supporting her?

'I don't think I'm being too optimistic,' she replied, brow furrowed.

'Just saying,' Cassie said. 'It won't work.'

Olivia had to do everything she could to hide the hurt she was feeling. *Why is Cassie being like this? I've spent all this time telling the others how wonderful Cassie is, and now she's acting like this!*

'No, I think you're on to something here, Livs,' Alf said. 'What's your thinking?'

As he uttered her name, Olivia saw a flicker of annoyance flash across Cassie's face.

Please, Cassie. Please.

'My proposal is this: an online campaign encouraging people to share why they think it's important to read with pride. Why books should be accessible, why we should all be able to read about characters like us. Why that right should never be denied us. We'll share our personal stories and encourage people to share theirs too. We can make a website and an Instagram page, start a hashtag. We need to get people talking! This is so much greater than us: we might think we have it hard at school, but think about the places all over the world where people have it harder, where books are banned on a wider scale and there are greater consequences for being queer. So many people will be able to relate to our story and our mission to enact change; so many people, I'm sure, will want to help us.'

'You do know that sharing your stories will mean you'll have to come out, don't you?' Cassie said. Was it Olivia's imagination or did she look smugly satisfied?

She's doing this on purpose.

'There's no way we can do that,' Nell said quietly. 'Too risky. You know some of us aren't out – what if someone we knew discovered what we were up to? I get where you're coming from, Olivia – we all knew what we were entering into when we started this, but this is a step too far. Once something's on the internet, that's it. It's there for ever. There's no coming back from that.'

'I get it,' Olivia said, 'of course I do. But I wouldn't do anything that would endanger this or would out us. I'm not that careless!' *Have some faith in me.*

Oscar messed with the spine of his book. 'I'm not ready to come out yet.'

'You don't have to, Oscar. We care about you too much to make you do that,' Alf said, and Oscar blushed.

'Alf's right,' Henry said. 'Those of us who haven't got anything to lose can take the responsibility. It would be safe for me, it would be easy. I shouldn't sit here and expect all of you to take the fall, if there is one. That would be unfair; we have to be good allies too.'

'I won't dispute that,' Nell said. 'I want things to change as much as all of you, and have wanted that all along. I just feel there's too much at stake.'

'But there's too much at stake if we don't at least try,' Saffy said, with a shrug. 'When the bullying was at its worst, all I wanted was people to listen to what I actually had to say. They had this idea about who I was, and I would have loved to have been able to correct that. I've never had the chance, though.'

'Can I say something?' It was a small voice. Too small at first for Olivia to realise where it had come from. It was Ed, though, who had spoken. He shifted about, looking down at the table, messing with his drained mug. 'I don't think I've ever . . . Well, maybe a few times . . . But being here with all of you, I feel like I've got something to say. It might not be important in the scale of things, but I get why this needs to be done. Because I'm not straight. I don't know what I am; I don't know who I am. I just know that I'm attracted to people regardless of their gender and I haven't found a label I'm comfortable with or feel like it fits me, but I think that's okay. So yes. My name is Ed and I am *not straight* and that is OKAY.'

As he'd spoken, every single one of the group had listened in awe at the determination in his voice, unable to take their eyes off him as he pushed through.

'Oh god, I'm so proud of you!' Tabby said, throwing her arms around him and resting her head on his shoulder.

'I can't believe I just shared all of that!' he said, hugging her right back.

'I can,' Tabby said. 'You're amazing, Ed.'

'Okay,' Nell said, putting her hands up in defeat, 'okay, we can do it. If we're all on board, we've got to at least try. As long as we all pledge to keep it as anonymous and as controlled as possible. No risks that we don't all agree to.'

'Agreed,' everyone echoed.

'I can create a website,' Rocky said. 'I've needed an excuse to put all my coding knowledge into practice.'

'And you will, of course, project manage, Livs,' Tabby said. 'The rest of us who don't have specific jobs, you can make sure we're all helping everyone else, make sure we're on task and working productively.'

Olivia grinned. 'That is basically my perfect job. Is this a thing, then? Are you all on board? Because I mean it: if you're not all on board, then we can rethink it; I don't want to do something that goes against your principles.'

Nell nodded. Only once, but it was enough. 'I'm in.'

'Wooopp!!' Ed fist-pumped the air. 'Let's go, team!'

'So, how does this sound?' Olivia said, leaning over her notebook to make sure she mentioned everything. 'Oscar and Alf, how about you two set up an email account where people can submit their stories if they so choose, and monitor any responses we get? We can encourage anonymous messages, just like we'll be sharing, so that everyone will get the opportunity to have their voice heard.'

'I love that idea,' Alf said, while Oscar enthusiastically nodded, not meeting Alf's eye.

'And Nell, you've done so much already and it's been clear from the start how passionate you are: would you like to draft up some rallying text to make sure that we have the best possible chance of it being shared by as many people as we can?'

'It would be my pleasure.'

'Oh, and Morgan! We're going to need someone who can keep track of everything we're doing and the progress we're making – you won't have to read all the messages that come in, especially if we get any hate, because I know how awful that would be, but do you think you could look at the maths side of things: analytics, data, all the stuff I wouldn't even know where to start with?'

'Thank you, Olivia, thank you. I'd love to!' She'd already turned to her phone and Olivia could see the Notes app open, where Morgan was jotting down bullet points.

'And finally . . .' She'd intended to take a deep breath to compose herself, but instead it came out as a huge, tension-relieving giggle. 'Eeeek! We're doing this! Sorry, I just had to say that. We're doing this! It's real! Okay, I'll stop now. Finally . . . everyone else, are you okay to be designated tasks and help everyone else as we go along? There'll be moments when some people need more help than others, so it would be great to be able to flit between jobs as and when it's needed.'

'I'll do anything you want, Livs,' Henry said. 'Within reason, of course. I only say that because I know Ed's bound to make some silly comment, so I'm just covering my back.'

'I'm not *that* predictable.'

'Something tells me you are,' Rocky said, giving him a pointed look.

'Hey! I thought you'd be on my side!'

Now that's sorted . . . 'How do we feel about book shopping?'

'Woo!' Rocky said. 'I feel very enthusiastic about that! Bonus points if you can find me something K-pop related.'

Morgan, smiling, said, 'Okay, let's see if you can pick out something that I'll enjoy. And I promise, if you do, I'll read it.'

They moved out from their booth and out of the café, into the main bookshop.

'Don't you think it would be great to work here?' Ed said, gazing around at the bookcases all around them.

Tabby had hold of his arm. 'You should ask,' she said. 'It wouldn't hurt to try.'

He shook his head. 'They'd never have me. Nobody else will.'

'Don't give up,' Henry said. 'You'll find something.'

'Yeah, when someone's stupid enough to take pity on me.' Olivia hadn't realised how down Ed was getting about not finding a job – he sounded so despondent!

As she watched her two worlds interact, clustered around the bookcases in Woolf and Wilde and chatting over books, Olivia felt like her heart would burst. *This is what it means to read with pride*, she thought, *and this is what everyone should have the opportunity to feel and do. It's magic!*

They could do this. If they did all they could, their plan would have to work.

They would be unstoppable.

Olivia: I've put the petition up!

Olivia sent a link.

Olivia: It would be great if you could all sign it!! We can start gathering everything together this weekend, ready to begin with our big plans next week. Is that okay with everyone?!

Alf: I've just signed and am also working with Oscar to get the email working this weekend.

Olivia: Amazing!!

Rocky: And I'm working on the website but we might have to begin with the petition only first before I get it to a point I'm happy with

Cassie: graphics are underway!

Olivia: We have got this!

Ed: Yes we have! GO TEAM! (I've decided that my job is going to be Chief Motivator)

Rocky: You're doing an amazing job already, I feel so full of motivation

Ed: I hope that wasn't sarcasm! Sarcasm is the enemy of the Chief Motivator!

To Do:

READ WITH PRIDE

- ~~Finish poster wording~~
- ~~Print out posters~~
- Write personal story to share

HOMEWORK

- French -ir verb table – Tuesday
- English Literature essay on portrayal of Beatrice in *Much Ado About Nothing* – Tuesday
- ~~Maths fraction questions – Thursday~~
- Religious studies definitions – Friday
- Biology questions on biodiversity – Friday

Chapter Fifteen

Will everyone please shut up already?

Kimberley had invited some friends round and they were blasting out music in her bedroom down the hall. There was no way Olivia was going to be able to get her *Much Ado About Nothing* essay done, and she highly doubted Shakespeare had ever had to contend with rowdy teenagers singing to Ariana Grande when he was writing the play.

Olivia: How was your day?!

Cassie: it was all right, it's college, isn't it? that says it all. But i was only in for two hours, so i came home and worked on my sketches.

Olivia: At least you can work! Kimberley's friends are here and they are UNBELIEVABLY LOUD. There's only so much laughing and screaming I can take!

Cassie: i can come over if you want, keep you company?

Olivia: I can't, sorry! Too much to do!

She put on her noise-cancelling headphones, but even then, she could feel vibrations on the floorboards – they must be dancing around, and it was not an environment conducive to productivity.

Once this was done, she could move on to her Read with Pride jobs, working out a strategy she could discuss with the others to launch the petition campaign, but until then, her best friend would have to be Shakespeare.

Although if Kimberley carries on like she is, I won't be getting anything done.

She leant back in her chair, reaching her hands behind her head to stretch, and gazed out of her bedroom window. Across the road, she watched as someone scaled a ladder to wash their windows, battling with a sponge attached to a long stick and rattling about.

The next minute . . . *BARK! BARK! BARK!*

'Lizzie,' she groaned, as she pictured exactly what Lizzie must be doing: standing on the back of the sofa, her whole body shaking as she showed her curiosity and fear at the strange person up the ladder.

Seriously?! Can I get no peace and quiet today?!

Growling in frustration, she stood up forcefully and shoved her stuff into her backpack – pencil case, exercise book and notes, Read with Pride notebook – and pledged to get out of there as quickly as she could.

There's no way I'll get anything done here with this racket. No chance!

She didn't know where she'd go, but anywhere would be an improvement. When she got down the stairs, stomping her way to prove a point, Lizzie was waiting for her at the bottom, wagging her tail.

'You're evil, you know that?' Olivia said, giving her the side-eye. 'You may look cute, but it's all an act!'

She wrapped her scarf around her neck and shrugged on her coat, and when she got outside, down the street and away from home, the relative quiet was bliss. The afternoon was grey and overcast, with a slight chill in the air, but she was glad of it.

She headed for town, not sure where she'd go but knowing that was her best bet. She'd find somewhere that was better for working, and she wouldn't end up screaming at Kimberley in the process.

Cassie: how's work going?

Olivia: Ask me later when I'm done! Until then I don't want to jinx it!!

Cassie: you'll do great! sure you don't want me to come round? or if not, i can come round another night?

But when? I can't think of even a spare second I have at the moment. Every little bit of time is accounted for!

She'd have to put Cassie off. She wouldn't be good company anyway and she got far more done when she was on her own.

> Olivia: Honestly, I'm so busy here! I'm just taking a study break at the moment for 2 minutes and then I'm back to it! Got to keep going!!!

She put her phone back in her pocket and kept walking. The streetlights were switching on as she got into the centre and, due to their olde worlde style, they made Olivia feel as if she were walking through a Christmas advert, everything lit up to a glow.

She didn't allow herself to become distracted by the stationery shop, and passed the turning to Woolf and Wilde quickly, so as not to be lured in by the promise of books.

Up the high street she went, never faltering.

The lights of Brain Freeze and the sugary treats inside beckoned her closer and she peered through the window, looking around for a spare table. Even though it wouldn't be dead silent, it was the kind of background noise she could handle, and the ice cream would sweeten the compromise.

Plus, I bet Shakespeare would approve. Ed would definitely say so.

There! Tucked along one wall was a spare table for two, where she'd be able to spread her stuff out and have room for a sundae glass. It would be perfect and, now she'd seen it, there was no way she could walk on past.

The bell tinkled as she entered and she headed straight for the table, where she took out her pencil case and exercise book, marking her territory by putting them on the table, before going up to the counter to order herself a drink and a chocolate brownie sundae. With extra cream and chocolate sauce. Because why not? She would need the energy if she was going to get this essay done!

I just hope that Brain Freeze doesn't actually freeze my brain – it needs to get working!

When she went back to her table, she got out her favourite essay-writing pen and smoothed open her exercise book, hoping that the writing flow would reach her and she'd be able to walk out with a complete essay.

In Much Ado About Nothing, *Shakespeare portrays Beatrice as* . . . Olivia bit her pen lid – not something she wanted to make a habit of – as she thought of the right adjective to use . . . *as a cynic regarding love*, she wrote. *In Act 2, Scene 1, her insistence that she will not marry 'till God make men of some other metal than earth' sets her apart from the stereotypical view that women at the time were only interested in marriage and shows that* . . .

With every paragraph she finished, she permitted herself a few mouthfuls of her sundae, and she knew then that she'd made the right decision to come here. In fact, she thought it would be a good idea if school moved to Brain Freeze permanently or built its own ice cream parlour on the side. She'd get so much more done! Ice cream was the key to productivity.

In conclusion, it is my belief that . . .

She added the final full stop, put her pen down, and took an extra mouthful of sundae this time to celebrate finishing. Now to read through and check she was happy with it!

'Olivia!' She jumped as she heard the voice and, turning, met Morgan's pleased smile with one of her own.

'Hi Morgan! What are you doing here?'

Morgan half-gestured to the empty seat on Olivia's other side, and Olivia nodded. Of course she could sit down! Morgan took off her beanie hat, her hair underneath turning static, which she smoothed down with a laugh, and sat down. 'I can't resist the temptation of ice cream,' she said, her cheeks rosy from the cold, 'and I was going to grab a tub to take home for my mum, too. She's been working night shifts for the last few weeks, so I like to treat her – she's always asleep when I'm at home.'

'And there's no better tasting ice cream,' Olivia pointed out.

'Too right.'

'I was just going to start some Read with Pride work, actually, so you've turned up just in time!'

She reached down to her backpack and got her notebook out. While Morgan went up to get a small pot of ice cream – and paid for the tub she'd take home later – Olivia went through her notes.

PETITION → How to get people to care or at least notice?
IDEAS:
• Social media – although how do we get enough people to see and why should they listen to us?
• School – but what to do that won't reveal who we are?

PROMOTION IS KEY

When Morgan got back, Olivia was scowling down at the notebook.

There was a scribbled diagram on the page with arrows pointing in each and every direction off the points she'd made, but none of it seemed right. There was something missing, and she couldn't put her finger on what.

'It's about working out how to get kick-started,' Olivia said, her head resting in her hand, her elbow on the table. 'How do we actually get going with it all?'

'I keep thinking we need to do something extreme,' Morgan said. She took a scoop of ice cream. 'We've got to make people realise that this is something they should be thinking about. Right now, it's easier for them not to because they don't think it affects them, but there's bound to be people who will feel like us and haven't realised it yet.'

'But what? You're right, but I can't think of a solution.'

Morgan thought for a while, staring down at her hands, palm down, on the table. 'That's the million-pound question, isn't it?'

Olivia doodled stars on the page, trying to get her brain thinking.

'A poster wouldn't work, would it?' Morgan said. 'Who actually looks at those things and pays attention?'

'They might look, but it doesn't mean they'd act on signing the petition.'

'Unless . . .'

'Unless?'

'Unless there were so many posters that people *had* to pay attention! So many posters that they were impossible to ignore!' Morgan let the idea carry her away, so that Olivia wasn't sure if she was even aware of her presence any more.

'Go on,' Olivia said. *I'm liking this!*

'We could create a snow-storm of Read with Pride posters and drop them around school; it would cause chaos! It would make a real statement!'

'A poster drop,' Olivia repeated. 'You know, I think that could work! Morgan! You are a genius! That's such an amazing idea!!'

'Well, I do try.' Morgan grinned.

'I'm happy to sort a poster out if you can coordinate the others?' Olivia suggested.

'We'd have to get lots printed and work out who would drop them – but I really think this could work!'

SORT OUT POSTER, Olivia added to the to-do list at the back of her notebook.

'I want it to work,' Morgan said, and she sighed. 'I want it to work because I want to feel like I have some faith in the school. I don't think they're bad people, but they've acted in this clueless way and now we're having to face the consequences. And for me, the consequences feel huge.'

'What do you mean?' Olivia asked, watching as Morgan's expression betrayed the inner turmoil she was facing. A few moments passed and, in that time, Olivia bolted down the remainder of her sundae. The pull to lick her lips was great, but she decided on a politer wiping of the side of her mouth with a napkin. She didn't want to scare Morgan away!

'It's such a huge thing,' Morgan said, and lowered her voice, 'and sometimes I have doubts because it's all I've ever wanted, but if we get the result we want and the school shows that they're supportive, I'd like to, well, I'd like to start transitioning. Openly. I know things won't always be smooth, but I'd just love to get to the point where I can go, *I'm Morgan and I'm transgender and that's okay.* I feel so much better since I've found friends who understand me for me, who don't refer to me by my deadname and know that I'm a girl. It's given me the confidence to do this.'

She could see how much it meant to Morgan; loved the soft happiness that came over her.

'Transitioning is different for everyone,' Morgan explained. 'Some people want to transition medically – so through hormones or surgery or both – and for some people that's something they don't need. But I think if we get our result, it will give me the courage to decide what it is that I want. I'll feel like I can be supported.'

'And you know you've got us, supporting you all the way.'

'I know.' Morgan smiled. 'I feel very lucky that we all found each other. Hey! Did you know that Saffy is an amazing dancer?! She was messing around the other day after school and she has serious moves!'

'Actually, I can see that!' Olivia said.

'Rocky wants her to teach them how to do that thing where you spin around like the speed of light on your back, but somehow I don't think that's a good idea.'

'Can you imagine?!' Olivia laughed. 'That's typical Rocky.'

'Luckily, Nell managed to convince Saffy how dangerous that might be. Otherwise, who knows what might have happened!'

'You'll have to get Oscar to try instead,' Olivia teased.

Morgan snorted. 'I'd like to see that.'

It was by chance that Olivia looked up at that exact moment towards the window, mid-smile. And it was by chance that she met the eyes of Cassie, who was looking in.

The smile fell from her face; it had completely vanished by the time Cassie had dashed off.

'Morgan, I've got to go, I'm so sorry.'

'Everything okay?' Morgan asked, confused.

'I think I've really messed up,' Olivia said. 'I'm sorry! I'll see you at school, okay?'

She rushed to gather her stuff together and was out of the door in moments, with one final, hasty wave to Morgan.

But where was Cassie? She had to find her!

There! Her retreating back, weaving through the other shoppers, walking as fast as she could.

Please be okay. Please be okay. PLEASE be okay.

Chapter Sixteen

'Cassie! Wait!'

Olivia knew she'd heard her: she'd shouted loud enough, but Cassie gave no sign of stopping.

'Wait, please!'

Cassie turned right down a side alley that was a shortcut to the next row of shops over. This was her chance! Olivia sped up, nearly tripping over numerous feet and shopping bags as she darted closer and closer, trying not to lose sight of Cassie. It was touch and go for a bit, especially when Olivia had to manoeuvre around a row of pushchairs.

'Cassie, stop!' She was out of breath and wanted to give up, but she couldn't now. Finally, Cassie yielded to her pleas – she came to a standstill down the empty alley, and leant against the exterior wall of a shop. She exuded anger and it made Olivia walk a little slower, not wanting to face the music.

'Busy, were you?' Blunt, unforgiving.

'Cassie, let me explain.'

'Just so you know, I've never heard anyone utter the words "let me explain" before who then followed it up with a valid explanation. Why didn't you just say you had no interest in seeing me? That would have hurt less than these lies.'

'Because I did want to see you!'

Not the right thing to say. 'Well, not enough, obviously.'

Cassie spun on her heel and was about to storm off when Olivia reached out to touch her forearm in a bid to halt her in her tracks.

'Please, Cassie. I know you don't like it but *let me explain.*'

Olivia drew her hand away. Cassie stopped, turned back, and inspected her nails – a ruse, Olivia expected, to make it seem like she didn't care, when really she couldn't bear to look Olivia in the eye.

'I didn't mean to,' she tried to clarify, but suddenly any coherence had evaded her. 'It was completely unintentional that I bumped into Morgan – I was trying to work!'

'Why lie to me, Livs? Why lie *all the time* about where you are and what you're doing?! You never have any time for me any more! How do you think that makes me feel?' Olivia looked around to see if anyone had noticed Cassie's voice rising to dangerous levels. 'I just want some honesty.'

'Excuse me, Cassie, but when you were included at Woolf and Wilde, you just tried to make things difficult. You never showed *any* kind of understanding.'

'I didn't make things difficult,' Cassie denied.

We clearly have different versions in our head, then.

'You just don't like the thought of any of us being happy around other people! You were the same when Tabby came into our lives! Stop being so protective, and get over yourself, Cassie! We can have other friends; we don't have to be with each other twenty-four hours of the day!'

'That's the biggest lie I've ever heard – why wouldn't I want you to be happy?! I can't believe you'd say that. I want you to be happy more than anything!'

'Just listen to what I'm saying, *please*.' Olivia ran a hand through her hair, sighing. She didn't know how she'd ever get through to Cassie.

'I am listening,' Cassie said, but she turned away again.

Olivia tried to muster up the words, to really think about how she was feeling and what she wanted out of this. She'd known all along that Cassie was insecure, especially after her dad's death, but it had never come between them before. She knew that Cassie could be difficult to warm to and that her spiky façade hid the hurt that was inside, knew that Cassie felt so out of control that her friends were the only thing left – but where did that leave them?

Neither of them was happy. Not like this. And it couldn't go on.

'Kimberley had some friends round and they were making so much noise that I had to get out of the house and Brain Freeze was the first place I went. Morgan came in once I was done, and we got talking. I don't want you to be jealous of Morgan. We were just chatting about Read with Pride. I didn't choose her over you.'

Please believe me when I say that.

'It's not jealousy, Livs, not like that. And I don't care that you were with Morgan – I like Morgan. She's cool. But you seem to have so much time for everyone else, and I'm your best friend *and* girlfriend, and never, for as long as we've known each other, have we spent less time together.'

'I'm sure that's not true.' But when she thought about it, maybe it was. They'd hung out before Ed's birthday party but not for long, and seen each other at Woolf and Wilde, but she couldn't remember the last time they'd hung out just the two of them and her brain hadn't been caught up on something else. It had been weeks and weeks.

'You really hurt me, Livs,' Cassie said. There was pain in her eyes and a rawness to her voice, and not just because she'd been shouting before. 'I waited outside your house for you that night and then to hear that you were at some party having this amazing time with your amazing new friends, and there was me, a sad loner, with nothing. I didn't know what I'd done wrong, or if I was wrong for even caring.'

Nell's party. And did Cassie really think she had nothing? Olivia thought of the fun she'd had that night, the dancing and laughing and joy of getting to know Rocky and Nell better, of meeting Alf, and she knew right then: *I should have invited Cassie. I should have just turned around and said, 'I've been invited to a party, do you want to come?' Why didn't I do that? I wouldn't have minded her being there.*

'I keep trying to see you, I keep suggesting things, but you never want to do anything with me any more. I'm at college, you're at school, we don't have as many Paper & Hearts Society meetings. I *knew* everything would change once the magic of the summer was over. I knew it!'

She raked a hand through her hair, her head hung in frustration. Her eyes had lost their earlier heat and now looked cold, sad.

They reminded Olivia of the first time she saw Cassie after her dad had died, when it was as if all the hope had been drained out of the world and nothing was left. It had broken Olivia's heart then, and it broke it now.

Her voice cracked as she said, 'Cassie, I've never meant to push you away. I tried to push *everything* away, but I didn't realise that in the process of doing so, you'd be the one who was affected the most.'

Cassie shrugged. 'Maybe you haven't meant to, but that's how it's come across. This is tearing us apart, and I can't bear it.'

'This is so stupid,' Olivia said, throwing her hands up in the air. 'The whole point of Read with Pride is to join people together, and we're out here arguing over being "torn apart". If we just stopped to listen to ourselves for five seconds, we'd realise how trivial this is.'

Cassie risked a smile. 'I can see how much it means to you, and I don't want you to think I'm coming between that or stopping you. I'm not controlling the way you live your life, I'm just asking – okay, maybe not *nicely* because I realise my reaction hasn't been small – but I'm asking that I'm included, too, if it means we get to spend time together.'

I'll try. I'll try to make this work and I'll make the time for us.

She realised then, standing opposite Cassie, who was so close, yet seemed so far away, that the hard part of a relationship wasn't the getting together bit: a good relationship took hard work on both sides, a commitment, and she hadn't understood that she needed to keep working at it. It wasn't just enough to want it to work – it took effort, too.

Olivia hoped she conveyed a question in her eyes as she looked into Cassie's: *Can we hug this out?* She was too far away; they needed to be close again.

They gravitated closer and closer, closer again, until their bodies were touching and Olivia's arms wrapped around Cassie's middle.

'I'm sorry, okay? I really am. I know I've got to stop worrying so much,' Cassie whispered. 'And no more projecting my insecurities on our relationship.'

'You do need to stop worrying,' Olivia said. 'But I'm sorry, too. I just can't seem to make everything work in unison at the moment. My head feels so muddled.'

They drew apart slightly, no longer hugging, but their arms still touching.

'Muddled? But you're so organised, Livs. Have you not got every single minute planned out in an elaborate bullet-journal calendar? That's not like you!'

She laughed. 'How did you find out about my bullet journal?'

There was no bullet journal or calendar and she didn't think she really had a grip on organisation, but she let Cassie hear what it would help her to hear.

'Do you know, when I spoke to Ed about this, he said what I really needed to do was take you on a date to this cat café that's opened up in the next town over, but I didn't think that was such a good idea.'

'Thank goodness our romance isn't in his hands! Wait. You went to Ed for advice?!'

Cassie grinned. 'He's not so bad, you know, when you catch him in the right mood. He also advised me to stand underneath your bedroom window and throw rocks at it until you came downstairs, but I thought that might have been a bit too expensive. I would have thrown a boulder by mistake and you'd have ended up with smashed glass.'

'So romantic!' Olivia giggled, and linked her arm in Cassie's. They began to walk back, out of the alley, and away from town. Neither wanted to let go of the other.

'I'll help, you know. I'll do whatever you need me to do to make sure you get the result you need.' Olivia knew Cassie meant it, too.

'Well, there is one thing you could do for me,' Olivia said. She thought of Morgan's poster idea – of course Cassie was the perfect person to design it. 'Would you like to be instrumental in our latest idea, the big poster drop?'

Olivia was over the moon when Cassie agreed. 'I'll make it the best poster the world has ever seen.'

As they got to the point where they had to part ways, Cassie pulled them to a stop.

'I love you, Livs,' she said. 'You're the best thing in my life.'

There were no words. No words! The *L* word?! 'Cassie!!'
Cassie laughed. 'It's true!'

'Do you really? Even though I basically ignored you and didn't see you and left you hanging around outside my house while I did the Macarena?!'

'Yes, even then,' Cassie said. 'You're worth it. Wait – the Macarena?!'

'Long story. I'll tell you another time.'

Tucked behind the bus stop, nobody could see them. Olivia reached up and cupped Cassie's face with her hand, smiling widely. 'Despite the fact that you're the moodiest person I've ever known and really need to chill out sometimes, I love *you*, Cass.'

It was the sweetest kiss they'd ever shared – when their lips met, love spiralled around them. Neither of them were particularly happy when Cassie's bus pulled up, but they drew apart, still smiling.

'I am not moody!' were Cassie's parting words as she boarded the bus.

Olivia's laugh covered the distance between them. 'Oh, yes, you are!'

Cassie: <3

Olivia: <3 <3 <3 <3 <3

Cassie: (i'm sorry)

Olivia: (And I'm sorry so we balance each other out!)

Olivia: Although next time you're taking me to the cat café!!

Cassie: do not tell ed!

Morgan: Listen up my pals! We're launching our petition with a BANG with an unforgettable poster drop! We need to work out who's doing what

Oscar: w8, wts a pstr drp?

Rocky: Ooh a poster drop! I like it!

Alf: Oscar, it is impossible to take you seriously when you write like that!

Nell: Let's get out there and make a statement! But yeah, what's a poster drop?

Morgan: So we get loads of Read with Pride themed posters with a link to the petition and pin them up all around school and then create a snowstorm of posters to throw at people so they can't ignore them

Oscar: Yeah, that could work! I don't really want to be the one dropping but

Morgan: Oh so you'll stop for Alf but not for me, your best friend? RUDE

Henry: I'm happy to help! :)

Alf: Hahaha I'm glad I have some influence! My eyes
    couldn't take any more

Oscar: Watch it or I'll start again!

Ed: OH DAMN I WANT TO BE PART OF IT but I don't think
    the school will let me in, not after I dropped that Bunsen
    burner on someone's blazer by accident on my last day

Tabby: Wait, I have not heard that story!

Ed: 🔥

Rocky: That's AWESOME

Cassie: i just emailed the poster over to you, hope it's okay
    x

Olivia: !!!!!!!!!!!!!!!!!!!

Olivia: IT'S AMAZING!

Chapter Seventeen

Furtively, Olivia took the posters from her locker, double-checking to see she hadn't left any behind. She'd spent the previous evening printing them out, using way too much paper and ink, and with each copy the printer spat out, she felt the nerves build within her.

It will all be fine and it will all work out and we will make the impact we need, and I've just got to keep my fingers crossed that it all goes according to plan. It will be FINE!

She hid them under her blazer, holding the stack tight under her arm, and tried to look casual and not like she was about to commit a terrible crime. Which, in a way, she was. It was an act of protest; it was a challenge against the school, and everything she'd ever been taught advised her – and Read with Pride – against their next actions.

But she thought of all the students who had come before her, who had protested and gone on school-strikes and fought passionately for what they believed in, and it gave her the spur she needed to take the first step towards rebellion.

Olivia headed casually – far too casually – downstairs to the meeting point they'd agreed on, tucked into a corner of the stairwell where nobody would be able to see them convene. She steadied her breathing and focused her concentration on the task at hand, attempting to let calm wash over her.

It became easier once she turned the corner at the bottom of the stairs and found Saffy, Nell, Alf and Henry gathered; the others were taking refuge where they could see what was happening but wouldn't be seen to be involved.

She untucked the posters from under her blazer where she'd been hiding them.

'Are we ready, team?'

'As we'll ever be,' Henry said. Olivia hadn't expected him to be anything other than calm.

'So we'll each take separate areas, but try to stick together too, especially in the main corridor. That way it should be harder for anyone to work out where – or who – the posters are coming from. Sound good?'

She gave them each an equal pile of posters.

'So there's five of us: two in the main corridor, throwing the posters over the stair bannisters and the balustrade, and then the three remaining can take the science, music and IT corridors, where most people will see them. Nell, do you want to take IT and then come back down to support us once you've finished? Then Henry, you can take the music, and Alf the science corridor. So, Saffy – happy to help me in the main corridor?'

'Yes!' Saffy said. She clutched the posters to her chest and smiled. 'I'm small enough to escape quickly if something goes wrong!'

'Perfect!' Olivia said. 'Although hopefully everything will go according to plan.'

'It will,' Henry said, 'and if there's any trouble, don't all meet up back here again: it's best if we just continue as normal, so that we don't all attract attention to the group of us.'

'Good thinking,' Nell said. 'Carry on like we have no idea what's happening.'

'Be safe,' Alf said, and they split off into their groups: Olivia and Saffy headed one way up the stairs, and the other three headed to their respective corridors, where they would plaster the walls with their posters.

'Nervous?' Olivia asked Saffy, squeezing her arm for support.

'A little,' she admitted, but smiled nonetheless.

'Me, too, but it will be fine and we can do this. And we've got each other, every step of the way.'

The main stairs leading from the large corridor to the upstairs corridor rose in two parts: while Saffy went to position herself on the one side so they would cover all bases, Olivia took two stairs at a time to stand in the middle. She leant against the metal barrier and looked down at the students milling around, chatting in groups and laughing.

She took one last glance at Cassie's beautiful poster on the top of her pile. *Right. I can do this.*

LET US READ WITH PRIDE

The recent introduction of permission slips in the library is discriminatory and restricts access to those who need it most.

If you feel as passionate about this as we do . . .

Sign the petition to show your support!

Follow us on Instagram and tell us your #ReadWithPride stories

---

Glancing up at Saffy, who looked as ready as she'd ever be, Olivia nodded with a steely determination. Just once. Big enough so Saffy would see.

And then they were off. Without a second's hesitation, Olivia took a handful of posters and flung them over the bannister, ducking back as soon as she heard the first scream. And then it was mayhem, her arms aching as she threw the paper missiles into the air, scrunching some up so they'd make more of an impact, others free-falling and landing on the ground, on people's heads, at their feet and on their shoulders.

Everywhere around them, students were shouting in disbelief as they reached their hands to the sky to grab for the hundreds of pieces of paper floating around them. It was the same on Saffy's side: nobody was safe. Between them, they'd managed to make a statement. And they were only aided by the ricochet effect that took place: the more paper that landed, the more other people grabbed the balls and began to throw them at each other, or began to make hasty paper aeroplanes and take part in the tomfoolery. And, Olivia noticed, some began to read what was on the posters.

'WHAT IS GOING ON?' The pandemonium subsided slightly, only slightly, for a few brief seconds, as the voice of Olivia's Head of Year, Ms Ryding, boomed over them. She was strict at the best of times, but now, thundering along the main corridor, eyes scanning the crowd for culprits, she looked murderous. 'ALL STUDENTS, DOWN FROM THE STAIRS! IF I SEE EVEN ONE

PERSON START THIS UP AGAIN, YOU'LL BE IN INSTANT ISOLATION. DO YOU HEAR ME?'

By this point, the paper storms had ceased but the ground was littered with poster upon poster upon poster, some untouched, others trodden on and squashed underfoot. Now that Ms Ryding was parading back and forth, looking for the source of the commotion, a hush had descended. Everyone had ceased movement, all wondering what would happen next.

Olivia managed to get away by sneaking past a group of incredulous students on the stairs after dumping her last batch of posters, and skirted round more of the gathering to position herself on the other side of the corridor, away from the action.

Her heart was racing! It was exhilarating! She felt alive! The risk!

The only sound that had started up was the crackling of Ms Ryding's walkie-talkie, gripped tightly in her hand. 'Incident in the science corridor!' it called. 'Another incident in the music corridor!' a second voice exclaimed.

'That was Nell and Henry,' Rocky said, with a tap on Olivia's shoulder. 'That means they did it!'

'Shhh!' Olivia said. 'Someone might overhear!'

She was happy to see Rocky, though, glad to see the familiar face. She just hoped that Saffy had managed to get away safely.

'Sorry,' Rocky corrected themself. 'My bad. I'm just so happy that it worked. I had my doubts, right up until the last few seconds.'

'There's still time for it to go wrong. We're not out of the woods yet.'

But even if it does go wrong now, Olivia thought, *this was the first step.* The first step towards change. People had to take notice; they had to see what was going on. And even if they didn't care now, Read with Pride would have to make them.

'I WILL FIND OUT WHO HAS BEEN PART OF THIS, AND YOU WILL BE IN SERIOUS TROUBLE IF YOU DON'T HAND YOURSELVES IN. THIS IS NOT HOW WE BEHAVE, IS IT?'

Ms Ryding waved an accusing finger between the groups of students; they were beginning to get bored, shuffling about and leaving the area. And once they were moving, there was nothing else that could be done.

'You know,' Olivia said, just as the warning bell for the end of break went, 'I think I could get used to being a rebel. A rebel in the name of books. Let's teach this school what reading with pride really means.'

She and Rocky shared an enthusiastic high-five.

It may have been daring, but she'd do it all over again, without a shadow of a doubt.

Chapter Eighteen

The thrill of the poster drop didn't leave Olivia for days afterwards. It was a secret she carried around with her as she walked past the few posters the teachers had forgotten to take down, as she listened to the rumblings of discontent from students who were waking up to their cause.

They'd done that. They'd started something worth talking about.

The best part had been sitting in the library one break-time, listening as people went up to Miss Carter's desk and asked things like, 'Is it true, what we're reading about on these posters? Are you really stopping us from taking out books with LGBT characters?'

She could have sworn Miss Carter turned to look in her direction, but Olivia had gone straight back to the revision notes spread out in front of her – a mish-mash of copied definitions from her religious studies textbook, diagrams for biology, and answers to French reading comprehension questions.

She'd savoured the memory of exhilaration as she monitored the online activity, hoping for a pick-up in followers to their social media pages and more signatures to their petition. It kept her going, even through the headaches she kept getting when she returned home in the afternoon, the ones that were more a numbness than pain. She spent more of her time trying to push through and keep going than she did anything else – her books were gathering dust, and her bed had hardly been slept in. There had even been a few nights when she'd woken at her desk, not sure where she was, what time it was, how long she'd been asleep.

She was still thinking about it now, as she made Cassie a cup of tea in the kitchen.

'How is the petition going?' Cassie asked, sitting round the kitchen table. 'I keep meaning to check in.'

In a bid to be the better girlfriend she'd promised to be – and to give Cassie the chance to be involved further with Read with Pride – she'd invited her round for a revision session, which was the only way Olivia had been able to fit everything in.

'Well . . . Not terribly?' Olivia shrugged, and put the mug of tea she'd made in front of Cassie, taking her own seat opposite. 'These things take time, I guess. We've barely got started, so the thirty or so signatures we've got so far is amazing, I think!'

'And you have to start somewhere,' Cassie pointed out.

'True.' Olivia went quiet as she sorted through the stack of paper she'd brought down from her desk, ready to put the homework that needed handing in tomorrow into her bag.

Trying to cross-reference the paper with her homework planner proved trickier than she'd expected because when she turned to this week's spread it was to find an indecipherable mess. Half of what she'd originally written had been crossed out, with arrows zigzagging the page and replacement details written in an agitated scrawl.

Ugh, this is impossible. Why can't I work out what any of this means?! I'm the one who wrote it!

Turning to the page before yielded the same results. She had to strain her eyes to be able to make out even a single word.

'How's your mum?' Olivia asked, giving up on the planner for now.

Cassie stared down into the depths of her tea. 'We've had some good days,' she said, 'when Mum has left the house and been fine with it and I've been able to go to college, but there are still bad days when she won't leave her bed or can't stand the thought of me leaving her side. Those days have been *rough*. But . . . I don't know, I want to feel hopeful? I keep thinking that if the good days can one day equal the bad, that will at least be something, and then maybe we can look to getting her some more help. I

237

know she doesn't want to be like this, but I think she's forgotten how to live without my dad. I'd like to show her that there's more than the four walls of our house.'

'She's lucky to have you,' Olivia said, and meant every word.

'And I'm lucky to have *you*,' Cassie said. She reached her hand across the table and Olivia linked fingers, feeling the unnatural warmth stolen from her hot mug. 'Thank you for forgiving me when I was being so ridiculous.'

'And thank you for forgiving me when I basically abandoned you.'

This time, Olivia picked up her homework planner in an attempt to decode the scribbled language, putting the pages close to her eyes to work it out one letter at a time.

'So ... I think ... this means French? A French ... worksheet? Cassie, can you look through the pile there for a French worksheet of some kind?'

She pushed the paper pile over to Cassie and moved on to the next scrawl down. She cursed her past self for being so jumbled.

I'm glad I know Rdvdegis *isn't a word because right now it is the only thing I can make out.*

She'd have to make a concerted effort to do better.

'Livs ... this is half-finished.' When she looked up, she saw Cassie frowning down at the worksheet. 'There are loads of gaps!'

'Are there?' Olivia asked, sliding it away from Cassie so she could see. 'I could have sworn I'd done it.'

She rubbed at her temples – she'd done it yesterday, hadn't she? Or maybe it was the night before . . . or . . . 'I must have done it. I must have.'

Cassie shook her head. 'I don't think so, Livs.'

'But . . . !'

Although, when she thought about it, when would she have had time yesterday? She'd been checking in with Rocky to see how the website was going, and making a list with Nell of what they needed to do by the end of the week to reach their targets. 'Oh, give it here, I'll have to do it now.'

'You don't have to sound like you're under duress, Livs; it's only French, and hardly any French at that. You literally only have to fill out some boxes.'

Olivia grumbled at that. It wasn't only some boxes! It was some boxes she thought she'd already done and was not in the mood for now.

She made sure to shake her head and grumble even more as she carried on where she'd left off, just to show Cassie how distasteful the thought of French was to her right now.

From her side, her phone lit up.

Alf: Hey Olivia! Everyone's been sending in their
Instagram submissions to the Read with Pride email.

> I've just forwarded them on to you so you can take a look. :)

Olivia: Ah, thanks so much for that! I'll have a read now!

'Ooh, look, Cass! The first stories are in!'

Olivia got out her laptop. She clicked open the first email and Cassie came around to her side so they could gather around the screen.

'This is exciting,' Cassie said, and Olivia relished the feeling of their bodies side by side, the closeness of them.

'Ready?' Olivia said, more for herself than Cassie. She didn't wait for a response before she began reading.

Subject: Fwd: SAFFY'S STORY

#ReadWithPride is important to me because it's about more than just the books: it's about acceptance. Before I got involved with the campaign, I didn't think anyone would ever accept me for who I am. Once, a boy found my diary after it fell out of my locker and I came into school the next day to find that his whole group of friends had read it. They started spreading it around that I was gay and called me names that I never want to hear again in my life. After that, I found it

difficult to trust people and, even when I tried, I
didn't know why I couldn't make friends.

But then I met other people who were just like me
and knew how important it was to #ReadWithPride.
For the first time in my entire life, I knew that
I'd been accepted.

  It's okay to be me.

'Oh, Saffy,' Olivia breathed. 'That's . . .'

She could hardly explain how it made her feel to read those words, to hear them in Saffy's voice, shy as she'd been when they'd first met but now growing stronger. She was finding her voice – and her people.

And it gave Olivia a sense of satisfaction, too, to think that a small conversation they'd had by chance was giving Saffy so much. That's why she was doing this, and she had to store that feeling away to use when things felt difficult, when she thought she couldn't carry on any more.

She'd see this through. She wasn't just doing this for herself any more: she had to do it for them, too.

It's okay to be me.

'I'll have to get a box of tissues because I don't think my tear ducts will remain dry through all of this,' she said to Cassie, who promised to wipe the tears away with her sleeve.

'As long as they're pure tears – no mascara stains, please.'
Olivia opened up the next email.

Subject: Fwd: ROCKY'S STORY

I #ReadWithPride because I believe it's the only
way anyone should read. Nobody should ever be
made to feel ashamed for their sexuality or
gender orientation, and reading is one of the
best ways to build empathy and understand that,
at the end of the day, we're all just human.

I hope that our #ReadWithPride campaign will show
people that anyone can make a difference and even
a small action can transform someone's day. It's
about standing up for yourself and other people,
using your voice when you're able to, and never
giving up on the promise of a better future.

We have to believe that we can change the world.

'Rocky's great,' Cassie said. 'And they're right – not
everyone has to make some grand gesture. Even little
things add up, if everyone does them.'

'I love the line about empathy,' Olivia said. That's what
had stood out for her. 'Reading puts you in other people's

heads and makes you think outside of your own experience. I wouldn't be half the person I am today without it.'

'An alternative universe where there's an Olivia who doesn't read?' Cassie pretended to shudder.

Olivia grinned. 'It doesn't bear thinking about!'

'What are you going to write for yours?' Cassie asked. She nodded to the screen.

The truth was – Olivia didn't know. When she thought about it, it was like the contents of her brain emptied and she forgot how to form words. Seeing her new friends' stories typed out on screen, imagining what they would look like once they were posted, only made her feel more hesitant: what could she say that could possibly sum up her experience? How would she ever be able to articulate how much this meant to her?

'I'm working on it,' she said. And she would, when she was ready. When she had the time. She wouldn't let them down, she just needed to think about it. To consider what it was she had to say, and how she'd ever condense all her thoughts down.

'Alf's turn now,' she said, and opened the last email.

Subject: Fwd: ALF'S STORY

When I first realised I was bisexual, I kept thinking I'd made it up. I felt like I'd gone through my whole life knowing who I was and what I wanted, and suddenly everything was different. I was the same person, and yet I was terrified at what it might mean for me or what people might think.

Here's what I learnt about myself since I realised: being bisexual doesn't mean that you're fussy or can't make up your mind; it doesn't mean that you're greedy; it doesn't make you confused about your sexuality; you're not bisexual because it's trendy or cool. And no matter who you love or who you go out with, nobody should ever invalidate your sexuality.

Anyone can identify as bisexual and every bisexual person is different. There is no one way to be bisexual.

It just means that you're attracted to more than one gender. That's all there is to it.

#ReadWithPride — always.

'I feel like my heart is going to explode with all the emotions that are racing through my veins right now,' Olivia said, clasping her hands to her face. 'These stories – they're so amazing! And if even one person reads them and feels understood, that's what it's all about. Cassie . . . are you . . . crying?'

Cassie sniffed and scowled. 'No, I just have something in my eye. I am *not* crying.'

'Are you . . . sure?' Olivia didn't want to push but she could have sworn she saw a tear or two in Cassie's eyes.

Cassie leant back in her chair. 'Fine. That got me. Reading that . . . I know that I come across as confident when it comes to my sexuality and that I seem in control all the time, but that still doesn't make it easy. There are still days when I question or doubt myself; there are still times when you stumble across someone online saying any one of those harmful, stereotypical things, or overhear a conversation from some ignorant person who hasn't stopped to think about the real life people they're assuming things about. Sometimes it affects me. I try hard for it not to, but it does.'

Olivia put an arm round Cassie's shoulders and rested her head on the one person who knew her inside out. 'You could write a story for us, you know,' she suggested.

'I'll think about it,' Cassie said. 'In the meantime, I am looking forward to reading yours.'

'But first,' Olivia said with a groan, 'I better get on with this French worksheet. It won't do itself.'

But there was a little question in her mind that grew bigger and bigger: *If I've missed out this worksheet, what else have I missed? I'm in for another late night, I think.*

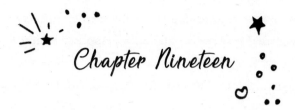

Chapter Nineteen

Under the auspices of a 'revision club', Read with Pride had managed to steal the computer room next to the library for themselves for the duration of their lunch break. Olivia thought that there was a distinct possibility, due to the fact that it was at Miss Carter's discretion that students could use the room, that their true motives had not gone undetected, but there was little time to worry about that today.

She'd got there as soon as her previous lesson was let out, sneaking in five minutes' worth of revision before everyone turned up. She had a religious studies test coming up and had a whole list of definitions to memorise before then, and when she got home she would have to do Read with Pride work, as well as maths and English homework. She didn't know how she'd ever fit it in.

But I can't think about that! Just got to keep going!

She copied out the definitions from the textbook she'd borrowed, on to a fresh set of cue cards that she could carry around and use to test herself on whenever she had a free moment. Learning from her earlier mistake, she concentrated especially hard on making her handwriting legible.

I can't have a repeat of that again. Poor Cassie kept finding so many half-finished pieces! It was never-ending!

The door opened and in walked Oscar.

'Hey Olivia,' he said, taking the seat opposite her. 'What you up to?'

She pulled a face. 'Just revision.' She barely looked up from the page as she finished off the definition she was writing out.

He pulled his blazer off to reveal his crisp white shirt underneath, and from the pocket took a somewhat squashed book. 'On to the next *Heartstopper* volume!' he said. 'I've had to get Morgan to take it home with her because I can't risk my mum finding it. I'm just glad it's so worth the hassle.'

Olivia put her pen down – there was no point carrying on now. She'd have to finish them off later.

One more thing to add to the list. But IT'S FINE. I CAN DO THIS.

'That's nice of Morgan to do,' she said, 'but can you not leave it in your locker? Won't that be easier for both of you?'

A little sheepishly, he replied, 'I like reading it on the bus to and from school. Morgan gets off at the stop before me, so I give it to her then, and that way I don't have to go ages and ages without reading.'

'I know how you feel: I can't imagine going without a good book!'

An unintentional lie. She couldn't remember the last time she'd read and, really, she didn't know how Oscar felt. She'd never had her reading censored before, had never not been allowed to read a book because of its contents. She guessed that Oscar's mum thought she was protecting him, but Olivia thought that was a flawed argument, one that didn't take his feelings into account whatsoever.

The door swung open again and Rocky and Saffy arrived, giggling together. Rocky slapped Oscar on the back and gave Olivia a thumbs up, while Saffy said loudly, 'Hi Olivia! Hi Oscar! I'm so excited for today! It'll be great!'

Just seeing how happy she was made Olivia's smile refuse to disappear, even when she had to stuff her revision cards in her pocket, out of the way.

Once everyone was in, gathered around the table – Morgan perching on the table itself to point at the progress plan she'd outlined on two pieces of A3 paper Sellotaped together – it was time for their meeting to start.

'Right then, pals,' Morgan said, 'as official progress tracker, here's what's been going on: we're up to sixty signatures on the petition. We didn't have a major spike after our poster drop but it got everyone talking so it doesn't matter too much. It's early days for the social media campaign, but so far, so good. We just need to ramp things up now, I think, and make sure we're working a hundred per cent.'

'Have you heard any more about the poster drop?' Saffy asked. She bit her lip. 'It was the most rebellious thing I've ever done!'

'We managed to get away with it,' Olivia said. An echo of the thrill she'd felt went through her, and she grinned. 'It was the most rebellious thing I've ever done too!'

'Sixty signatures doesn't seem many, though,' Rocky said. 'That's, like, a ridiculously small percentage of the students at school. It doesn't seem like it will hold much weight.'

'I want to tell you to be more optimistic,' Nell said, 'but I think you're right. We've got some serious work to do if we're going to get even double that.'

Even double that? Olivia's heart sank. Was that really what they were aiming for, at a push? Maybe this was all too much for them. Maybe they'd never get anywhere. Maybe they should just give up now.

No.

But it would be so nice. So nice to sleep at night without the thoughts whirring in her brain, so nice to catch up on all the revision she had to do, not to feel like she was paddling for her life in an ocean of exam preparation.

No, Olivia. She snapped herself out of it.

'We've still got the stories to post,' Alf pointed out. 'The best is yet to come, in my opinion.'

Olivia cried, 'They were all so brilliant! I just wanted to squish you all into a big hug!'

'No squishing,' Morgan said. 'Squishing is not a productive use of our time right now. The squishing can come later!'

Oscar cleared his throat. From his blazer pocket, he took folded up bits of paper, and pushed them into the middle of the table. 'You know the, uh, the stories? Will you – would you read mine for me before, we, um, before we post it? I don't know if it's all right.'

'Of course we will!' Olivia said, at the same time as Nell. And at the same time as Alf. The spooky unison brought a grin to all their faces.

It's strange and amazing all at once how quickly we've grown close, she thought. *I can't imagine my life without them in it now.*

Each taking a printout, they began reading. The only noise to be heard was their combined breathing and the flickering turns of paper against skin.

Subject: OSCAR'S STORY

The first time I read a book with a gay character in, it was like someone had peered into my soul and written all about it. Before then, the only time I saw gay people on TV or in films, they were known as 'the gay best friend'. They were only good for offering fashion advice to the main character, they didn't really have lives when away from their friend, were loud and outgoing, the life and soul of the party, and seemed to know exactly where they were going in life.

Which is fine if that's who you are, but not every gay person is. Take me, for example: I'm so shy that sometimes it feels like my face is being set on fire when I have to talk out loud, and I didn't want to just be the best friend. I wanted to think that I could be a main character too, if I wanted that.

To begin with, I struggled with feeling proud
because everything to do with pride was rainbows
and fun and people who seemed confident. As I
learnt more about myself, though, and as I've
made friends with other LGBTQ+ people, I've come
to understand that pride can be quiet and
unassuming, too, and that everyone deserves to be
the hero of their own story.

Even I can be the hero.

I didn't realise how strong I was until I began
to #ReadWithPride. And I want everyone to know
their own strength too.

'Oscar, it's amazing!' Nell said, the first to finish. She grinned warmly, radiating delight. 'You did a great job!'

'Oscar!!' Olivia squealed.

'Awesome!' Saffy said, in awe.

'And to think you had all of that in you all those times in IT when you told me to stop distracting you with my guinea pigs in sombreros gifs.' Rocky laughed. 'You go, Oscar!'

'So I don't have anything to worry about?' Oscar asked. He wasn't looking any of them in the face, staring down at the table.

'You've got absolutely nothing to worry about,' Alf reassured. 'You should be so pleased with what you've written: it does you complete justice.'

Oscar blushed brighter than he ever had before, and his words sprung to her mind: *I'm so shy that sometimes it feels like my face is being set on fire*. But maybe that wasn't as bad a thing as he thought it was: fire was fierce and passionate, it was determined. Oscar never had to be embarrassed again. He was as strong as he now knew himself to be.

'I was so scared writing it,' Oscar admitted. This time, he did allow himself to look up and survey the concerned faces watching him. 'I kept thinking my mum would burst in at any second and find out what I was doing.'

'Have you spoken any more about . . . what happened?' Rocky asked. Somehow, there was an unspoken agreement between them that they wouldn't press Oscar on topics concerning his mum. They let him speak in his own time, when he was up to it.

Oscar sighed. 'She hasn't stopped going on about it since she complained. She wants to know that "justice has been served" and that a permanent change has been made. I don't even like to think about all the things she's said because it hurts too much.'

Morgan huffed. 'No offence, Oscar, but I have no clue

where you came from. You have more tolerance in your little finger than she does in her whole body.'

'I know,' Oscar said, resigned. 'I've kind of accepted by now that she might not ever accept me for who I am. But I've only got to wait for a while before I can leave home, go to university, and in the meantime, I know that you lot will love me for who I am, so I know that there are other people out there who will, too. You can't choose your family, but you can choose your friends and I'm glad I've chosen a bunch like you.'

'Don't!' Nell said, putting a hand up. 'Stop right there or I'll get emotional!'

Rocky teased, 'You love it really, Nellykins. Admit it!'

'Well, maybe just a little bit,' she confessed.

'Who wants to upload the first story?' Morgan asked.

'I'm happy to do it!' Olivia said, beginning to make a list in her notebook. When she looked up from the page, Rocky was giving her a funny look.

'Aren't you already putting the final touches to our Twitter account tonight?' they asked.

'Oh, it won't take me two minutes to do that,' she said. She didn't see what the problem was. 'It makes more sense for me to do it, while I'm logged into the accounts. I can do it in one go.'

'If you're sure,' Rocky said. 'But let us know if you want one of us to do it.'

She batted them away. 'I'm sure! Anyway, you've got enough on your plate with the website and you already did such a good job with your story to share. So it's the least I can do!'

She didn't think about her own overflowing plate. Wouldn't think about it. If she just ignored it, it wouldn't be an issue.

Ed: Another day, ANOTHER JOB REJECTION I AM SO
   ANNOYED

Henry: What was it this time?

Ed: Working in the pet shop in town because apparently I
   don't have enough experience even though I AM A
   PROUD CAT FATHER

Cassie: the catfather

Tabby: Awwww Ed, you'll get there eventually!

Ed: Eventually isn't good enough! Like I don't have enough
   experience with animals. I have to deal with Mrs
   Simpkins's litter tray, don't I? THAT is experience

Henry: It's their loss and I'm sure something better will
   come along that's even better suited to you

Ed: Maybe I'll become a ventriloquist

Cassie: i'd pay good money to see that!

Ed: See! I better start training now. Hey, Tabby, do you want
   to be my ventriloquist's dummy?

Tabby: Should I be insulted right now?

Henry: Hey, Olivia, how are things going?

Olivia: Sorry!!!! No time to type!!!!!!!!!

Nell: Sent you some words to put on social media, should
   help with getting a few more petition signatures

Olivia: Hold on! I'll just check now!

Olivia: Got it! Do you want me to post it tonight?!

Mum: I'm resorting to texting you because I've been
shouting up the stairs and you obviously can't hear me.
Are you coming down for some food?

Morgan: Olivia, are you posting another story tonight?
We've had a few extra signatures this evening and I think
it would be a good idea
Olivia: Sorry I didn't get to this sooner! I had to eat! What an
inconvenience! Nell's sent me some good information to
go alongside the graphic that Cassie made. Shall I swap
them over and do another story tonight, then this
tomorrow?
Morgan: I think that will work!

Morgan sent a photo.
Morgan: And a motivational photo of Michelle the giant snail
for you!

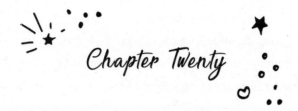

Chapter Twenty

Olivia: I've overslept this morning – you can walk on without
me because I don't want to make you late!!
Tabby: Everything okay?! We've barely seen you the last
week or two!

Yes, everything is fine but I REALLY NEED TO GET GOING.
I AM SUPER LATE ALREADY.

Somehow, she'd slept right through her alarm and
should have left the house ten minutes ago, but was still
in her pyjamas, frantically brushing her teeth, messaging
Henry and Tabby and buttoning up her school blouse,
all at the same time. One brush of each tooth equalled
one button equalled one word of her message, which
she mistakenly thought was the most economical way
of doing it.

She had to speed-walk to school, making it to tutor
group first thing by the skin of her teeth; she only just sat
her bum in her chair before the first lesson bell went,

luckily saving her from a late mark next to her name, which she really didn't need.

She took the time in tutor, while Mr Joyce went through a presentation on exam techniques, to catch up on the last few maths homework problems she hadn't completed yet, tapping away at her calculator under the table and scribbling down the answers in her exercise book. All the numbers were outside of the little boxes they had to write in, and she gave up on showing all of her working out after a while, not even sure herself how she'd got to the answers she now had.

She still felt like she was in a rush when she got to French, where she sat next to Tabby and collapsed in a heap on her shoulder. 'Ugh,' she said.

'Is everything okay?' Tabby asked, looking concerned. She patted Olivia's head in a slightly awkward manner, but Olivia didn't mind.

'I overslept, I am behind on everything, and I feel like I'm running on a hamster wheel and I'm annoying even myself!'

'You'll get there,' Tabby said sympathetically. 'French is bound to make you feel better.'

Tabby was still surprised that Olivia was so good at French. 'I never knew you had a secret love of languages!' she'd said the first time she'd heard Olivia speak French, and she still repeated it every lesson. 'I can't believe I didn't know that about you!'

Olivia shrugged and with a silly, sarcastic tone said, '*J'adore les langues!* What can I say? I'm very talented, Tabby, you should know that by now. There's nothing I can't do.'

'Well, of course, I do know that by now. You and your scheming!' Tabby gave her a pointed look but turned quickly back at her exercise book as their teacher, Madame Heger, walked past. '*La semaine prochaine, je voudrais lire mon livre ...*'

'It's not scheming,' Olivia said as Madame Heger moved on to another table. 'Well, not exactly ... There's just so much to do!'

She filled Tabby in, as quickly as she could before Madame Heger made a second rotation of the classroom, on her break-time activity: checking over their personal story submissions, sharing the few messages other people had contributed on social media, and redoubling their efforts.

'You're amazing, Livs,' Tabby said and patted Olivia's hand. 'I don't know how you do it all, I really don't. I wish I could do it! To make a real difference: that's special.'

'I haven't done it yet, that's the thing. There's still plenty that could go wrong.'

'*Je bois en vous!*'

'Do you mean "I believe in you"? Because you just said "I drink in you" and that does sound a little creepy.'

'Ha!' Tabby said. 'If I ever go to France, I'm taking you with me.'

'Next time, we'll go on a bookish road trip to France,' Olivia said with a smile to her friend, 'and it will be perfect.'

There was a knock on the door and a younger student was ushered in with a note in their hand – a student runner, a job the younger years were given to deliver messages around the school. Olivia had hated doing it when she was in the years below because it had always meant missing her favourite lessons.

'*Oui?*'

In a nervy voice, the boy said, 'I have a note for Olivia Santos.' He handed the note to Madame Heger, who squinted down at it.

'Olivia, you're wanted in Ms Ryding's office immediately,' she said. And with a shooing action, 'Off you go.'

Her heart skipped a beat. What could Ms Ryding want with her? Her Head of Year had never wanted to speak with her before.

'Good luck,' Tabby said, and Olivia nodded. She collected her stuff and stood up, aware of all the eyes on her as she left the room. The quiet of the corridor only made her feel worse as she slowly walked the empty space to the opposite side of the long building where Ms Ryding's small office was.

There's only one thing I can think that she might have to say to me. And it can't be good.

She could see all the mayhem with the posters, hear the anger in Ms Ryding's voice, and braced herself for what was about to come.

And I will have to remain dignified and take what I'm given, in the hope of protecting everyone else. That's what I promised and I'll keep my word.

When she got to the office, she found that she wasn't the only one: Nell and Henry were also there, seated in two of the three chairs. Henry had his long legs stretched out and was twiddling his thumbs; Nell raised her eyebrows when she spotted Olivia, and her nostrils were flaring. Anger.

Ms Ryding, stern-faced, nodded to the remaining chair, and Olivia took her cue to sit.

'Thank you for coming,' Ms Ryding said, looking like she meant anything but. 'I think you all know why you're here.'

Olivia did, but she wished she didn't. Maybe it was inevitable but a tiny part of her had hoped ... Maybe it was stupid to hope.

Maybe this whole thing was a ridiculous idea. We were just kidding ourselves.

'I must say that I am very disappointed in the three of you. When we looked back at the CCTV footage, none of us could believe what we were seeing, especially from students like you.'

What's that supposed to mean? Olivia thought, offended on behalf of the other students who she would have expected it from. *Because we might be seen as academic students, you mean? That's not discriminatory* whatsoever *against those other students.* She wanted to roll her eyes.

'What do you have to say for yourselves?'

She could feel Nell bristling next to her and wished she'd protest, but also that she'd keep quiet and wouldn't make it worse for them. If Ms Ryding believed they were sorry, they could still keep this going; if they aggravated her further, it could make things worse.

Silence. 'Nothing?' Ms Ryding said. 'Not one of you has anything to say? Are you even *sorry* for the disruption you caused?'

She tutted as they remained quiet.

'Olivia?'

Her mouth felt dry; she didn't think she could have spoken even if she'd wanted to.

'Henry?'

'We feel passionately about the library, Ms Ryding,' he said, and Olivia snapped her head up in shock as he spoke his words with defiance. 'It may have caused disruption, but it was all my idea. Nell and Olivia were only doing what I told them to.'

Ms Ryding looked bored. 'Girls, you are both fifteen and old enough to know your own minds. I don't for one second believe you did this unwillingly.'

Olivia felt bad when neither of them spoke, but she also felt like they'd been backed into a corner. She didn't want Henry to completely take the fall, but she also didn't want to incriminate Nell if she contradicted him.

'Well . . . As none of you have been in trouble before, we won't be giving severe punishments and won't be informing your parents.' *Phew.* 'As long as you promise to stop everything you've been doing and cause no more trouble. If there's a next time, we won't be so lenient.'

Give up?! Give in?!

Olivia and Nell shared a glance, anguish paining both of their expressions.

'But will you be looking into the issue we have with the new library system?' Henry said.

'Henry Gillingham, I am very close to changing my mind on being so lenient when you choose to speak to a teacher like that. That's not a student matter, so I will not answer. I mean it: no more nonsense from any of you. You are extremely lucky right now.'

Lucky?! This isn't luck! Luck would be the school listening to what we have to say, not shouting us down. We are allowed a right to protest!

'I'm glad we could sort that out,' was the last thing Ms Ryding said before she kicked them out, shut the door behind them and they were left in silence, with only their turmoiled thoughts to keep them company.

'It is *not* sorted out,' Nell said, under her breath. 'Far from it.'

Where do we go from here? Olivia gritted her teeth to fight back the tears. *What do we do now?*

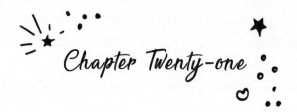

Chapter Twenty-one

Rocky: Nell filled me in on what happened! Are you all okay?!

Ed: What?!?! What's happened?!?!?!?!

Olivia: The school found out who left the posters. They want us to stop.

Nell: Fair play, Henry was magnificent in there. My blood feels like it's boiling!

Ed: Henry?! In trouble?! Wow, I didn't think I'd EVER SEE THE DAY

Morgan: I'm sorry, I feel like this is all my fault, coming up with the idea of the posters in the first place. Maybe it was too risky

Saffy: It worked though! We got people talking!

Oscar: Was it scary in there?

Nell: Put it this way, I love horror and zombie films and even I was terrified

Olivia: Where do we go from here? Do we stop?

Alf: We can't stop now! If the teachers are acting like this, it means they know they're in the wrong. They're scared. We can't give up!

Oscar: I'm with Alf. We can't stop now

Rocky: It must be serious if Oscar isn't using text speak any more

Oscar: nt n e mor

Ed: Hahahaha that's a good one!

Cassie: don't give up, let it spur you on, you've gone too far now to stop

Olivia: It's not my decision to make. I want to carry on but you've all got to be okay with it too

Nell: I'm still in. We've got to take this all the way

Morgan: I finished my story and emailed it over to the RwP account. Can we put it up tonight?

Alf: Let's do it

Olivia: We've got this! We've just got to keep going!! We can do it!!!

Subject: MORGAN'S STORY

Even though I'm not a book lover, I #ReadWithPride because without the stories of others I would never have had the courage to begin transitioning. These personal stories made me feel hopeful even when it seemed like the

world was against me. At first, when I realised
that this was what I wanted to do, all I could
see around me was newspaper articles and TV
interviews and bad headlines written by people
who would never be able to understand what it's
like to be trans but tried to tell me how I
should be feeling. What I should be doing. They
made me feel like it was wrong to be myself. I
didn't know where to turn, but eventually I found
the place: the truth. I listened to people who
knew exactly what it was like to be in my
position, I sought out every little piece of
information I could, and even though I still
have bad days, those bad days aren't so terrible
any more.

So I #ReadWithPride for all my fellow transgender
people, for the moments when we've been made to
feel like we shouldn't be proud of who we are.

We should. We deserve to be happy too. <3

Tabby: That's so lovely, Morgan <3
Rocky: Really lovely, I'M PROUD OF YOU MORGS
Alf: Go Morgan!

Morgan: I loooveeeee you all

Oscar: u r the best

Morgan: Apart from you, Oscar

Morgan: Do you think we should tag people in the
comments who might take notice and spread the word
more??

Olivia: Great idea! Let's get thinking and then we can tag
some in previous posts too!

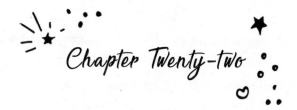

Chapter Twenty-two

'And that's it for today!' Miss Forster said, just as the end-of-the-day bell ricocheted through the classroom. Olivia grabbed her things, tucking her copy of *Much Ado About Nothing* under her arm, and filed out behind the rest of her English class.

Her head was swimming. *Got to go home and walk Lizzie because everyone else is out this afternoon and then I've got to upload the next campaign post and then I've got to finish off my chemistry homework for tomorrow which I haven't done yet and really should have done last week when we got given it and then I have to prepare tomorrow's campaign post and then ... Well, I'm sure there will be something else to do!*

She had about five to-do lists on the go, all of which were in various states of completion.

Her locker was only opposite the English corridor, so she headed over and put everything in her bag, making sure her books didn't get crushed under the weight of everything else.

She turned her phone on, popping it in her blazer pocket in case a teacher came by and saw – they were still funny about mobile usage, even though technically school was over for the day. Her fingers were itching to check how the campaign was getting on, but her hopes weren't particularly high. Nothing had happened so far that was worth getting excited about.

'See you tomorrow!' Olivia heard Ife say, who then patted her on the back as she passed to go to her own locker down the corridor.

Olivia slung her backpack over one shoulder, pulled her skirt down as she stood up, and weaved her way around the other students to get out of the corridor.

I'll have to do some revision tonight too, but maybe I should spend that time drawing up a revision timetable so then at least I'll know if I'm on track or behind. Or am I better revising a little bit as well as *doing the timetable?*

As she felt the first blast of cold air against her face, some of the tension, but not all, left her body. Her shoulders relaxed, although they felt constantly tight these days, like the muscles were an elastic band waiting to snap; the thought of going back home helped to focus and calm her brain.

I've got to do this – school – all over again tomorrow, though. And the day after that. And that.

She'd never thought about it before, but suddenly the days stretching ahead of her were too long, too many, and she couldn't see how that would ever change.

I'll just listen to some music on my way home – that will sort me out and then I won't feel this weird.

She shook off whatever this was she was feeling. She didn't know what. It was new. Too new – and, admittedly, a little frightening.

When she got her phone out of her pocket, it was lagging.

That's strange, she thought. *I've never known it this slow before.*

She stopped just outside the gate as she stared down at the flashing screen, not quite believing what she was seeing. Because hundreds of notifications were pouring in, and Olivia had no idea where from.

'Oh my,' she whispered, lifting a hand to her head.

Read with Pride has been tagged in a post.

I #ReadWithPride because everyone deserves to see characters like themselves and to know that they're not alone.

This isn't one of our posts! None of us wrote this!!

She exited the post to look at the notifications screen and couldn't believe it when she was able to scroll down so many – likes and follows and comments, a few mentions. Actual interaction!

The ReadWithPride hashtag had pictures in it that weren't any of the official ones they'd been posting, and their followers were going up by the second. Soon to be in three digits!

WOW!

By chance, Nell and Rocky were coming through the gates and Olivia just about managed to garble out a quick, 'You need to see this!' before losing it completely and letting out the biggest, most excitable squeal she'd ever made in her life.

'Someone else posted!' Rocky exclaimed. 'We've done it! The campaign is working!'

'Can't believe it!!' Nell twirled around in a circle, arms wide, like she was Maria von Trapp in *The Sound of Music*. 'Woo hoo!!!'

She wasn't sure who first initiated it, but somehow they ended up in a group hug, squealing in glee, squeezing what felt like the life out of each other as they rejoiced in their happiness.

By the time they'd gathered everyone else, the rest of the school was quiet, only a few stragglers yet to leave – and the teachers. They huddled around their phones, all with huge grins on their faces, an electric atmosphere between them.

'It was all down to you, Morgs,' Oscar said. 'You were right about tagging people!'

'Not down to you and your text speak, you mean,' she joked. 'Nah, it wasn't just me: it was all of us. We've all played our part.'

Olivia noticed that Morgan kept looking at her own post, tracing a finger over a selection of comments that had gathered there.

Saffy was refreshing the page, giggling every time a new notification came in. 'A second post!' She was the first to notice and the celebrations started afresh as she read it aloud.

Read with Pride has been tagged in post.
I #ReadWithPride so one day everybody on the LGBTQ+ spectrum can have access to books that offer a safe space. #ReadWithPride, people!

'This is amazing,' Oscar said in wonder. 'I never imagined this would happen. I hoped it might, but I never allowed myself to think about it actually being a thing.'

'And there's a few more petition signatures,' Nell said. She waved her phone in all their faces. 'More petition signatures!'

'Read with Pride! Read with Pride!' Rocky chanted.

'Shhh . . . somebody might hear!' Oscar fussed.

'All right then . . . RwP! RwP! RwP! Woo!!'

Olivia laughed. 'This is all too exciting!'

Olivia was giddy when she got home, putting music over her speakers in her bedroom and dancing around to the happiest songs she could think of. Her arms in the air, she let herself go, wiggling along and letting herself be as silly as possible. No inhibitions, no time to be self-conscious: just dancing.

When she finally stopped, some of the energy had left her and she turned the music off and put her phone away to listen to the sound of her heavy breathing, to run her fingers along the spines of her books in silent thanks.

It's really happened. There's no turning back. This is bigger than just our little circle now.

And whilst that was exhilarating – it was also petrifying. This wasn't a poster drop or just them sharing their stories. This was the internet and people knew they existed.

It's not us in isolation. Our stories are being read by people who don't even know us, and will never know us. We've just got to hope that they'll listen to our words.

She dropped on to her bed, hugging her knees into her chest. What a day! Olivia knew she'd never forget it for as long as she lived.

She saw her phone flash on her bedside table and jumped to pick it up, wondering who out of Read with

Pride it would be: Rocky sending an incessant round of excited gifs? Nell singing a celebration song she'd made up and was recording for them? Or maybe Alf, who was trying to get them all to remain composed in the face of such delight.

She looked at the notification. Clicked on it. Read it. Blinked. Blinked again. She couldn't help it: she screamed. It was an involuntary scream, one loaded with disbelief and e xcitement, and she felt it ripple through her body.

Her bedroom door was flung open and Kimberley stood on the threshold, her eyes wide with worry.

'What is it?' she said, out of breath. Like she'd run from down the hall, just as Olivia would have done if she'd heard the same scream from her little sister.

Olivia shook her head. Reached her phone out to hand it to Kimberley, her fingers shaking. 'Look,' she managed to say.

Kimberley crossed the room, snatching Olivia's phone from her. Olivia watched as she bent her head over the screen, and began to read aloud. '"I #ReadWithPride because I want to believe that I can be a heroine too . . ." Wait, is this . . .?'

Olivia nodded. 'Uh-huh,' and her voice rose to considerable levels, 'only one of the biggest UK YouTubers out there who discusses what it means to be LGBTQ+, and she shared our freaking campaign! EEEEEKKKK!!!!'

'This is huge,' Kimberley whispered in awe. 'This is huge! Wow!'

'She has one million freaking followers! One million!'

In one swoop, Kimberley pulled Olivia from her bed and began to dance around with her, both of them giggling and whooping as they found the beat of the silent music.

'Ohmigod!' Kimberley cried. 'My big sister! She's going viral!'

Before Olivia could stop her, Kimberley grabbed hold of Olivia's legs and flung her big sister over her shoulder. She buckled under the weight, both of them collapsing on the carpet in another fit of giggles.

'My sister is an internet sensation! She's famous!'

'I didn't even look at the replies!' Olivia said, breaking away from their dance. 'Do you think other people are using the hashtag too?'

She picked up her phone from where it had dropped on the carpet and allowed Kimberley to watch over her shoulder. The picture that had been posted alongside the post featured the YouTuber with a big stack of books, many of which Olivia had read: *The Gentleman's Guide to Vice and Virtue* by Mackenzi Lee, *George* by Alex Gino, *More Happy Than Not* by Adam Silvera, *Release* by Patrick Ness.

'Ohmigod, look at all of these!!!!'

There were already loads of comments, with people

sharing their thoughts and feelings. Olivia didn't know where to begin: there were so many of them, some long, some short, others entirely in emojis, that her eyes flickered back and forth before she settled on one.

Omg I love this! Totally going to write my own #ReadWithPride story to post!

Her breath caught in her throat. This was what it was all about.

I basically never read books but your posts and videos always make me think I should start. Gonna check out some of these books now! #ReadWithPride

Ah, a new reading convert!

#ReadWithPride this is the BEST idea and I'm going to follow the account straight away thank you for sharing it love you so much and your videos

Who cares???

No, that one didn't count. It was one person. Just one person.
The rest of the comments were mostly the same nice messages of support, along with a sea of tagging at the

bottom. She didn't know how anyone would ever cope with notifications that were this busy all of the time!

> Cassie: ummmmm has anyone checked the read with pride page recently?
>
> Rocky: WHAT IS LIFE WHAT IS LIFE WHAT IS LIFE
>
> Ed: Well, that's a deeply philosophical question that might take some time to answer
>
> Ed: (Also I just looked and !! That's a BIG DEAL)
>
> Nell: WE'VE GONE VIRAL, BABY!!!!!!!!!!!!!!!!!!!!!!!!!!!!!!!!
>
> Saffy: Someone check Twitter RIGHT NOW YOU NEED TO SEE

'You look,' Olivia said to Kimberley, who was still lurking, still taking everything in. 'I can't bear it! I'll have to close my eyes.'

She gave her sister the phone. What now? If anything else exciting happened, she'd spontaneously combust.

Kimberley choked back her surprise. 'Um, Livvy? Open your eyes. Open them! Look!'

TRENDING UK TOPICS
4. #ReadWithPride

'Trending?!' Olivia cried. 'We're trending?!?!'

'Ahhhhhh!' Kimberley exclaimed, laughing with glee.

'Do you want me to pinch you?! This just keeps getting better and better! Remember me when you're living in your mansion with twenty bedrooms and five libraries, yeah?'

Olivia giggled. 'We're not quite at that point yet!'

Cassie: woah
Alf: I'm echoing Rocky here: what is life?!
Nell: Have you SEEN?!
Rocky: I JUST SAW

Rocky shared a gif.
Rocky: WHAT IS THIS DAY
Olivia: WE'VE GONE VIRAL!!!!!!!!!!!!!!!!!!!!!!!!!!!!!

And that was the moment Olivia Santos burst into tears.
We did it.

So why did it suddenly feel like the tears weren't all happy? Why did she suddenly have a pain in her chest that felt like she was being squeezed?

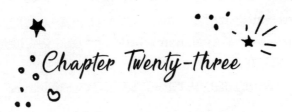

Chapter Twenty-three

'Have you seen this one?' Saffy was grinning from ear to ear as she looked down at her phone, twisting the screen so that Olivia, Oscar and Ed could look as she began to read it out. 'Look at the photo!'

Olivia looked on screen, as two girls – probably a few years older than her – had their arms around each other, faces so close that the sparkly highlighter on their cheeks joined.

Read with Pride shared a post.

I #ReadWithPride because, without books to show me the way, I would never have found the person who is my entire world. (We met in the university library in our first term.)

They were all gathered in Olivia's bedroom, the room feeling small with them all crammed in. Some, like Tabby and Henry, and Alf and Morgan, were pushed up against her bookshelves, while Cassie was stretched out on the bed, helping out by doing some preliminary sketches for the graphics she was creating. Everyone else had their own patch on the floor, except for Nell, who had taken over Olivia's desk. It was a squeeze, to say the least.

'So cute,' Ed said with a wistful sigh.

Things weren't moving quickly enough for Olivia: it was lovely that they were here, but there were constant distractions, things that took them off task and moved them far away from the meticulous to-do list she needed to complete.

I have to get through it or I'll be even more behind and I can't bear to think about that so it needs to get done, and sooner rather than later!

'Rocky, did you put the latest story on the website?' Olivia asked, looking down at the next thing on her list.

'Ohmigod, look at this one! Someone's drawn a little picture of them reading a book with Read with Pride written on it!' Rocky zoomed in on the picture and shrieked. 'I can't take it! It's just so lovely! The detail! Ah, I love it!'

The website clearly wasn't a priority. She'd have to come back to tick that one off the list. On to the next item . . .

'Ed, have you managed to read through the responses we got yesterday on Twitter to look for ones we might be able to use in some way?'

'Oh, it'll get done,' was Ed's response.

But when?! she wanted to scream at him. *'It'll get done' is no good to me right now!*

She felt a flutter of ... something ... go through her. She didn't know what. It started in her chest and rippled right up to her head, accompanied by a wave of nausea. She pinched the bridge of her nose, breathing out, before trying at composure.

'Alf,' and her voice was of a higher pitch than it had been, 'what's the story submission inbox looking like today?'

'I'm going to check it next,' Alf said, 'after Oscar's finished reading through the ones from the day before. We don't want to get muddled.'

'I'm nearly there now,' Oscar said, 'we've had quite a few come in!'

That meant she was at the bottom of the list and nothing had been ticked off. Nothing! She tried not to show her annoyance, but she couldn't help but let out a little huff, masking it by turning it into a yawn.

'Well, why don't I make some tea for everyone?' She had to step away from the bedroom, had to rethink her plans for the day.

'I'll have a very strong coffee, if you don't mind.' Rocky gave a thumbs up and went back to scrolling.

'Ooh, I'll join you in that one!' Ed said. 'Bring on the caffeine rush!'

'Trust me, Ed,' Henry said, 'I don't think you need a caffeine rush: your normal state is caffeine rush.'

Ed pouted. 'Can't you just let me have one nice thing in my life, Henry?'

Morgan grinned. 'Just put decaffeinated in without telling him and he'll never be able to tell the difference. The placebo effect!'

Ed deepened his pout, like a petulant child. 'You don't *all* have to be mean to me!'

Tabby got up from her place by the bookshelf, stretched, and said, 'I'll come and help you carry the mugs up, Livs.'

Olivia smiled gratefully. Maybe she'd even be able to add *make tea* to her to-do list so she'd have something to tick off.

Lizzie jumped at their heels as they got downstairs, desperate for attention. Not that she hadn't had any – she'd been spoilt today with everyone arriving, and they'd doted on her.

If we don't get these bits sorted by the end of the day, we'll be so behind and right now the most important thing we have is momentum and if we don't have that, everything will fizzle out and it will all be for nothing.

Olivia didn't realise how forcefully she was getting the mugs down from the cupboard until Tabby intervened and took them from her.

'Are you okay, Livs?' Tabby asked as they waited for the kettle to boil. She must have been staring off into space without realising, trying to ignore the tightening in her chest.

'I'm fine,' she said, and then shook her head. She lowered her voice as she continued, 'Don't tell the others because they'll get all worried, but I've got this weird numb feeling in my head and it feels like my skull is being squeezed. It's nothing.'

Tabby frowned. 'How long has this been going on?'

She shrugged. 'I don't know, really. A few weeks? Like I said, I'm sure it's nothing. It goes away for a bit and then comes back.'

'You'd say if something was bothering you, wouldn't you?'

'Bothering me? No, I just need to get this stuff done. There's no fairy godmother to sweep in and do it all for us.'

'No, *you're* the fairy godmother,' Tabby said.

But I don't have a magic wand that I can wave, and maybe the fairy godmother finds all of this exhausting too.

Tabby must have thought she was helping, but it didn't make Olivia feel any better, just more aware of her position.

If she didn't do it, who would? There was no other fairy godmother.

Keep going. Her motto. The words she muttered to herself for most of the day and then at night, when there was always one more thing to do.

The kettle clicked as it finished boiling.

'Here, I'll pour it,' Tabby said, and Olivia let her, staring out the window into the leaf-strewn garden. A blackbird kicked about in the autumnal litter, his beak a beautiful orange, and not for the first time Olivia wondered what it would be like to be a bird, with only the pressure of finding enough food and avoiding the neighbourhood cats. Maybe things were a lot more complex for them, but it seemed a simple existence, and there must be something freeing about soaring through the air on wings that could take you anywhere.

Why, when everything was going so well, did she feel this empty? She wanted to share in the excitement, she wanted to again experience the initial high that going viral had caused, but it was like it was long gone. She wasn't sure if it would ever return.

Tabby handed Olivia the first tray and said, 'Go on up and I'll finish this lot. I don't mind.'

She took the tray, careful not to spill any tea, then Tabby said, 'And Livs?'

'Yeah?'

'You don't need to take this all on by yourself. That's why you've got us. We want to help.'

Olivia shook her head, but smiled – to reassure Tabby more than anything else.

As Olivia came back into her bedroom, Alf said, 'We had this one come through on the email yesterday.'

She put the tray down for them each to take their mug, and then settled against one of her bookcases at the edge of the room.

'Oh, this one was good!' Oscar said. He smiled at Alf. 'Read it out for us!'

'Oh, all right,' Alf said, and began.

Subject: ANONYMOUS

I'm aromantic asexual which basically means that I don't experience either romantic or sexual attraction. My journey hasn't been easy, and I've had to put up with lots of family members who think they're well-meaning, asking 'So when are you going to get a boyfriend?' or saying things like, 'You'll find the one for you one day, don't worry.' Until I found out what it meant to be aroace, I wondered why these sayings always bothered me because the truth was I didn't want

to find 'the one' and the idea of there being
someone out there who was supposed to complete me
didn't feel right.

I want to share my story because it can be
difficult to #ReadWithPride when you're surrounded
by love stories and the feeling that a love story
is something you should want. We're taught that
the worst thing in the world is to be on your
own, but slowly I'm learning that that's not
true.

You don't need to be in a romantic relationship
for the world to keep on spinning. It shouldn't
be the default.

I don't just want to #ReadWithPride. I want to be
proud of myself too. And I am.

Olivia closed her eyes as she listened, feeling each word:
while she wasn't aroace herself, she could see the
similarities with her own experience of being demisexual
and she wanted to reach out through the screen Alf was
holding and say that she understood, that she got it.

'I'm just popping to the loo,' she said, making a
hasty exit from her position on the floor. The more

stories she heard, the more her brain seemed to jumble up. She could feel the emotion dripping from each word, felt it deep in her soul, until it threatened to pull her under.

She stumbled down the hall and locked the bathroom door behind her, sitting down on the closed loo seat.

And breathe . . . And breathe . . . And breathe . . .

But her breathing was too fast and she had to slow it down, had to stop the jumbling in its tracks.

I'm so tired.

She could close her eyes now, take a power nap, be back in five minutes and they'd be none the wiser.

'Livs? You've been a long time in there. You all right?'

Or not.

She opened the door for Cassie; anyone else she would have dismissed, but she had to let Cassie in. Literally and figuratively.

She splashed her face with water and felt fresher, more alert, and let Cassie step inside. She was frowning.

'Livs,' she said, seriously. 'You've got to slow down.'

'Cassie—'

'No excuses. I know you, Olivia, and you look shattered. You've been working at five thousand miles per hour and it isn't right – I've been watching you all afternoon and you haven't known what to do or where to go next. Promise me you'll start to take it easy?'

'If you know me so well,' Olivia said, attempting a grin, 'then you must surely know that I never take it easy. You're all worried but you've got no reason to be. We're nearly there now, so things will calm down soon.'

Or that's what I'm hoping for.

'Come on, let's go back,' she said, and took Cassie's hand, giving it a little squeeze. Cassie went a step further and pulled Olivia out of the loo, into the hallway, and into a hug.

'You're doing an amazing job, Livs,' she said into Olivia's hair, and Olivia grimaced, because she knew Cassie couldn't see it. There were only so many times everyone could say she was doing an amazing job; she was detached from it, separating their praise from the work she was doing. 'You really are.'

Olivia pulled back. 'I want to see these sketches of yours! Come and show me what magic you've been working on!'

'I'm on a caffeine high!!' Ed cried as they got through the door. 'This is thrilling!'

As Morgan had predicted, the placebo effect had worked: Olivia had gone for decaf over caffeine.

Kimberley appeared in the doorway, surveying the scene with a smile. 'I was going to walk to the shop to pick up some study snacks. Does anyone want anything while I'm there?' A look of surprise came over her. 'Oh, hi, Saffy! I didn't know you were friends with Olivia.'

The excitable energy had left Saffy and her mouth hung open slightly before she built up the effort to speak. 'H-hi Kimberley.'

'We have geography together, right?'

Saffy nodded a little too enthusiastically for it to appear casual.

'Cool!' Kimberley nodded, and with that nod, Olivia hoped that Saffy might be able to make a new friend. Or at least be accepted by the people she'd always wanted to be accepted by. 'So anyone need anything?'

'Chocolate wouldn't go amiss,' Olivia said, and got up to get her purse from her bag, handing Kimberley some change. 'Get the biggest bar you can find and we'll divide it up between us.'

Kimberley grinned. 'Coming right up!'

'Right then,' Olivia said, turning back to the room, 'let's crack on with the next few days' worth of posts. They won't get sorted by themselves!'

'Let's do this!' Nell said, punching the air. 'Go team!'

After Read with Pride and The Paper & Hearts Society had all left, Olivia trudged back to her desk, where she settled down for a night of catching up on revision. She wasn't sure if she'd even be able to remember her name at this moment in time, never mind write out a set of key chemistry equations. The writing on the revision cards swum in front of her eyes, but she pushed on and on until eventually she heard her parents go to bed and the nearby church's clock strike midnight.

With a yawn, she clambered into bed, only to be met by nightmare-filled sleep.

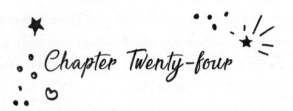

Chapter Twenty-four

The mirrors in Olivia's bedroom had had to be covered; when she went in the bathroom, she had to close her eyes or turn off the light and shut the door. She couldn't bear to look at her reflection: she hadn't washed for days on end and her greasy bird's nest of hair, paired with an old, faded grey T-shirt she'd found at the bottom of her wardrobe and some pyjama bottoms, were too much to take in.

She wasn't exactly a sight for sore eyes. And speaking of which, hers were definitely sore. Her left eyelid kept twitching, she could barely focus on anything other than the pile of work in front of her, and she had to stop herself from falling asleep at every opportunity.

Communication had also gone out the window. She could only force one-word sentences, and even they were tricky. She'd taken to communicating in vague gestures and movements of her hands, but abandoned even these once she became frustrated at everyone's failure to understand what she meant.

I'm so behind, was all she could think. *I'm never going to get this finished, but somehow I've got to keep going! I haven't got any other choice!*

The petition signatures were creeping up by the minute and she couldn't stop sneaking glances, refreshing the page constantly at all times of the day.

We're getting so close to five thousand! FIVE. THOUSAND. WHAT?!

'I can't go to bed now,' she'd tell herself. Out loud sometimes, because she'd also taken to talking to herself outside of her head. 'We could get another influx of signatures and I'll miss it.'

She knew everyone else was busy and she tried to delegate tasks as best she could to lighten her own load, but her plate was still overflowing with work.

Just last night, she'd stayed up responding to interview questions she'd been sent by an LGBTQ+ university-student-led blog who had offered to lend their support to the Read with Pride cause and spread the word about the petition. It was an opportunity they couldn't miss out on, but thinking about original answers to the questions she'd been sent took way longer than she'd anticipated. By the time she'd got into bed it was 5 a.m. and her mind was whirring so much that it felt like she'd barely closed her eyes before Lizzie came into her bedroom, jumping on her bed and licking her face. There had been no point in going back to bed: the household was beginning to stir, and she needed complete silence to sleep these days.

I don't think my head is supposed to hurt this much. She'd taken paracetamol but it was still pounding.

Sitting at her desk, crouched over her keyboard, Olivia was bashing out a writing exercise for French, but she knew it wasn't any good. She couldn't think of any of the right vocabulary, resorting to making stuff up and hoping for the best if in doubt. She had to finish it so then she could move on to—

Alf: We've had some good submissions to the email this
    weekend, can someone check them over before they're
    posted to Instagram? Olivia?
Olivia: Yes!! Send them over to me and I can upload! The
    graphics are all ready to go!

What did she have to move on to? She scattered a hand over her desk to look for the to-do list she'd scrawled on a scrap piece of paper, disturbing the thick, messy piles that had built up over the past few weeks. They floated to the floor to find a new home to gather dust in, but still the clearance couldn't uncover the to-do list.

Never mind. Just two more sentences and then you can come back to this essay later.

It was like walking through thick mud trying to get the words out, but she finished her two sentences and was able to put the essay down while she worked through her thoughts.

Morgan: Do you think we need to tweet the link to the
    petition again this afternoon? We seemed to get a lot
    more people signing it when we did the other day
Olivia: I can if you want! I think that's a good idea!
Nell: You sure? You're doing so much already
Olivia: Yeah it's fine!! It's easy – it won't take much to do!

I totally have control of this. Totally!

'Do you want to come and walk Lizzie with me?' A voice – Kimberley – said from the doorway. Olivia didn't turn round.

'Can't,' she said.

She heard Kimberley go and was relieved; she turned back to the screen and proceeded to tweet out the link to the petition Morgan had suggested, then clicked over to her email where Alf had forwarded her the next story. She didn't even get to properly read it before she'd copied it to her phone and uploaded it to Instagram with one of the ready-made graphics.

There was no time any more to read each tweet, each story, each message: they were coming thick and fast, impossible to keep up with. Between the group of them, they were managing to watch some of the conversation, but it was relentless: just when they thought they were up to date, people from all over the world, in different time zones, would add their voices to the conversation and they'd be behind again.

But I'm not complaining!

And then . . . *Where is that to-do list?!?!?!*

There was no hope: it must have vanished into thin air. She'd have to rely on her unreliable memory.

Saffy: we just had a reaaallllyyyy good comment on Instagram!! We should share it to our story! It's an anonymous account so I think it will be okay to share

Forget the to-do list. There were other pressing tasks to complete.

Cassie: one thousand signatures! you did it, livs! so proud

of you and everything you've achieved, that's huge! x

Cassie: livs?

Olivia: Thanks!

Cassie sent a photo.

Cassie: a picture of ed today at college with a 'GO OLIVIA'

sign he made just for you x

Olivia: Haha! Very motigbvgnw thanks!

Olivia: *motivation

Olivia: *motivational

GOOGLE SEARCH

Tips for feeling better after no sleep

What does no sleep do to you?

How long can you go without sleep?

Read with Pride petition

Chapter Twenty-five

'Olivia?'

Where was that voice coming from?

'Olivia?'

Where?

'Olivia, wake up,' the voice – deep, familiar – said. 'It's nearly time for you to go to school.'

How long had she been asleep for? She peeled her face away from her hard pillow only to realise that it wasn't a pillow at all and she wasn't asleep in bed, listening to her dad as an alarm clock, but bent over her desk, a small puddle of drool the evidence of her sleeping place.

'Livvy, are you okay?'

7:45 a.m.

She'd managed two and a half hours' sleep. And she wasn't sure if, even then, all her work was done.

Her temples pounded; her body screamed in discomfort. 'Fine,' she mumbled, forcing herself out of sleep. 'I'll . . . be . . . there . . . in two seconds.'

She pushed herself up from her desk, every tiny noise and sensation – the brushing of her chair against the carpet, the dropping of her feet to the floor, her hair tickling her face – making her want to scream out in pain.

By the time she'd got to the bathroom and splashed her face with water, she'd forced herself to wake up – if awake was what you could call it. She was more like a zombie than a human being!

I am never ever ever ever ever pulling an all-nighter ever ever again, even if I didn't realise that's what I was doing.

I could crawl back to bed and get under the covers . . .

'OLIVIA! Are you ready yet?!' It was Mum this time. She forced herself to move into action, but her body screamed in protest, in agony, as she went back to her bedroom and pulled on her school uniform. She fumbled with her tie so that it ended up skew-whiff, and had a near miss with her tights, nearly causing a ladder up one side of her leg.

No time for make-up today. No time to even brush her hair. She resorted to gum, too, which it hurt her jaw to chew, but at least she wouldn't have morning breath.

'Ready,' she said, finally getting down the stairs. Mum was waiting by the door to wave her off. The look she gave Olivia was one of disbelief.

'What?' Olivia said, feeling self-conscious; maybe she should have brushed her hair after all.

'Are you not taking your bag today?'

'Oh, yeah.' It delayed her by another few minutes as she trudged back up the stairs to get it, chucking in everything she could find from the surface of her desk, just in case she needed it. No time to organise!

She made the trek back downstairs, where Mum was still waiting.

'Your dad and I will be at home all day today if you need us.' She never said that usually. Why would Olivia need them? It was all fine! She'd only be a little bit late.

'See you later,' Olivia said, and left before her mum could say anything else.

She made it into her French seat just as the bell went, out of breath from the speed-walking she'd done, and Madame Heger fixed her with a steely glare. Punctuality was Madame Heger's closest friend, and Olivia was pushing it.

'Are you all right?' Tabby asked.

'Great,' Olivia mumbled. She turned to the board to check what they were doing today, ready to write the date and objectives in her exercise book, when she realised . . .

'Do you not have your book with you?' Tabby stared down at the empty space on their desk where Olivia's exercise book and pencil case should have been.

'Oh, that!' For some reason, she couldn't muster her usual nonchalant giggle. It just wouldn't come. 'Right, that. I'll get it now.'

She didn't know how she got through the rest of the lesson, but it was safe to say that not a lot of French had been understood.

They were coming out of the classroom when Olivia was spotted by Nell, who was leaving the German classroom opposite.

Nell waved and came over, her sleeves rolled up to her elbows like she was about to get down to business.

'Hey, Livs, do you have your story to put up?' she asked. 'I spoke to Alf earlier and he said he hadn't had anything from you yet. Nearly done with it?'

Another student behind her was laughing as if nobody else could hear and they had to keep laughing and laughing and laughing until it grew louder and louder and she couldn't take it, she wanted to clamp her hands over her ears, but instead she had to ignore it and push out, 'I'm working on it, Nell, it will be with Alf and Oscar soon,' and was she overheating, or was it her imagination?

'Okay,' Nell said. Her face was looming right in front of Olivia's, it seemed huge, and Tabby was standing so close, right by her shoulder, and other students from younger years pushed and shoved as they struggled out of the corridor, and for a moment, Olivia lost where she was. 'Are you all right? You seem a bit out of it.'

WHY DOES EVERYONE KEEP ASKING ME THAT?! I AM NOT A CHILD! I DO NOT NEED TO BE ASKED EVERY MINUTE OF EVERY DAY IF I AM OKAY!

'Just hungry!' she said. It was the first thing that popped into her head. 'Got to go – I've got maths next! Yay!'

She moved so fast that she left Tabby behind, but she had to keep going. Tabby would understand. Of course she would.

If I ignore the fact that my eyes are burning, I think I'm doing pretty well on minimal sleep.

At lunch, she hid herself away so she didn't have to see anyone, squished under the stairs where nobody would find her. No reading, though, not today: instead, she meditated. Or called it 'meditating' because anyone else would refer to it as a failed attempt at power napping.

At least I don't have to waste my energy talking to anyone, because that would be disastrous.

When it came to meeting up with Tabby and Henry at the end of the day, she tried to act breezy. Casual. Not sleep-deprived.

'I'm going to stay after school to clarify this question I had for religious studies,' Olivia told Henry and Tabby. She waved them on. 'See you tomorrow!'

I can't even remember what the question is but I'm sure it will come to me by the time I get up there. Then I'll be back home in time for a few hours of revision and Read with Pride work and then I can fall into glorious sleep.

But Olivia didn't make it to her religious studies classroom. Stopping suddenly in the middle of the corridor, unaware of anything else going on around her, she burst into tears.

I can't do this any more. I can't carry on like this!

It had all got way too much, way too fast.

Olivia stumbled through the school gates, desperately trying to keep her eyes open, watching where she was going through a tide of tears. She made it out of school, but she wasn't sure what she was doing.

I don't know why I'm crying but everything feels so overwhelming and it's like I'm drowning in life and I don't know what to do and I don't know how everything can feel so crushing!

She pulled out her phone and dialled the first number that came up in her contacts. It rang and rang and then . . .

'Ed, I know this is really weird, but can you come and pick me up?' Her voice quavered as she spoke down the phone, blocking out everything else except from Ed's breathing down the line. She didn't want to wait to give him the opportunity to talk or she might hang up, chicken out.

'Are you okay?!'

'I don't think so and I could really do with a friend right now but Tabby and Henry have already left because I told them to go on but I didn't mean it and then it was too late and I don't even know how I'll get home, I don't know – I just don't know!!'

Her eyes were leaking tears and she rubbed furiously at them, betrayed by her own emotions.

'I'll get in the car now and I'll be there within ten minutes, okay?' She hated to panic Ed like this. 'I can't stay on the line while I'm driving, but I promise I'll be as quick as I can. Never fear, Olivia, your knight in shining armour is coming for you!' He gave a nervous laugh. 'Do you need anything else before I hang up?'

She shook her head, and then realised he couldn't see her. 'No,' she sniffed. The line went dead, then, and she was alone. She walked up the road a bit, not sure where she was going, but looking for somewhere quiet, somewhere to rest.

She slid down a tall garden wall bordering the pavement opposite the school, tucking her legs into her body and resting her heavy head on her knees. So heavy . . . so easy to sleep . . . so . . . tired . . .

The more time that passed, the more her tears subsided: there was no energy left in the tank even for them.

Eventually, she looked up to find Ed's car pulling into view. He scrambled out, the door slamming shut behind him, and took bounding steps towards her. In no time, he was by Olivia's side, pulling her up from the pavement. At any other time, she would have commented on his dishevelled hair and panicked expression, but not today. Definitely not today.

'Oh, Olivia!' he cried, wrapping his arms around her like a shield. 'Let's get you home, Livs. It's okay, it's all going to be okay.'

She let him lead her to the car and gather her in, even going so far as putting her seatbelt on for her. She found that she couldn't move unless she was being aided, that even the simplest of movements made her brain hurt too much. The numbness had spread and reached down to her whole body; it smothered her in a claustrophobic embrace, but she couldn't fight it. She didn't know how.

Ed, looking nervous, drove right up to the speed limit on the way home, trying but failing to hide his frustration when he was stuck behind other, slower drivers. She put her head against the window, not caring about the droning noise that rushed into her ears, or the vibrations as the old car moved.

There was no caring any more.

'We're here,' Ed said, and chucked his seatbelt off as soon as he'd twisted the key in the ignition. 'I'll come round and help you out.'

She let him; she wouldn't know how to resist. He led her like she was a little child, and she thought that maybe it would be better if she was, if she could shrink down and go back to being eight years old, when she had her whole optimistic future ahead of her, with nothing to think about but the books she was going to read and the people she was going to play games with at break-time.

The front door opened before they got there, and Mum came rushing out.

'Livvy! Livvy, what's happened?! Ed, thank you so much for bringing her home. Thank you.'

'I don't know what's happened,' he said, and she was glad they were talking to each other because there was no way she could. 'She just rang me and asked me to pick her up, but she hasn't said anything.'

'You're a good friend, Edward,' Mum said. Olivia would have giggled at the added 'ward' any other day.

'I hope you feel better soon,' he said to Olivia as he turned to leave.

She nodded once. Gave in to her mum's cajoling and made it into the hallway. Gave in to the rising pain. Mum shut the door and Olivia's composure left her.

'Oh, baby,' Olivia's mum said, scraping her hair back from her face, where it was sticking to her tears. 'There we are, let it all out. Let all that emotion go.'

'I've worked so hard, Mum!' she cried. 'Harder than I feel I've worked at anything before! And it still isn't enough! I thought I could do it all, but I can't!'

I don't know how I can keep going on, I don't know how I can even think about breathing, never mind doing anything else, and it was all going to be fine and I was going to work it out and I can't, I couldn't, I'll never be able to.

'What's going on?' Mum said, helping her up. She allowed herself to be guided along because to do otherwise would be too difficult.

But Olivia couldn't talk to tell her. There were only tears.

'Let's get you into bed,' Mum said. 'I'll bring you up a hot water bottle. The best thing for you at the moment is rest. Go on, up you go. You can tell me all about it once you can think straight.'

Her movements numb, Olivia did as her mum said, trudging up the stairs like a great weight was attached to her legs and she had to drag it along with her.

She somehow managed to make it into her bedroom, pulling off her uniform as she went and finding the pair of pyjamas she always kept on top of her bed. It seemed to take her years to get them on, but she did. She pulled back the duvet. Got in. Buried her head against the pillow. Hauled the duvet back up. Over her body.

Can't think. Too much emotion. Too much sadness, too much disbelief.

She wasn't sure how much time had passed before her mum came up, tucking the covers around her shoulders.

'Try to get some rest,' Mum said, kissing her daughter tenderly on the forehead. 'There's time for talking later, but now you need to switch off your mind.'

Sleep seemed impossible, especially once Mum was gone. Olivia felt so alone, stranded. Dark shadows were cast on her bedroom floor and she felt like a little kid again, wondering if the monsters under the bed would come out and gobble her up.

If I were a Victorian literary heroine, she thought, *this would be the thing that would do me in. I'd be so full of emotion that I'd either be sent to an asylum for being a dramatic young woman or I'd lie on a chaise longue and DIE.*

The thought made her start crying again.

Kimberley snuck in later that evening, lifting up the duvet and creeping inside. Olivia didn't roll over to face her sister, but she did reach out a hand behind her to let Kimberley know she was awake.

'Forget about it now,' Kimberley whispered in the dark. 'Just sleep, Livvy.'

Before Olivia eventually fell asleep, she could feel Kimberley's body heat against her, better than any comforting blanket.

'Wake me up for school in the morning, I can't miss it,' she mumbled, before giving in to Kimberley's reply.

Can't miss it. I can't. Got
to
keep
going.

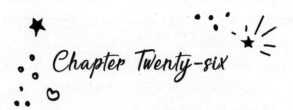

Chapter Twenty-six

Sunlight against her hand where it rested on her pillow. An awakened sense of energy. The same numbness that had filled her days, yet it felt sated, now that she'd cried some of it away.

She guessed she'd been asleep for a good fifteen hours, but when Olivia reached out to twist her alarm clock around, she found that it was 9:30 a.m. and she'd slept for seventeen. No wonder she was itching to get up – there's no way she'd make it to her first lesson in time!

But she couldn't. Not today. She had no desire to step out of the confines of home because she didn't want to let the outside world in.

She wrapped her dressing gown around her middle, over her pyjamas, and after refusing to look at herself in the bathroom mirror, padded downstairs to face the music.

Although hopefully it won't be loud music.

Her parents were in the living room, talking in hushed voices, and stopped as soon as she walked in, Lizzie sitting innocently between them both. She took the sofa opposite theirs, and waited for them to speak. She didn't know how to begin.

'You slept well,' her dad said. She appreciated his attempt at small talk.

'Like the heaviest log,' she tried to joke, but it wasn't a very good one and nobody laughed.

'Olivia – we need to talk,' Dad said.

'We're worried about you, Livvy,' Mum added.

'You and everybody else.' She rolled her eyes. 'But you don't need to be. I'll be back to normal tomorrow.'

'That's what concerns us,' Dad said. He and Mum glanced at each other and then he continued with, 'What's been going on, Livvy? You don't talk to us any more – you don't tell us anything. You're just up there in your room, crouched over your desk, never stopping.'

'I wish it did me good, all that work.'

'What does that mean?' Mum asked. She readjusted her position on the sofa, as if bracing herself.

Here it was. Olivia couldn't keep it to herself any longer.

'I failed a test,' she said, and the weight it took off her shoulders to admit it felt better than anything else she'd done recently. 'I really badly failed. I couldn't tell you because I knew you wouldn't be happy and I know I should have worked harder and I'm so disappointed in myself.'

'We know you did,' Mum said.

'You know?' But how?! She'd been so careful!

Mum smiled. 'Do you think Kimberley doesn't tell us stuff too? She was worried about you, but I knew you'd tell us when you were ready to talk about it.'

'And we aren't mad at you,' Dad said. 'We couldn't be, even if we tried, because it sounds like you've been very mad with yourself over it, and that's bad enough. One negative test result isn't going to erase all the other good work you've done.'

She fell back into the sofa, letting the tension go. She heard their words, but they didn't quite go in. 'But it's not just one negative result – I felt bad about that, I felt rotten, but it's everything else, too. Everything feels too big, like I'm scaling a mountain and will never get to the top unless I crawl on my hands and knees, but I don't have any protective gear and the further up I get, the more it hurts and by this point I basically have no knees left.'

She stopped as Lizzie left her parents and came to sniff around her, jumping up on the sofa and pushing her nose into her as if to say, 'What's wrong, Olivia?'

'I feel so awful,' she said, stroking Lizzie absent-mindedly, and now she'd started, it all came pouring out. 'We've had all this success with Read with Pride and I want to enjoy it but there's always more to do and even when I cross everything off my to-do list, there are always five more to-do lists left. I'm weird! Everybody else can manage! Why can't I?!'

'Olivia, you aren't weird – you're burnt out!' Mum cried.

'Burnt out?' She was confused. What did that even mean?

Mum gave her a knowing look. 'You've been working *too* hard – pushing yourself past your limits, letting go of everything you love, ignoring your mind and body when it tells you to slow down, to stop. You've hardly been sleeping, you don't read any more.'

'You're the textbook definition of burnt out,' Dad added. 'Actually, let me get my dictionary out and I'm sure under the "burn-out" section, there'll be a little description that just reads, "Olivia Santos".'

'Ha ha,' Olivia said. This was not the time for dad jokes – although she was tempted to crack a smile.

'I'd argue, too, that you can't possibly say that everybody else is managing. There will be so many other people who are experiencing the same thing as you, but nobody ever talks about it or, like you've done, they dismiss their emotions.' Mum was on a roll now. 'The pressures you kids have on you these days from so many directions is immense. It's not just about exams, you have to think about friendships and relationships and growing up and your home life, and it's not easy.'

'But what can I do?'

'Right now?' Mum said. 'Right now, you do nothing. You have nothing to worry about today and nothing that you need to do. Just take the day to be *you*. Then, when you're ready, however long that takes, you can slowly start reintroducing things that bring you joy again. Reading, seeing your friends, taking Lizzie for walks. Whatever it is that makes you feel like yourself. And then alongside that, you work out a balance for the things that you have to do, like schoolwork.'

'But what if I don't have time for everything I want to do?'

'That,' Dad said, 'is what got you into this mess in the first place. It isn't about what you want, but what you *need*. It's about asking yourself every time you think of something to do, "Is this going to make me feel better, or worse?" It's tough, but we're here to support you. You're not alone in this.'

'No, I know,' she said, 'and I'm so grateful. Thank you. And thank you, Lizzie.' She scratched her little dog behind the ears. 'I promise I'll take you for a walk soon.'

She had some thinking to do. Changes would have to be made, and they wouldn't be easy.

What is it I need right now?

She was curled up on the sofa, watching afternoon antique programmes on the TV, when the doorbell went. Mum, who said her own work could wait for now and had camped out for a relaxing day with Olivia, got up from the sofa and went to answer.

I bet Kimberley's forgotten her key again.

'SURPRISE!' she heard. She could recognise that mix of voices from anywhere. She relieved her mum's astonishment by going out to the door and rolling her eyes at the gathered group, who were standing around a bouquet of flowers.

'You really didn't have to,' she said, changing tack when she saw Ed's disappointed face. 'But thank you.'

There they were – her best friends, The Paper & Hearts Society, all beaming at her as if Ed hadn't seen her have a breakdown in his car yesterday.

'Ed picked them out,' Cassie said, and grabbed the bouquet from him to hand to Olivia, 'which explains why half of them are dead and the other half are squashed.'

'I don't mind that,' Olivia said, and the first thing she did on taking them was lean down and give them a hearty sniff. 'Oh . . . okay, maybe I do!'

'Oops.' Ed held his hands up in the guilty position.

'We're never trusting you with the get-well-soon present again,' Henry said, clapping him on the back. He and Tabby were wearing their school uniform, while Ed and Cassie still had their college ID badges hanging from their necks. They must have come as soon as they'd got out.

'Well, you'll have to come in to arrange them for me to make up for it,' Olivia said, and beckoned them in.

'I'll leave you to it,' Mum said, and went out to the kitchen. Olivia went back to her spot on the sofa, and let the others work out where they wanted to sit. Cassie took the space next to her, while Henry, Ed and Tabby took the other sofa.

'I should have brought doughnuts,' Ed hissed at Tabby. 'They would have got a far better reaction than flowers!'

Olivia didn't allow for any more conversation. She wanted to get in there first before they could stop her. 'First of all, please don't ask me how I am,' she began, 'because, right now, I don't know. I thought I was fine, but it turns out I wasn't, so I don't know what to think any more.'

'We were starting to realise you weren't fine,' Tabby said, 'but it wasn't soon enough – we're sorry. You should have said something, though, and you know we would have helped relieve your load.'

Olivia shook her head. 'That's the thing: how could I have asked for help when I didn't know I needed it? I wish I had, so I wouldn't have ended up in this mess.'

How had she not seen it? The *just keep going* attitude had masked any sign on her side that something was up.

'You don't need to dwell on that now,' Henry said. 'Hindsight is a marvellous thing, as usual. Just like with hindsight we would have given someone other than Ed the task of getting you a present.'

'Are you ever going to drop that?' Ed muttered.

Tabby answered for Henry. 'I doubt it.'

'Nell and Rocky send their love,' Henry said. 'We caught up with them earlier and let them know you weren't well. Rocky said they're happy to coordinate the Read with Pride pages until you're ready to get back to it.'

'That's nice of them,' Olivia said. It was good to know that she'd been missed, that they were thinking of her.

Maybe she missed herself, too, that part of her that had disappeared among the chaos her brain had turned into. She missed the version of Olivia she was around The Paper & Hearts Society, how bright and exciting everything usually was; she missed the knowledge that every day is a new day of adventure, full of possibility.

'You know I love you all, don't you?' she said, and promised herself she wouldn't cry. 'I haven't been loving myself lately and I don't want our friendship to have suffered for it. I get that you might be annoyed.'

'The only thing I'm annoyed about right now,' Cassie said, 'is that the five of us aren't in the middle of a group hug. Because I feel like that's something all of us need.'

'GROUP HUG!' Ed cried, and pulled Tabby and Henry up with him as he divebombed Olivia and Cassie on their sofa.

Olivia felt their love envelop her as she suffered under the weight of their group hug, cursing their combined weight. But it was amazing.

'I can't believe you just initiated a group hug,' Tabby said, high-fiving Cassie.

Cassie shot her a smug smile. 'We're all capable of change, Tabby. Don't act so surprised.'

'I can't take it!' Ed joked. 'Cassie, it's too sudden!'

'Shut it,' she warned him.

'That's better,' he said. 'I was worried for a second that you'd had a personality transplant.'

'What's the next step?' Tabby asked Olivia as they settled back into the sofas. 'Do you have a plan?'

'Yes,' she said, and it was true. As she'd listened to their banter and felt their unconditional love, it had come to her. There was only one way forwards.

A few months ago, when all of this was unheard of, everything had seemed so simple. Olivia had her love of books, her friends, her family, and she was happy.

Then Read with Pride had started and while she was still happy – to have met the group, to feel like she was making a difference – the happiness was increasingly becoming eclipsed by having to do more and more, and suddenly there was no enjoyment any more. It had all gone.

She hadn't finished a book for a long time. She never

felt truly present when she was with her friends. She was hiding stuff from her family.

I don't know who I'm becoming, and if I keep on going as I am, there'll be nothing left for me to give.

Her strengths had turned into her flaws. She'd allowed her fight for change to consume her.

Read with Pride feels so close now to our end goal and I've done everything I can. I've put my heart and soul into it. I'll never turn around and think to myself that I haven't tried.

So, yes, she had a plan. A plan that would bring her back to her true self and restore some balance to her life. She had no doubt that Read with Pride would be to each other what The Paper & Hearts Society was to her.

'I know what I've got to do.' It almost killed her to say it, but she had to. 'I've got to step back from Read with Pride.'

It was the only way.

To: Read with Pride
From: Olivia
Subject:

Hi everyone,

It's me. I don't know how I'm writing this really
because I've sat down to type it out for the past
few hours and I keep getting up again and finding
something, anything else to do. My dog, Lizzie,
is very worried because I'm disturbing her sleep,
and my sister has shouted at me to stop pacing
the floor because I'll burn a hole in the carpet
with my feet.

So I suppose I'll have to start writing.

Read with Pride has given me so much: not just a
whole new group of amazing friends who I hope I
know for the rest of my life, but also a purpose
and a cause. I've always known how much I loved
books, but I didn't realise just how far I'd go
in the fight for access to them. Now I know that
I'd travel to the ends of the earth if it meant
everyone could read a book that has the ability
to change their life.

Being able to have the conversations I've had with you — being able to speak in a safe space, where you know everyone will get how you feel, and learning more about you all as amazing individuals — has been an experience I only ever could have dreamt of before. Somehow, we all found each other, and against the odds, we've allowed countless other people to make their voices heard.

Who would have thought that our tiny ambitions could turn into something so huge?

But I've been hiding something from you, and from myself. The thing is, I haven't been coping very well. I've been filling every single second of my day with work, missing homework tasks and having to complete them at the last minute, failing tests because none of the revision is going in. I hurt people around me, I made them worry, and I let everything go because I thought that if I just do *one more thing*, everything will be okay. I'll turn a corner and it will be fine. *I'm fine* is a saying I seem to have stuck on repeat, and now I've managed to unstick it and I know that I'm far from fine.

I'm so proud of Read with Pride and I'm so proud of all of you. Nell — who would have thought that bumping into you that day in the library would have started all of this? I didn't think anyone would ever listen to a bunch of teenagers because why should they? But people haven't just listened — they've added their voices too. We haven't just started a little campaign; we've started something that we'll have for the rest of our lives, and we've made people really think. That's invaluable.

I'm devastated that I can't continue as I have been doing, but I'm so burnt out that if I don't stop now, with it being my own decision, the choice will be out of my power and I'll still have to stop.

You are all amazing and so, so capable. I want the victory to be yours — because I know that the tide will turn in our favour and we'll have our library back. I couldn't see it before, when we were in the midst of it, but I think we've made a real difference.

With so much love and all the pride in the world,

Olivia x

PS. Will you do me one last favour? I've attached my story and I'd love you to share it for me.

OLIVIA'S STORY

All my life, I've been surrounded by happily ever afters. A prince kisses the sleeping girl, she wakes up, and they get married. A lost slipper fits. A beast's curse is broken. The couple run off into the sunset, blessed by fairies and elves, mice and fairy godmothers. That's what happily ever after means.

As I got older and my peers started putting posters up on their walls of the celebrities they fancied, and gossiped in the corridors about who had a crush on who, I started to feel like there was something wrong with me. I didn't understand how anyone could ever fancy someone they knew nothing about or lust over someone they'd known for five seconds. How did that make sense? And if I couldn't understand it, did that mean I was broken in some way?

I didn't want to be different. I would make things up — pretend I had crushes when I didn't even know what that would feel like. I found posters in magazines like my peers had and when they came round, I would put them up, just so I seemed like them. So I fitted in.

Then one day I found someone online who mentioned they were asexual and everything clicked into place. It wasn't weird and I wasn't broken — I just didn't experience sexual attraction like everyone else. For a while everything was fine, but something still felt off.

Because there was one person who I was beginning to like in a way I'd never felt before. I'd known her for so long that I knew her better than anyone else, and I knew I'd do anything for her to feel the same way about me as I did about her.

I was finally able to figure out who I am: I'm demisexual and I wouldn't have it any other way. I'm only attracted to someone if there's a strong emotional connection first, and that is absolutely, one hundred per cent okay.

I #ReadWithPride to reinvent the meaning of happily ever after and to show the world that I deserve mine too, even if it doesn't look like it does in the movies.

Two Weeks Later . . .

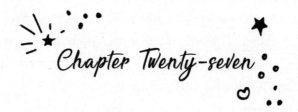

Chapter Twenty-seven

She'd done everything as she usually did: taken her stuff to her locker, neatly prepared the books she needed for her first lessons – pleased that her attention to detail was back in full force – and headed to tutorial, where she was currently chatting away to Ife, who was bemoaning the English homework she'd spent all night doing.

'I actually didn't mind it all that much,' Olivia said, 'because it's the memorising quotations I find difficult. At least with that, you could refer to the text.'

'I'll never understand why they make us memorise the quotations,' Ife said. 'It's a crime: when else will we have to know two hundred Shakespeare quotes?'

'When you're playing the lead role of Beatrice at the Globe?' Olivia giggled.

There was a knock at the classroom door, and Olivia was surprised to find Miss Carter's smiling face peering around the door frame. 'Could I borrow Olivia, please, Mr Joyce?' she asked.

Me?! Olivia thought. A kind of dread began to spread through her. There was so much that could still go wrong.

'Go ahead. Olivia?' He gestured from her to Miss Carter, giving his permission. Olivia scraped back her chair and headed towards the door.

'You might want to bring your stuff,' Miss Carter said, 'we might be a while.'

That doesn't sound good. Olivia tried to calm her heartbeat, which was speeding up so rapidly she was able to feel it in her ears, but there wasn't really any way of doing so.

She had to face the inevitable music. And, if she had to, she'd take the fall. She couldn't get anyone else in trouble.

After picking up her stuff from the table, she retraced her steps back towards Miss Carter. Olivia never minded being watched, but something about leaving the tutor room made her conscious of all the eyes on her. Following her every move.

'It's nothing to worry about,' Miss Carter said as she shut the door behind them. Olivia followed her as she led the way down the series of corridors; she recognised that they were heading towards the library.

Easy for you to say! she wanted to pretend-joke. Or, in her tiniest voice, ask, *I'm not in trouble, am I?*

She wanted to at least be prepared if she was.

'This way,' Miss Carter said, walking down the stairs. 'How are your lessons going?'

Olivia gulped. 'Good,' she said, not trusting herself to say any more.

Miss Carter seemed to detect something was up. 'Read anything you've enjoyed recently?'

'Do revision notes count?! Otherwise, I've just started *A Quiet Kind of Thunder* by Sara Barnard, which I think I'll be recommending lots. It's very good!'

'Ah, yes, I know that one! Excellent choice.'

They went downstairs and across to the library, the halls eerily quiet as everyone was in lessons. In ten minutes, though, it would all be different: the halls would fill and it would be impossible to move except at a snail's pace, as everyone crowded into the same space.

The eerie quiet permeated into the library too. They walked to the far end, Miss Carter leaning over to pick up a thickly bound black notebook from her desk before taking Olivia through to the adjoining room at the back.

The computer room that joined on to the library was not a massive space, but big enough to fit a row of ancient computers. In the centre, tables were pushed together to form one big table, and around the edge were separate desks with numerous computers. The walls were lined with posters on internet safety and the dangers of social media. Olivia had always wondered how many students paid attention to the rAnD0m password combinations or 'stranger danger!' warnings they advised.

'Take a seat,' Miss Carter said, gesturing to the chair across from where she'd just placed herself. From the notebook she'd picked up, she took out a folded piece of paper, and drew out the process of opening it up and sliding it across the table to Olivia.

'Have a look at this.' As Olivia began to read the printed-out email, she could feel that Miss Carter's gaze was unfaltering.

To: ALL STAFF
Subject: LIBRARY

Dear Staff,

After reviewing our previous procedure re the tightening of library loans, the Senior Leadership Team have come to the decision to withdraw the new system and reinstate the old one. This will mean that all students are able to take out all books, and the so-called 'warning' cards that have been instated will be removed, with immediate effect. We have come to understand that our original decision was taken without the consideration of the welfare of certain students within our school community, and we are sorry for any inconvenience caused.

As always, the views of our students are
extremely important to us, and we hope that
students who attend our school feel comfortable
enough to express these views, as they have done
on this occasion.

Tutors — please let your students know the change
in policy.

Senior Leadership Team

Olivia looked up from the paper, unable to see clearly any
longer for the tears clouding her vision. 'They've changed
it?' she said, not able to believe what she'd just read.
Maybe it was a sick prank, all a dream and she'd wake up
in a minute and find that she'd imagined it.

'They've changed it!' Miss Carter said, and there were
tears in her eyes too as she smiled the biggest smile Olivia
had ever seen. 'And it's all down to you, Olivia! I've
suffered in silence since the start of the school year, trying
to get it to change, but I couldn't. And then you came
along, and your campaign sealed the deal: there was no
way they could ignore it. Not when there was such uproar.'

Olivia laughed, a joyous, bright laugh full of promise
for the future. 'Do you really think so?!'

'Think so? I know so!'

Olivia held the paper in her hands, and she kept looking at it – not reading, just looking and looking, thinking of the power it held and how she'd played a part in that.

We did it, she wanted to scream, to let the whole world know that she'd fought so tirelessly for something she felt utterly passionate about, and she'd won. *We did it!*

But she didn't scream. Instead, she said, 'Miss Carter, would you mind doing me a favour?'

Ten minutes later, after the bell for first lesson had gone, Olivia jumped up as the door to the computer room burst open and she was faced with the emotional, excitable, totally overwhelmed figures of the Read with Pride group.

She didn't say anything – no words could convey how they were all feeling – but simply held her arms wide open and shut her eyes against the impact of all of them being pulled into a group hug. The best group hug, carrying with it all the stress and toil and strife and emotion that they'd had to deal with over the past few months. Olivia knew, even though there were no words, that the others felt the relief and delight like she did. It wasn't exactly happiness – they'd had to go through a lot to get here – but it was close enough. It was just as sweet.

When they finally pulled away, it was Oscar who spoke first. 'I can't believe it worked,' he said. 'Even in my wildest dreams, I didn't allow myself to imagine that it would.'

'And all it took was going viral, making headlines, and fighting off a few angry trolls,' Rocky said. 'All in a day's work!'

'A day?!' Olivia laughed. 'It was a very long day if so!'

Morgan added, 'I still don't love books, but I do at least like them after all of this.'

'Result!' Olivia said, lifting Morgan's hands in the air in victory. 'RESULT! See! I did say that everyone has the opportunity to live their best bookish life!'

'Did you?' Alf said.

'Hm, maybe not, but I definitely should have done. Are you sure I didn't say that? It's a very me thing to say. To be honest, I still feel so sleep-deprived that I can barely remember my own name.'

'Okay, time's up,' Miss Carter said, 'I can't get away with keeping you all out of class any longer, I'm afraid.'

'Thank you, Miss Carter,' Olivia said. 'You don't know how much it means to us.'

'No,' said Miss Carter. 'Thank *you*. What you've all done – what you've achieved and what you've had to go through to enact this change – has saved our library for the better. Now I can make sure that the right books get into the right hands, and I wouldn't be doing my job properly if I couldn't do that. You've saved the library.'

'Library superheroes!' Saffy said with a giggle. 'We could have our own comic!'

'I think this superhero might take a break before her next duty,' Olivia said, grinning. 'And that goes for all of us: we deserve a rest! I don't know about you, but I'm exhausted.'

'Lightweight,' Alf teased.

Olivia pushed his arm playfully. 'Oh, all right then. I'll dust off my cape. What are we saving next?!'

Chapter Twenty-eight

Returning to the library for the first time since Miss Carter's announcement, Olivia felt a thrill go through her for the first time in a long time. It was the same satisfying feeling as when you get to the end of a really good book and turn the final pages to discover that everyone has lived happily ever after. And while she knew, practically, that this was only a tiny sliver of happily ever after – hers certainly wouldn't be the last school in the world to act as they had done – for now, she could remain happy that they'd managed to change things for their student population.

Maybe it was because she was so happy, maybe there really was change in the atmosphere, but the library felt different today: the electricity was back in the air, there was no tension lurking under the surface, everyone seemed to be laughing or animatedly chatting or surfing the bookshelves with glee.

Not literally surfing because that may be a little different, Olivia rectified as that thought popped into her head.

Miss Carter was in one of the stacks, helping a student to find a book. 'Olivia!' she said, on catching her eye. 'Come over to my desk when you're ready, won't you?'

She waited until Miss Carter was done by browsing the shelves – now that Read with Pride was complete, she was looking forward to gathering a big reading pile to work her way through. She'd missed out on so many books! She deserved some quality reading time after everything that had gone on.

Picking out a few to take home with her, she took them over to Miss Carter's desk and slid them across the counter.

'Good choices,' Miss Carter said, scanning them through the system.

'I can't wait! I think I'll be reading on the way home, walking along the street gazing down at my book.'

'Don't walk into any lampposts, then. Maybe I should supply a bandage with each book?'

Olivia laughed. 'Good idea!'

'To say thank you,' Miss Carter said, and she reached under her desk and pulled out a bag, slowly handing it over to Olivia on the other side. 'I was clearing out my shelves at home and found these. Do you think they'll come in handy?'

Olivia opened up the tote bag and lifted the books out

– to find beautiful old copies of each of Jane Austen's novels, tied up with a fading red bow.

'They were my grandma's, but I've always been more of a George Eliot girl myself. They're yours, if you'd like them.'

Olivia gasped. 'Are you sure?!'

'I'm certain,' Miss Carter said. 'I can't think of anyone more worthy.'

Olivia grinned. 'Thank you, Miss Carter. You are the *best* librarian!'

Miss Carter laughed. 'And you, Olivia, are one day going to make the best book editor the world has ever seen. Think how much you've already achieved: you managed to rally thousands of people into believing in our cause, you gathered a group of your fellow students and made them feel as passionately as you do. I am a very proud librarian. Remember me when you're a famous editor, won't you?'

And to Olivia, that meant the world. 'Always!' Olivia said. 'Although that might be a little way off yet ... I've still got lots of work to catch up with that I didn't do a very good job on. But I'll get there. I'm learning to slow down and take things one step at a time.'

'That's what I like to hear!'

As she turned to leave, Olivia saw Morgan sitting at a table on her own, engrossed in a book.

'Hi, Morgan!' Olivia said.

'Look!' Morgan said. She held the book up in her hands, the plastic wrap crinkling under her fingers. 'I just took this out!'

Olivia grinned. 'Yes!! Amazing!'

'And I'm enjoying the book even more because it feels like such a win to be able to take it out – and to be able to take it home!'

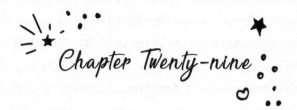

Chapter Twenty-nine

Olivia never usually felt self-conscious but, dressed in her rainbow-striped short-sleeved top, a bright pinafore dress and with rainbow make-up applied by Cassie, she couldn't help but feel slightly exposed as they walked down the high street.

'This must be an important photoshoot,' Olivia had said as they got ready in her bedroom. 'I don't know if you've ever made me look this fancy before – or bright! You won't be able to miss me.'

'It's very important,' Cassie said.

'Is it a big part of your final grade?'

'Huh?'

'This project. How much of your final art grade is it worth? I thought you were working on something else, anyway. Is this new?'

Cassie tutted. 'You ask too many questions. Now close your eyes and let me sort out this eyeliner of yours. I don't want to get it everywhere if I can help it.'

For both their sakes, Olivia didn't ask any more questions; not when they'd left the house, or now that she was obediently following Cassie to wherever she was taking her.

She wasn't often roped into modelling for Cassie: usually Cassie preferred candid shots for sketching from, rather than anything posed. Cassie's drawing was all about being in the moment and Olivia had often heard her complain, over the years, about having to do anything that wasn't spur of the moment.

But Olivia went along with it anyway, knowing how much Cassie relied on the expression art gave her. And knowing, also, how nice it was to be in each other's company, how much she owed it to Cassie to spend quality time with her.

'I look like I'm going to a party,' Olivia joked, linking her arm with Cassie's.

'Too bad it's going to be way less exciting than a party. Honestly, you'll be bored by the time I've finished with these photos – and I know you don't get bored easily.'

'Boredom, here we come!' Olivia giggled.

They looked a right pair, a collision of rainbows. Cassie had said Olivia might have to take some photos of her, too, and so she'd also dressed up in her brightest clothes. For once, Cassie didn't look ultra-stylish – instead, she looked like she'd raided a toddler's wardrobe and gone for the most fun she could muster, even going so far as getting some neon pink leg warmers from somewhere. Olivia couldn't begin to guess where! They certainly weren't a wardrobe staple.

Cassie came to a stop outside the village hall on the outskirts of the town centre.

'What are we doing here?' Olivia asked.

'Oh, I just have to pick something up,' Cassie said. 'There's a Women's Institute meeting or something today and I've bought something from a member for this photoshoot I need to do.'

'Okay, cool,' Olivia said. She leant against the railings at the bottom of the path leading up to the entrance door.

'Aren't you coming in then?' Cassie asked. She twisted round to look at Olivia, holding her hand out.

'Oh, I thought I'd just wait here. You don't need me, do you?'

Was it her imagination or did Cassie look annoyed? 'I might need your help carrying, I can't manage on my own. You'll have to come in.'

Okay then . . . She took Cassie's hand. As Cassie pushed the door open, Olivia squinted to look inside: she couldn't see anything. It was completely dark.

'Are you sure we've got the right place?' she whispered to Cassie.

'I'm sure,' Cassie said, and there was a laugh hidden in her voice that Olivia couldn't work out.

'Maybe we should turn back—'

'SURPRISE!'

Olivia jumped out of her skin as the main lights switched on and everything came into bright, sharp focus. Balloons everywhere, paper bunting hanging from the ceiling, and so many people, more than she could count.

In the middle, though, were the people she was most happy to see: Tabby, Henry and Ed, all grinning with excitement. Tabby looked gorgeous in a short sequin dress that caught the light and threw sparkly orbs on to the ground around her; Henry was wearing a garish Hawaiian shirt. And Ed? Well, Ed was wearing a fluffy pink tutu, a rainbow wig and a neon shirt, luckily paired with some neon pink shorts for modesty's sake.

Olivia burst out laughing. 'What is going on?!' She lifted her hands to her cheeks, trying to take in every tiny detail.

Cassie steered her body to the left, and she gasped, then squealed, as she took in the Read with Pride group: Rocky and Nell wrapped in a pride flag, Oscar and Alf, Morgan and Saffy. 'Everyone's here!!'

'Surprise!' they said again. And Nell added, 'Welcome to your very own pride party!'

'What is going on?!?!' she repeated. 'Ahhhhh!'

'We wanted to show how much we love and appreciate you,' Tabby said, 'and celebrate all the hard work you and

Read with Pride have put in. So The Paper & Hearts Society have been busy organising a celebration of pride in your honour!'

'Surprise, surprise, surprise!' Ed called.

'I'm in shock,' Olivia said, clutching hold of Cassie's arm and refusing to let go. 'For once, I'm actually speechless!'

Pop music was playing over the speakers, and there were round tables pushed to one side, leaving enough room for a good-sized dance floor, which people were already taking advantage of. There were members of her classes, the friends she'd made in English, in science and French, people she'd known for years. All here – for her!

'You like it, though?' Henry asked. 'We weren't sure if it would be too overwhelming.'

'Like it? I love it! I can't believe you did all of this!'

'It was Ed's idea, actually,' Cassie said. 'But we all helped. I gave the design direction, Henry and Tabby have spent most of today and last night decorating and organising, and Ed sorted out the invite list. It was a team effort!'

'I don't know what to say,' she said, scratching at the corner of her eye where tears threatened.

'Don't cry!' Cassie said. 'You'll ruin your make-up!'

'But what about the photoshoot?'

Cassie laughed. 'There is no photoshoot, silly! It was all a ruse to get you here! Here's to your pride party!'

'This is my kind of party,' Tabby was saying to Henry and Cassie. 'Not like the rowdy things that Ed hates but still insists on having.'

Olivia, clutching her hands to her face again in total shock, did a 360 spin in slow motion, wanting to drink in every single detail, wanting to capture every single moment to memory for the rest of her life.

Her heart was bursting! With love for The Paper & Hearts Society, with gratitude for Read with Pride for being with her every step of the way . . . and with pride in herself.

I actually did it. I fought for what I believed in – with the help of friends old and new – and I won. I didn't think it would ever work; who listens to anything teenagers have to say? But it did.

And, with them all by her side, she'd conquer the next step: seeing the library flourish, while concentrating on her studies and getting back on track, back to a place where she felt stable again.

And hopefully I'll never let myself get to a point where I take on too much again. No more burn-out!

Cassie pulled Olivia on to the dance floor, someone having turned up the music, and, laughing, she picked Olivia up, almost buckling under her weight. Olivia screamed with delight, giddy with excitement. 'Put me down!' she said through a peal of laughter. 'Cassie!'

With a spin and too much flourish, Cassie did as she

was told, and Olivia threw her arms around her girlfriend's neck, not worrying who was watching as she showered kisses on her cheeks. She loved the tinkle of laughter that burst from Cassie.

'I love you, Cassie,' she said, 'I love you so much. *Thank you.* I haven't always deserved this, I know that, but I'm so grateful. More than you can ever know!'

'I love you, too, Livs,' Cassie said, and Olivia could have sworn she saw tears glistening in the corner of Cassie's eyes. 'We're for ever, you and me.'

'For ever,' Olivia whispered into Cassie's hair as they hugged tighter than ever. 'And I promise that I won't abandon you again. I'll support you just like you support me. You're not alone.'

Cassie smiled softly, hopefully. 'I think things are turning round with Mum,' she said. 'Even in this last week, I've noticed a difference, and we're going to the doctor's next week to see what more can be done. I feel the best I've felt in a long time.'

'Cassie! Ah! Honestly, that is amazing.'

Cassie nodded. 'It is, but right now, can we just focus on dancing the night away?'

'Sounds good to me!'

The next song came on, apparently one of Ed's choices: Diana Ross's 'I'm Coming Out'. The dancefloor filled up further.

Somewhere along the way, she ended up sitting on Henry's shoulders, screaming out the words to all the songs and throwing her hands wildly in the air. People came and went – Tabby and Cassie danced together, Morgan and Oscar worked out their own routine, which they took great pleasure in demonstrating to everyone, Saffy and Nell chatted over at the food table, coming in every now and again for a quick boogie, and Alf, playing the cool card, watched on with Rocky, who was desperately trying to convince him to join in.

She didn't think she'd ever felt so happy before.

After the next few songs came and went, Olivia went over to the table where drinks were set up and poured herself a glass of water in a paper cup, breathless from spinning around on the floor.

Ed was already there, leaning against the side, watching everything going on.

Bless him, Olivia thought, *he always gets a little overwhelmed at parties.*

'Thank you, Ed,' she said, putting an arm round his shoulder and planting a sloppy kiss on his cheek. 'This is all . . . amazing. The best! I love you, Edward.'

'I love you, too, Livs,' he said, 'and that's me being sincere for the first time in my life. I will get choked up if I say any more, but we really are so proud of you.'

'Thanks,' she said, 'please don't get choked up because

once you get started, you'll flood the dance floor with your tears.'

He laughed, putting his own arm around her. 'I've got some news,' he said.

'Go on! What is it?'

'I got a job! I went for the interview last week and they rang me up yesterday to say I'd got it!'

'Ed! That's incredible! Tell me more, tell me more!'

She was genuinely happy for him; she knew how much this meant.

'It's at Woolf and Wilde,' he said. 'I'm going to be one of their young booksellers!'

'EEEEKK!!! Ed, that's so cool! You're going to work in a bookshop!! That is the DREAM!'

'I know!' he exclaimed. 'I keep having to pinch myself!'

She gave him a hug. 'I'm so proud of you, Ed. And I cannot *wait* to take advantage of your staff discount. That's why we're friends.'

'Hey, not allowed!' he said. 'Hands off my staff discount. You've got enough books as it is!'

'You can never have enough books – you should know that by now.'

As they wandered back into the fold, Olivia caught the eyes of the Read with Pride group on the dance floor. She was ready to catch up with everyone – this may have been a party, but she had enough energy for chatting, too.

'This is so cool!' Nell rushed over, holding out her arms to envelop Olivia in a hug. 'A pride party! Your friends did such a good job – they wouldn't let us help, said they had it all under control!'

Olivia looked behind her to find Rocky, Oscar, Alf, Morgan and Saffy coming over too, all dressed up so that they matched in their finery.

'We're having an amazing time!' Rocky called over the music.

'I feel very lucky!' Olivia called back.

Nell cleared her throat. 'We actually have some news for you,' she said, looking around at the others.

More news! Olivia thought. *This is clearly a night for partying and for news.*

'We've loved being part of the Read with Pride campaign,' she said, 'and so we hope that we might be able to carry it on, to make it a thing that lasts at school, even though we might have achieved what we first set out to do. We want to start a Read with Pride club, so that this past year won't be repeated and our LGBTQ+ books will never be endangered again.'

'Nell,' she said, 'all of you . . . that's amazing.'

Now it was her turn to stop herself getting choked up – she had The Paper & Hearts Society and knew that now she'd reached her goal, she needed her friends more than anything else, but that didn't mean Read with Pride had to come to an end. For Read with Pride, it was just the beginning.

'We hope we have your blessing,' Nell said, squeezing her hand.

'Of course you do!' Olivia squealed, squeezing right back. 'That's so cool! Imagine! Wow, I'm speechless . . . again!'

Olivia couldn't take the grin off her face as she partied the night away. At some point, she'd kicked her shoes off and flung them away from the dance floor, but she'd lost herself in the music and the movement, no longer having any control over what her limbs were doing. The shoes could be anywhere, as far as she knew.

It had been a weird time, for her and for The Paper & Hearts Society. But, despite it all, she didn't think she'd do it much differently if she could have her time again. It had all worked out in the end.

Olivia, Tabby, Henry, Cassie and Ed had gravitated towards each other as the party went on, until they were all dancing together and laughing at each others' awful moves. One of Ed's managed to trip Tabby up and she fell to the floor, only to grab his hand at the last second and drag him down with her.

'Group hug!'

'You're squashing me,' Cassie grumbled, but her hand found Olivia's and she squeezed.

'Hands in the middle,' Tabby said, and they created a circle with their bodies, arms into the centre. In three ... two ... one ... They raised their arms to the sky, all grinning as if their lives depended on it.

'To The Paper & Hearts Society!' Ed cried.

'And to our weird bookish friendship,' Cassie said.

'And to Olivia!' Henry said. 'Who we'd never be without in a million years!'

'And to reading with pride!' Olivia said. 'Because there's no other way to read.'

THE END

(Until next time . . .)

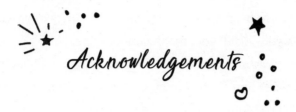

Acknowledgements

There were many moments during the writing of *Read with Pride* when I wondered if I'd ever hold the real book in my hands. While writing is far from easy at the best of times, I hadn't realised just how difficult the journey would be, and I'm immensely grateful to those people who made me believe in myself when I'd forgotten what it meant to believe.

Polly Lyall Grant, the best editor I could have wished for – words can't describe how special our working relationship has been to me over the course of *Read with Pride* (and *The Paper & Hearts Society*!). We really are the dream team, and I'm so grateful for your support, kindness, patience and passion. I can't wait to craft more silly cat jokes, fashion descriptions and bookish fun with you.

To Lauren Gardner, you are my hero and I'm so glad I can call you my agent and friend. I'm sorry for crying down the phone at you, (again, oops!), but at least I made it up to you by rescuing you from being stuck in Italy. It might have been a bit far to travel to meetings otherwise. Thank you, thank you, thank you.

To everyone else at Bell Lomax Moreton, including John Baker and Lorna Hemingway – thank you for being such an awesome, supportive agency.

I love being part of the Hachette Children's Group publishing family and it's such an honour to be published by a publisher who are working so hard to make the industry a better place.

In PR, I'd like to thank Emily Thomas, one of a kind publicist, for making sure I'm always where I should be, putting up with my weird food habits on tour, and recognising the power of a good hotel room. Please can you run my life for me? Everybody needs a publicist like you. Also huge thanks to Becci Mansell, as well as Katy Cattell, who I owe my newfound love of gelato to.

Natasha Whearity is a Marketing Wizard who is going to take over the world one day with her outstanding campaigns (not that she isn't already). I've also loved working with Naomi Berwin and Beth McWilliams, and I'm immensely lucky to have their expertise.

To Emma Martinez in Rights – thank you for helping *The Paper & Hearts Society* go international! And to Katherine Fox and Nic Goode in Sales – I'm still in awe of everything you do to bring books to readers!

They say you shouldn't judge a book by its cover, but I'm very happy for that to happen with mine. Alison Padley and Alice Duggan have done an amazing job with the *Read with Pride* cover and series branding. As someone with no artistic talent whatsoever, I only slightly envy their skill!

Thank you to the booksellers and librarians who have supported *The Paper & Hearts Society* so far – you work so hard to champion books and it doesn't go unnoticed. Special thanks go to everyone at Seven Stories; Elise from Waterstones Welwyn Garden City; The Book Shop in Lee-on-Solent; Martha and everyone at Waterstones Newcastle; Emma Suffield; Tamsin Rosewell from Kenilworth Books; and to all the Bath bookshops and booksellers who have supplied me with way too many books over the years (although I have no regrets).

Thanks also to all the bloggers and internet book folk who have left amazing reviews, taken stunning Instagram pictures, and sent generally amazing energy towards *The Paper & Hearts Society*. It's so weird to be on the other side now! I can't name you all individually, but I would like to mention Karolina from @come.book on Instagram, Ruby Granger for being so lovely, and send a hug to all the UKYA bloggers out there.

Yasmin Rahman – best motivational gif sender, The Good Place critic, and friend. I know you want me to dedicate the book to you, but please have this entire paragraph instead. I LOVE YOU. (And I'll dedicate a book to you one day. Promise.)

Aisha Bushby, you're one of the most talented authors I know and inspire me every day with your beautiful prose, positivity and, let's be real, out of this world style. Seeing your journey has given me the courage to continue with mine. You are amazing.

And to all my other author friends – the Nineteen Newbies, Bex Hogan, Lauren James, the terrible influences who are the Splinters, you make all of this worthwhile. I can't name you all because I will forget someone, but I'm so grateful to have you.

Mum and Dad – it's FINISHED! I know you'll be just as relieved as me to see the words "the end". You've lived and breathed this book with me and it hasn't always been easy, but we got there. FINALLY! I love you both more than you can imagine. Thank you for everything.

And because no book would be complete without animal companions, I can't forget to thank Izzy, Daisy, the guinea pigs, and the best man in my life, Digby, who makes the world a brighter place with his endless love. (Even if he does like to distract me while I'm writing.)

Finally, to you, reader: don't forget to READ WITH PRIDE!

For more information and support, Lucy Powrie recommends the following charities:

Switchboard – The LGBT+ helpline – a place for calm words when you need them most
https://switchboard.lgbt/

Stonewall – working to let all lesbian, gay, bi and trans people, in the UK and abroad, know they're not alone
https://www.stonewall.org.uk/

School's Out – working to make our schools safe and inclusive for everyone
http://www.schools-out.org.uk

Gendered Intelligence – working with the trans community and those who impact on trans lives
http://genderedintelligence.co.uk/

LUCY POWRIE

Lucy Powrie is an award-winning author,
blogger and BookTuber from the UK, and started
writing the first book in *The Paper & Hearts Society*
series while she was still at school.
To date, her YouTube channel has attracted over
35,000 subscribers and over one million views.
When she's not reading, Lucy enjoys cuddling her
herd of guinea pigs and her three dogs,
but let's be real: she's almost always reading.

YOU CAN FIND LUCY AT:

▶ LUCYTHEREADER   🐦 @LUCYTHEREADER   📷 @LUCYTHEREADER
LUCYTHEREADER.COM